RENEGADE

THE GRAY ASSASSIN TRILOGY BOOK TWO

RENEGADE

To Kait— and thanks for coming. See you at Horbonton!

Gregory A. Wilson

GREGORY A. WILSON

Detroit, Michigan

RENEGADE

Cover Illustration by Peter Tikos
Interior Design by G.C. Bell

Edited by E.D.E. Bell

Published by Atthis Arts, LLC
Detroit, Michigan
atthisarts.com

ISBN 978-1-945009-98-3

Library of Congress Control Number: 2023939139

To Clea, Senavene, and Calen:

Soul, heart, and spirit.

PROLOGUE

THE snows would come with a fury.

Sweeping down from the Scales over the Glacalta, the wind would cover the villages and towns of eastern Silarein, and their sometimes complacent residents, in a retributive blanket of white. Everyone in Elskeg said so, and most of them had seen enough winters to make the claim credible. But the snows had not yet come, and in truth, if one had fallen asleep for months and suddenly woken now, they could be forgiven for believing it was still summer, even barely two months until the turning of the year. It was hot enough that the workers trudging back from the Iron Reaches were sweating by the time they reached Elskeg, even in the evenings.

Hot enough that I'll take this swill that passes for ale, thought Ress sourly as he took another deep drink of diamond tear brew from the stained wooden mug in front of him and sighed. Everyone in Elskeg also claimed that the water here was more pure than the center of the Glacalta, and Gods knew that was a lie to end all the others. But at least it was cold, and that was a mercy in itself.

Ress sat at a table in the almost empty common room in The Mountain's Heart, one of two taverns in Elskeg, and by far its oldest. The other, The Fan and Feather, had only been in Elskeg for two years, and by all accounts had taken over much of The Mountain's Heart business ... a bigger fire, better ale, and, according to rumor, "other services." That might explain why finding a seat (or a room) there was well-nigh impossible, but had he heard tell of a hundred free chairs, Ress would likely have avoided the Feather anyway. The Mountain's Heart had been a fixture in his evenings for two decades, and he would be damned if fancier people and a more palatable drink would sway him from it. Besides, the Heart's bartender Gallard was always nicer to him on pay days, and as Ress glanced over at the mostly full bag of coins sitting near his mug, he knew he would have a few more hours of as much diamond tear brew as he could stomach.

He had just allowed himself the smallest of smiles when the front door to the tavern flew open, smashing against the interior wall with a bang as two soldiers stumbled into the room. Ress's smile vanished as he saw the uniforms they were wearing. *That's what you get for thinking you've got everything under control, Ress. Ain't nothing stays the way you think it will.*

The two men, staggering more or less in the direction of the bar, wore leather armor, with swords at their sides and shields on their backs; ordinary soldiers by any passing account. But their tabards were decorated with green and gold, dominated by the image of a tree in full leaf and covered in golden blooms. The colors of Arginn.

"Bartender!" the taller soldier shouted as they reached the bar, as if summoning him from the Depths instead of the space five feet away from where the men stood.

Gallard, sandy-brown hair and life-worn eyes over a crooked smile, nodded patiently, placing a mug he had been drying on the counter. "Gentlemen," he replied. "Warm night out. What can I—"

"Ale," the taller soldier roared. "Ale for the both of us, if you serve any in this outhouse you call a tavern."

Gallard blinked, but his smile didn't waver, and without a word he took the mug from the counter and filled it from one of the barrels on the rack behind him, repeating the process with a second mug before placing both in front of the two men.

The smaller soldier snatched his mug up and drank, some excess rolling down the sides of his dark beard. "Swill," he finally proclaimed, following up the observation with a loud belch.

"Aye," the other agreed. "But what else can you expect, Kester? We're hundreds of miles from anywhere with something real to drink." His bloodshot eyes scanned the tavern briefly, perhaps looking for any potential signs of resistance, but with only Ress, Gallard, and old Callish in the back corner of the room as a silent audience, he soon gave it up and turned back to his companion. "Never should have been out here in the first place. If the captain had done her job—"

"Pheh, Rannik," said Kester, with something between a laugh and a cough. "Captain ain't worth that scratched armor she wears."

"Aye. But as I say, if she'd done her job, we wouldn't be here to begin with."

"Or if Calarginn had bowed down the way they should have," Kester replied. Ress's hand tightened around the handle of his mug.

"We should have made 'em bow. Could have ended this stupid war months ago if we'd just marched straight to Calarginn and shown them what we do to traitors and scum that act above themselves." Rannik drank deeply before continuing. "But no, we can't be 'foolish,' the captain says. 'Got to fight smart, boys.' Pheh!" He spat on the floor with gusto, ignoring Gallard's look of surprise. "Fighting smart ain't coming out here to knock sense into a bunch of half-breed sheep herders. We're wasting our time."

"Aye," replied Kester. "Could have gotten things done even faster if Tellisar had taken our side, the way it could have."

"Tellisar," snarled Rannik, slamming his mug down on the counter for emphasis. "Tellisar ain't ever taken any side but its own. Tellisar's happy to see us fight for what scraps it decides to leave us. Anyhow, rumor has it Tellisar's leaders ain't the only ones calling the shots . . . they got others telling them what to do now, from the shadows. I hear tell," he said, only slightly quieter, "that when we're done sending Calarginn back to the Depths, Tellisar's next."

"Pah," Kester scoffed, "you're drunk, Rannik. Tellisar ain't a rotting waste like Calarginn. Enough for us to worry about giving Calarginn what it's been asking for."

Ress set his jaw. *It ain't worth it*, he thought. *Don't matter what a couple of drunkards have to say.*

"Eh, won't make a difference to us, anyway," Rannik said. "Either way we're stuck out here, halfway between the cow-lovers of the highlands and the dirt-eaters of the Depths. Gods know what I ever did to deserve being stationed in this dunghole." He drained his mug and turned back to Gallard. "Another."

"Certainly," Gallard said pleasantly enough, though Ress could tell his smile was now more than a bit strained. "First ones'll be two coins each, though . . . gotta make sure we keep ahead of the tax collector, you know." He chuckled a bit at the joke, but Rannik did not return the laugh, digging into a small pouch at his belt. He fumbled around for a bit longer before pulling out a single coin.

"Kester, throw in a couple for us, lad."

Kester raised an eyebrow. "With what? I ain't got a coin left after giving you something for your fun at the last place."

Rannik's red eyes blinked. "Ah. Well." He looked at Gallard, then back to Kester, and finally surveyed the room as Ress turned away, focusing his attention on his drink. "You!" he finally exclaimed.

At first Ress didn't respond, but when he heard footsteps drawing close he looked up to see the two Arginnian soldiers standing above him.

"You don't talk?" Rannik asked. Ress didn't respond. "Well, I was talking to you," Rannik went on, his voice suddenly quieter. "Still am. Couldn't help noticing that you've got a pouch of money next to you . . . lot more than you could ever spend, unless I miss my guess. My friend and I seem to be a bit low on funds, and we'd appreciate a bit of assistance."

Ress still said nothing, even though he felt his face growing hot; he simply shook his head and turned away.

"Don't think you heard my friend here," Kester said, more loudly. "When he asks for help, he aims to get it. Just a few coins will do. But you act as dumb as you probably are and we'll take the whole bag, and leave you a few reminders of causing us the trouble."

"Now gentlemen," Gallard said, coming out from behind the counter. "We can work out some—"

"Shut your mouth, barkeep," Rannik said, cutting him off. "We don't want to have to shut this place down, but we'll do it, if only to teach you dirt-eaters what it means to have some respect. Now I'll ask one more time, old man: coins."

Ress's knuckles were now white as they curled around the mug's handle. "Eat spit," he muttered.

Rannik laughed. "Oh, some spirit, eh? That's something different, for a change. Nice to finally have someone show at least a bit of a—*spine*." With this last word he grabbed Ress's shoulder and pulled him backward hard, knocking his chair over and him with it. "Now you're going to give us the whole bag ... and now we're going to teach you a lesson," he said, drawing his sword and standing over Ress as he struggled unsuccessfully to pull himself to his feet. Behind the foul-smelling man, Ress saw Gallard step back.

"I think he made it quite clear he wasn't interested in giving you any of his own money, friend," a low voice said. Ress twisted around to see a hooded figure standing alone in the shadows by the door. He couldn't remember anyone else besides Gallard and Callish in the common room—there was no second floor, and he would have heard the front door open for a newcomer the way it had for Rannik and Kester. But there he stood, hands by his sides, eyes glinting in the reflected lantern light.

"Don't recall asking you for an opinion, *friend*," Rannik said, a slight sneer playing over his face. "In fact, don't recall asking you for anything at all. So I'd keep your mouth shut and find another place to do your drinking."

"Those places seem to be hard to find around here," the stranger replied. "Wherever I go, someone's ordering someone to do something they don't seem to want to do, and convincing them with a fist or a blade. Makes mealtimes ... unpleasant."

"It'll be a lot more unpleasant if you don't do what you're told," Kester barked. "Get out."

Without bothering to see the result of their command, the

two turned back to Ress. "Now that you've had the chance to think it through, let's have the—" Rannik began as he lifted his sword, but his sentence ended with a yelp of pain as he staggered sideways, the blade clattering to the ground as he grabbed his wrist. Out of the corner of his eye, Ress saw a metallic ball roll over to rest against the table leg.

Kester and Rannik, still holding his wrist, turned to see the hooded man a step closer.

"I didn't think anyone here had fight left in them," Kester said, drawing his sword. "It's too bad we ain't got more around to see what it looks like . . . or what happens when you show it to an Arginnian soldier."

"Step off, Kester," Rannik hissed, crouching to pick up his sword from the ground as he watched the hooded man warily. "This ralaar waste is mine." He stood again, wincing as he held his blade in front of him; the hooded man remained motionless. "I don't know why you think it's worth throwing your life away over an old dirt-eater like this. But you made your own choices." The stranger said nothing, and after a tense few seconds, Rannik pulled his sword back and charged toward him.

Ress caught what might have been the glint of a smile from within the depths of the stranger's hood. Rannik swung as he reached the hooded man . . . but his swing passed through open air as the man was already gone, cloak swirling. Rannik whirled to find the man behind him, and swung again, but again the stranger was gone. Snarling, Rannik turned—but even as he did so, something connected with his face, and with a grunt Rannik fell heavily to the floor and lay motionless. The hooded man stood above him, holding a curved blade with the pommel outward.

For a moment there was dead silence; then Kester ran at the man, sword above his head, shouting wildly. The stranger did nothing until the last second, when he stepped out of the way of the soldier and—though it happened so quickly that Ress couldn't be entirely sure of what he was seeing—pushed him toward the wall of the tavern. Kester ran into the wall with a sickening crunch, and without a word he toppled backward onto the ground, his sword sliding out of his nerveless hand at impact and coming to a rest just a few inches from Ress's face. The whole business had taken, maybe, fifteen seconds.

What in the Hells?!

Ress crawled backward along the floor, eyes wide. But the hooded man took no further notice of him. He picked up the metallic ball from the ground and placed it within his cloak; then he tossed something to the equally stunned Gallard, who seemed to catch the object out of reflex. It made a jingling sound, like a pouch filled with coins. Then the stranger turned and left the tavern, the door slamming shut behind him.

For a few moments Ress simply stared, his brain struggling to process the wild-eyed Callish at the back table, the equally silent Gallard looking dumbstruck at the pouch in his clenched hand, and the two unconscious Arginnian soldiers. Then the thought came to him, urgent, overwhelming:

That's your chance, you fool. And you're letting it walk away.

Head aching, he scrambled to his feet, snatched his bag from the table, and ran from The Mountain's Heart into the night, following the stranger and his hopes.

PART ONE
DOUBT

There is no room for indecision, or uncertainty, or hesitation.
When the Hammer falls, it falls with absolute conviction,
and forges the metal it strikes whether it will or no.

—The Fourth Rite of Devotion

CHAPTER ONE

I paused for a moment outside The Mountain's Heart, letting the sounds of combat fade from my memory. Not permanently, of course . . . the sounds never went away entirely. But given time, they would sink into the gentle waters of the past, just a slight hum of shouts and curses and clashing metal which I generally ignored.

I took a deep breath. The fresh air felt pleasant after the stifling atmosphere of the tavern's common room, but that wasn't saying much. Even at night it felt more like late summer than mid-fall, though at least it wasn't humid the way it might have been at home.

Home. Well, yes, once.

I looked up at the faded wooden sign hanging by the tavern's weathered front door, the image of a road winding up a mountain barely visible in the faint, flickering light of the lantern hanging on the door's opposite side, and sighed. I had hoped to sleep indoors for a change, rather than bedding down in a patch of tall grass or trying to convince a farmer I could be helpful by hunting vermin in his reeking barn in exchange for a roof over my head. But The Fan and Feather had too many distractions (and too much traffic), and now I'd fought my way out of a room at The Mountain's Heart, even though I had dropped the innkeeper twice what it would cost to repair the damage.

Got no one to blame but yourself, I thought . . . *could have left well enough alone.* And in the past, that was exactly what I would have done.

Which had gotten me nowhere. Or to Elskeg, which was close enough to nowhere.

I pulled my cloak around me, despite the evening's warmth, and strode off down the street. Perhaps a bit of an ambitious description; it was more of a widened lane, really, with The Mountain's Heart on one end, a few ramshackle wooden buildings along the sides (out of which the traders, such as they were, plied their various wares), and on the far end The Fan and Feather. The house of Elskeg's theoretical leader, Wennish, a nervous man who had started as a prospector and became the head of the town when no one else wanted the job, was a luxurious affair by Elskeg's standards—two stories, with a sloped roof instead of a flat one—and stood next to The Fan and Feather. Outside of this "main street," Elskeg descended into an array of dirt-packed lanes, shacks and huts, and an occasional well filled with brackish water. For as much wealth as flowed from the iron and coal mines nearby to the Glacalta cities far to the west, it was a wonder Elskeg couldn't keep any of it for itself.

No, it wasn't much of a town, and not much of a place to find answers. Still, I hadn't been any luckier in that search with the empty waystops and nervous-eyed ranchers I'd encountered on the path here. I dodged a suspicious pile of something on the street, barely visible in the moonlight—Elskeg wasn't any more clean than it was rich—and sighed. How long had it been now? Six weeks? In the past I could count the passage of time exactly, but since leaving Cohrelle I had struggled to maintain a routine.

Too much musing, not enough movement, perhaps, though I had certainly come a good distance, through the Western Gap into Eastern Silarein, and toward the edge of the Glacal basin where Elskeg sat; a lot of ground to cover, even if the weather had not yet turned treacherous. Yet the people I had found along the way were few and tight-lipped . . . not unfriendly, exactly, but not overly generous to strangers either. At least in Cohrelle, I had people who were willing to talk . . . for a price.

But now I was in Silarein. And as I would not leave without my answers, I'd have to make do.

I stopped about two thirds of the way down the street from The Mountain's Heart and looked over my shoulder. Other than one lone figure just exiting the tavern, face indiscernible in the shadows, the street remained otherwise empty. I turned back, looking at the rapidly rising moon in the late fall sky. Despite the inn's uninspiring construction, something about the haze of the glowing moon as it rose over The Fan and Feather reminded me of the way Argoth's Cathedral had appeared over the Church District, silhouetted against the moonlight.

Cohrelle again. It was hard to imagine missing a city which had tried so much to kill me before I left it . . . but then I had known no other home for the better part of four decades. And, of course, I had done enough killing there myself that I could hardly blame a few of its residents for trying to return the favor. Yet despite everything, I thought of it often . . . and the people whom I had left behind within it.

Right now, I imagined, Rillia was slumbering in a room of Governor Jarrett's home—perhaps a plain space, the tapestries unhung and rolled into a drawer, with her secondary blade stuck into the far sideboard of the unadorned bed. I imagined her, next to the kicked-off covers in a hastily thrown on sleep shirt, exhausted after a long day of advising the Governor and avoiding being killed. I smiled in spite of myself; she wouldn't appreciate the joke, but she would understand the sentiment.

I gripped the hilt of my cucuri. Jarrett had promised to protect her, and the Order would take some time to regroup . . . and Rillia was a survivor. But after the events of the last two months, nothing was certain.

And what of Caron, the young leader of Varda's people—the one I saved, breaking the tenets of my faith to do so? Like Rillia, I trusted them to manage their interests. An unfair burden for a child . . . but what were these days except unfair?

I imagined them, seated on a wooden bench in plain robes, continuing training with their "teachers," their guides in the Cloud, the brow of their smooth, brown-hued face wrinkled in concentration while they were working on developing their techniques as a sensate. Such an odd thing to consider, the Cloud . . . the idea that we lived in a kind of obscuring fog while Varda's people lived in a world of clarity and foresight. I still wasn't entirely sure I believed it, but there was no doubting Caron's abilities . . . I owed my life to them. And my new path was one they had helped set.

What path? I thought, suddenly angry. *What exactly are you doing out here, in a broken-down mining town, beating up guards from a city a hundred miles from here to save a local you don't even know?*

I had easy answers for this, and I settled into them, retracing each for reassurance. Governor Jarrett had told me I couldn't stay in Cohrelle; I would be in constant danger so long as I remained.

I was used to danger, but the reminder that I would bring more danger to Rillia and Caron had made my decision for me. I'd also known that if I stayed, I wasn't going to discover why the Order of Argoth, which I had served faithfully for many years, had suddenly decided to make a power play in Cohrelle. The Order's unquestioned leader, the Prelate, had gotten his orders from outside the city, and outside was where I needed to go. And so I kept my focus on that search . . . or tried to.

It was what my old teacher Caoesthenes would have told me to do. *Caoesthenes*. I closed my eyes, trying to summon a picture of him in his basement workshop, raising an eyebrow at me as he explained the use of the latest device he had created, or outside in the Gardens, training me in a particular technique with his usual combination of encouragement and sarcasm. But the image which blotted out all others was his dead, bloody form, lying still in my arms, his ravaged body a symbol of my own failure to understand the danger in time. I had visited my own form of judgment upon his immediate killers in Cohrelle . . . but that was only taking out my fury on the pawns who had killed him. The ones who had ordered the pawns—including, even, the Prelate—to act were elsewhere.

Yes, those answers were easy, but they were incomplete. Beyond anything else, what I was really searching for was much more personal . . . and nothing this repetition would help me calm.

Without Argoth—without the Order and the Service—who am I?

And so I had left Cohrelle and traced my path through the mountains into Silarein, following any half-heard whisper or drunken rumor, feeling as if I was wandering aimlessly from roadside campfire to sleepy farm to small village, watching both the path ahead and my tracks behind. I wasn't naïve enough, not anymore, to believe that the search was only in one direction. The Prelate's death might have thrown the Order off for a time, but it wouldn't last; even if Jarrett was as good as his word, he wouldn't be able to break the Order's hold on the city that quickly. Soon enough they would piece together what had happened, and then the Council would have to decide what to do next: either pull back, consolidate power, then gradually reemerge—or go after me, to set an example, to eliminate a potential threat. To prove who was truly in charge.

I had a pretty good guess what their decision would be.

So on I traveled until I found myself here, in Elskeg, between hopeless miners and ignorant farmers, where the path seemed to have come to an end. I'd seen an increasing number of soldiers from the cities of Arginn and Calarginn, locked in some kind of dispute I didn't care about, but hadn't paid much attention until I had heard the talk from the two drunken sots about Tellisar, Silarein's capital city, and taking orders from the shadows.

That sounded familiar.

"Oy," I suddenly heard a voice from behind me, and I whirled about, my cucuri drawn. Stumbling back a few steps, trembling hands up in apparent apology, was the man I had helped back in The Mountain's Heart—an older, grizzled man, stocky, slightly stooped, thinning white hair plastered to his sweat-covered forehead.

"Not smart to sneak up on people," I growled quietly.

"Sorry . . . sorry, sir," he gasped, voice thick and hoarse, hands still up in front of him. "I meant no offense. I . . . I just, uh, wanted to talk to you. To thank you, first off." I had heard that gravelly type of voice before—from those who had spent more than anyone should underground, breathing in coal dust instead of air.

"You're a miner?" I asked, lowering my blade.

"Yes—yes, sir," he replied, blinking as if confused by the question. "Been working in the Depths for nigh on twenty years now."

I nodded. "What do you want with me, then?"

"To thank you, as I said. The Arginn scum would have taken my wages for certain . . . and maybe done more, if you hadn't shown up."

"I've had to deal with a few drunks in my day. It's nothing."

"Didn't seem like that to me, sir. Like nothing, I mean." I glanced at him sharply, but he gave me a crooked smile, revealing at least three missing teeth. "You did for those Arginnians well enough, sir." Behind us, the door to The Fan and Feather opened suddenly, loosing two drunken patrons and a stream of music into the quiet evening, and I watched silently as the two men stumbled down the street past us. A high, trilling laugh was suddenly cut short as the door to the tavern slammed shut again, and we were left listening to the ambling men, trading verses in a popular drinking song I had heard many times in the taverns of Cohrelle, until they staggered out of view at the other end of the street.

I shook my head and turned away. "Good night to you."

"Wait," the man said, coming alongside. He had his head, hair shining white in the moonlight, bowed slightly, perhaps in respect . . . but not submission. "I . . . I hoped we could talk about something, sir. Might help both of us."

"Not looking for help right now."

"Begging your pardon . . . but I doubt that's true."

I narrowed my eyes. His face, covered with the dark wrinkles of a man who had spent too much time going from mines to tavern and back again, seemed innocent enough. But it had been a long time since I had made that mistake. "What?"

"Well . . . I know men like you."

"You don't know anything about me."

"I know you ain't from here. I know Elskeg don't show up on most maps of Silarein, and folks who come here are either running from or running to something." He looked up at me, tilting his head slightly. "Maybe both."

"You always get into the business of strangers?"

"No, sir. But when a stranger helps someone he don't know and don't ask for a reward . . . and when he takes out two soldiers in seconds—well, that ain't typical business." He waited for a reply, and when he didn't get one, shrugged and went on. "Name's Ress. Like I said, I'm a miner. Lived in Elskeg since I was a young man."

I folded my arms. "Grayshade." I had decided against any concealed identities in my weeks clearing the pass; an Acolyte-cloaked man of my age would be distinctive enough in Silarein, and whatever else they could take from me, my name was my own. "What were *you* running from when you came here?"

Ress smiled grimly. "Myself, sir. Leastways, the myself I was afraid I was going to be if I *didn't* run here. Been here ever since." He walked past me, looking at The Fan and Feather. "Ain't been much change over the years, 'cept maybe a new building once in a while. But the folks here are steady, anyway . . . you know what you're getting." He turned back to me. "Used to, anyway."

"I'm sorry to hear it," I said, getting impatient. I had no use for Ress's nostalgia, and I still didn't understand his angle . . . even though he was clearly aiming for something. "But as you've said, I'm not from here, and it's about time I move on."

Ress's eyes widened. "But sir—"

"Best of luck to you," I said, turning away and moving off. But I only got a few steps before Ress ran in front of me, hands up. "Get out of my way," I said firmly.

"Not until you hear what I have to say."

"This isn't a discussion," I said. "Now get—"

"I know what you're looking for," Ress said.

I was silent for a moment, staring him down. "I don't appreciate being played with," I said finally. "You don't know anything about where I'm from or where I'm going."

"I know a lot about this part of Silarein, sir. And I know people who know more than I do. I can get you your answers."

Damn.

I stared at Ress, but his gaze didn't waver. Either a gutsy liar or a true believer, then. Dangerous either way . . . but it wasn't like my other leads had been any more solid. I pondered, then sighed. "You've got one minute."

Ress grinned. "Figured you weren't the hasty type." He drew closer. "It's like this, sir—I know some people, and they're looking for men like you. Men with a particular talent, as it were."

"I'm not a sellsword, Ress."

"Figured that when you dropped those two in the tavern, then gave Gallard money to fix things up. A sellsword wouldn't have cared about me or a tavern owner . . . would have been interested only in his wallet. The people I know—" He hesitated. "Well, they ain't looking for that."

"Who are these people?"

"I can't tell you, sir. They've asked me not to draw attention to them with others who wouldn't understand what they were all about . . . their cause, you might say."

True believer it is, then. "And the cause?"

Ress pursed his lips and drew closer. "Justice," he whispered, looking around as if waiting for something to leap from the shadows.

"Look," I began . . . and then stopped. For a brief moment I remembered Caoesthenes's face, his dead eyes staring at mine as he lay in my arms in the basement of his home, victim of an attack I should have prevented, and my anger flared. I took a deep breath and shook my head. "Nine times out of ten, people say 'justice' when they really mean revenge, Ress. I'm not your man for that, or anyone else's." I started to turn away, but he grabbed at my arm, and I only just managed to suppress the reflex to throw him aside.

"I don't know what you're looking for, sir . . . not exactly," he said, a note of desperation in his voice. "But these people have connections in Silarein—in the cities. Whatever you need to find, they can probably help you do it . . . I swear it."

I shook my head. "I'm sorry, but I—"

"It's for my son," he said suddenly, lips trembling.

Damn it all. "What?"

"My son, sir," he repeated, clutching my arm. "I can't find anyone in this Gods-forsaken hole to help me, not even people

I've known since I got here. They don't want to get wrapped up in the war. But these people—if I can find someone to help them, they say they can help my son. I ain't got no one else . . . and he's a good boy."

A high, raucous laugh floated from an open window on the top floor of The Fan and Feather. "How old?" I said after a moment.

"Twenty, sir," Ress replied. "If you come with me, I can tell you the story . . . after we see them."

More wasted time, more delays, and the very real possibility I could be walking straight into a trap, I thought. But waiting for someone to save you from Arginnian soldiers in a sleepy tavern in Elskeg struck me as a very odd way to find potential victims. And somehow this didn't feel like a setup to me. Either my six weeks away from Cohrelle and the Service had dulled my senses, or Ress was telling some version of the truth. If it was the former, I wasn't going to find the answers I needed on my own anyway.

I shook my head again. "How far?"

Ress's face lit up. "Not far, sir—maybe thirty minutes' walk to the west. Shouldn't run into anyone this time of night." His expression grew serious. "Sir . . . I ain't a thief, nor a liar. I'm asking for help, not to set you up. You've got my word."

How many words had I taken for truth in the past, only to be betrayed? But the alternative . . . to wander from here to the Scales until illness or carelessness ended me . . . or the Order found me . . .

I took in the moon rising over The Fan and Feather one more time, then turned back to Ress.

"All right, miner. I'll take you at your word . . . and if you're lying, I'll take you with me when I go. Lead on."

Despite his rundown appearance, Ress moved faster and with more agility than I would have thought possible, leading us confidently over the rocks and stones outside the town into the bordering scrub brush and bushes beyond. The area surrounding Elskeg was more akin to the mountains south of it, rocky and relatively barren of plant life, but it was on the edge of Silarein's basin, dominated by the waving green grasses of the numerous farms found there, and as we traveled on and the moonlight bathed the flatter landscapes, I saw the rocks and stony ground begin to recede. We were lucky to have the light, as it let us keep our lanterns burning low—this saved oil, and besides, I had no interest in attracting any more attention than necessary. I kept an active watch for potential sites of ambush, but unless bandits around here had learned to fly or dig shallow holes to lie in wait, the flat, plain route was a singularly poor one for an unexpected attack.

"How did you find these people, Ress?" I asked after a long period of silence as we continued to make our way. It felt odd to repeat his description, but I had nothing else to go on.

"They found me, couple of weeks ago," Ress replied. "I'd just come up after two shifts in the Depths, and was walking home with a bunch of the lads. Must have still been ten minutes away from Elskeg when we run into a few Arginnian soldiers. They stop us, start asking what we were doing at this time of night, who we worked for . . . that kind of thing. One of the others tells them we work in the Depths, and suddenly they get real friendly . . . start asking if we're heading to The Mountain's Heart, want to swap stories over a drink. 'If we swap stories,' I say, 'it'll be with each other, not some thieves with swords.'"

I chuckled in surprise. "Here I thought you didn't intend to upset soldiers."

He looked at me sharply. "Not all soldiers. And it was a stupid thing to say, but . . ." He trailed off, staring into the distance, then glanced back at me for a moment and shook his head. "Got pushed too hard that day, I guess. Don't know. Anyway, they get angry—but there's at least fifteen of us, three of them, and they ain't stupid. They won't forget me, they say, and move off. Later that night someone I ain't ever seen before sits down at my table at The Mountain's Heart, buys me a drink, and says she's heard good things about me, likes people who stand up for themselves. We get to talking, and eventually she tells me she can help me . . . and my son." He stopped and pointed. "In there, Grayshade . . . that's the Greenmark, we call it."

I followed his gesture to a dark patch not far away from where we were standing, a small forest set on a gentle rise. "Haven't heard anyone else talk about the Greenmark since I've been in Elskeg."

Ress nodded as we set off again. "That's because there ain't much reason to go there. Elskeg's a mining town, and the Greenmark ain't all that big. Folks get wood from the edges for fuel and building, of course . . . they say it used to be huge, parts going from the Glacalta all the way to the Depths, but that was a long time before even my grandfather was born. Now I reckon it makes folks sad." He looked over his shoulder at me and grinned. "Makes it a good place for people who don't much feel like getting found."

"And for jumping on people you want to rob."

Ress snorted. "They'd starve trying to rob farmers and miners, sir. Money goes through Elskeg, but it don't stay."

There are other things to rob besides money, I thought, but kept it to myself.

I didn't try to make any more conversation as we approached the edge of the Greenmark. Now that we were closer I could see evidence of the uses he'd described; branches and brush lay near and on top of stumps, and I could see a few piles of dead wood which had obviously been recently stacked. Ress held as straight a line as he could to the edge of the forest, weaving around the stumps as we drew closer. Finally we reached the edge of the living trees and stopped.

Ress took the lantern from his belt and turned the key on its side to raise the wick, holding it aloft as he did so. The light brightened and spilled into the shadows of the trees beyond, but it revealed little other than more trunks and greenery. "You might want to do the same, sir," he said after a moment of gazing into the dim light. "There ain't many creatures left in the Greenmark— leastways none that'd do anything to living men—but you can't be too careful."

"All right," I said, turning the wick and holding my own lantern higher. "How do we contact these friends of yours?"

"They'll contact us, sir," Ress said, stepping between two trees and into the greenery. I took one last look at the empty land beyond—if I squinted I thought I could still make out a twinkle on the horizon which might have been the lights from Elskeg—then sighed, turned away, and followed Ress into the Greenmark.

I've been in a few forests in my time—though not for long, and not since I was much younger. But as we made our way into the heart of the woods, the scent of pine and leaf-covered moss filtering into our nostrils, something struck me as odd about the place. It wasn't oppressive, exactly, and not really all that dense as wooded areas go; there was a reasonable amount of room to maneuver between the trees, and the ground, covered with a mixture of grass, leaves, and fallen branches, didn't seem particularly treacherous. Yet it seemed still, quiet ... almost silent in places, save for the branches and leaves cracking below our feet.

"Like I said, ain't many creatures left here now," Ress said, as if sensing my curiosity. "Probably they can't live very well when a forest's been cut back enough, and Gods know this one's been."

"Still, you'd think there would be something—movement in the underbrush, a moonbird twittering, something," I replied. "It's like the forest's dead, except for the trees."

Ress shrugged. "I ain't a woodsman, sir. But the Greenmark's alive, all right ... just mostly sleeping, I expect."

"I expect," I repeated. "But if your friends needed to find food, they'd have a hard time of it here."

"They seem to manage—ah, here!" Ress said, and with a smile and nod at me, he stepped forward between two trees and into a moonlit clearing, perhaps one hundred feet in diameter. The trees here were particularly tall, but there was no leaf cover, and as I followed Ress into the clearing I could see a few stumps surrounded by thick grass in the pale light.

"This is the place, then?" I asked. "Not the safest place I could think of to meet."

"No," a voice behind me said … but not Ress's. I turned to see a tall soldier in leather armor flanked by two others with their swords drawn. With the faintest whisper of footsteps, people emerged from all around the clearing until we were surrounded by a whole company—perhaps thirty or forty, eyes glinting in the reflected lantern light. "No," the first soldier repeated, gaze steady, "this isn't a safe place at all."

CHAPTER TWO

FOR a moment no one moved or spoke, and I started running through possibilities: take out the one in front with my reshtar and the two flanking with kushuri darts, then charge the outer circle ... if they're thrown off enough, I can break the line, then escape deeper into the forest ... Then I stopped. These were fighters ready for action. Maybe I could take out five or six of them ... ten, if I was on my game. But even on my best day I couldn't eliminate—or outrun—forty prepared targets in open combat by myself. So I lifted my chin, stared at the one in front of me, and waited.

Her face was grim, weathered perhaps more from action than age, and topped with graying hair pulled into a practical knot, over a steady gaze. Her sword was still sheathed, but her hands were open ... relaxed but ready.

"Well, uh," Ress suddenly stammered from behind me, and I almost flinched—for a moment I had forgotten he was there. He stepped next to me, licking his lips nervously. "A pleasure, Captain Kraes. I was looking for you."

"You found me," Kraes replied, still staring at me.

"Yes, ha, yes. I did. *We* did, begging your pardon."

Kraes let her gaze slip to Ress for a moment. "And who is this 'we'? What have you brought me, Ress?"

"Someone who can help, Captain," Ress replied with a

crooked grin. He glanced at me. "A weapon." I gritted my teeth at this—*what is Ress playing at?*—but said nothing.

The captain raised an eyebrow and looked back at me. "In my experience, weapons have wielders. Who wields you?"

I frowned. "No one. And I'm not a tool for use."

Kraes nodded slowly. "All right, an independent type. Then you can start by explaining what brings you to the Greenmark."

"No," I replied, folding my arms, "*you* can start by explaining why I'm here. Ress said he had people he knew who could get answers, and I'm looking for some."

Kraes chuckled. "I'm not sure you understand the situation you're in, friend. You're surrounded by my people, in the middle of a secluded forest where no one ever comes ... where the only place nearby with more humans than cows is Elskeg." She grinned without mirth. "Where no one ever comes either."

"Except me," I replied. "And now I'm here, and I'm asking the questions."

The captain's head tilted only slightly, as if in curiosity, but immediately the mood shifted. All around us I heard the sounds of people drawing themselves up, metal quietly sliding forth from leather, bowstrings tightening.

Ress held up a slightly trembling hand. "Let's all relax, now. Captain, you asked me to bring you some good people ... and I have."

"Is that so?"

Ress nodded. "Aye. This man—Grayshade—took down two Arginnian soldiers at The Mountain's Heart tonight ... didn't break a sweat to do it, either. If he wanted to, I'd wager he could have taken five more, easy."

Kraes shrugged. "I'm not looking for tavern brawlers, Ress."

"It ain't like that, Captain. He—" Ress glanced at me for a moment, licking his lips. "He *took them down.*"

Kraes stared at Ress for a moment, then turned her gaze to me. "A professional," she said after a long moment, her tone thoughtful. "A mercenary, then. Or—a trained killer. An assassin." I heard a few of the others start to grumble, and as I glanced around I saw eyes narrowing, lips tightening. For a moment I remembered the faces of the Sewer Rats, back in Cohrelle: a mass of bizarre, strange features, all staring at me, hostility radiating from them, bodies tensing and ready to strike. I blinked—and was back in the Greenmark again.

"My people don't much like assassins," Kraes said with a small smile. "We prefer to do things more . . . directly."

"Death is direct enough, no matter how it happens."

"True. The difference is we've got a cause that makes it worthwhile, instead of a purse that needs to be filled."

"Yes, very noble," I replied, growing angry. "Surrounding a stranger with forty people and then presuming to know his soul. When I was doing my work, I wasn't doing it for money. And I've seen a thousand soldiers with righteous causes. They died just as quickly as the ones getting paid to kill."

"They might not have felt the same way as we do when they were doing it."

"I wouldn't know," I said. "They were dead before I could ask them."

"You shut yer mouth, cutthroat," said the thinner woman standing to Kraes's left, her nose wrinkling as her brow furrowed. "You'll treat the captain with respect, or you'll choke out the rest of your worthless life on the end of my blade like the vermin you are."

"You'd be dead before the blade got within five feet of me," I said easily, "as would your captain. I'm much better trained than most vermin . . . and you."

The woman growled and took a step toward me, but Kraes held up a hand. "Enough. As you were, Fen. Grayshade, I don't know who you are, only who Ress says you are. And in the past, I killed men like you without a second thought. Now . . ." Kraes looked off and sighed. "Now, we find allies where we can. If you can be one of them, it'll be worth it to keep you alive. We should talk more . . . but not here. Follow me." She started to turn, but stopped as she caught a glimpse of my expression.

"Listen," she said, lowering her voice as she stepped close to me. "You've told me what you *won't* fight for, not what you *will*. But everyone fights for something. You ought to at least be willing to hear what I have to say, and answer a few questions on my end. If I like what I hear and you're able to help us, you've got my word I'll do everything I can to help you; if not, all you've lost is an evening. Beats knocking together a few skulls at The Mountain's Heart, eh?" She did not smile, but her gaze softened a bit, and I could hear Ress breathe an unsubtle sigh of relief.

I searched Kraes's expression for signs of deception, but saw nothing obvious . . . and I admit I found her intriguing. I had been a true believer once, and I knew the type: rigid, unyielding, uninterested in anyone else's beliefs but one's own. Kraes had mentioned her cause a few times, and her crew seemed to be behind her. But she also struck me as practical, which was an odd characteristic for an ideologue, and one worth examining further for someone with no allies or contacts otherwise. Besides, I didn't see that I had much choice; I doubted Kraes would just let me walk away without at least finding out more about my intentions.

I nodded. "All right, I'll listen. But my own search has to take priority over anyone else's ... I can't promise anything."

"Neither can I," Kraes replied, "so for now, we're even."

About a half hour later I was sitting near a campfire, or at least a version of one. In fact it was some kind of short, squat metallic device, looking a bit like the ovens I had seen in some of the better taverns and inns in Cohrelle; the burning wood was set on the ground below, the flame licking up into an open chamber in the heart of the metal device, which had a large open hole on each of its four sides and a fine metal mesh over the top through which smoke lazily floated into the air. "It's an eldur, designed by one of our smiths ... one of the few things we have out here which, as far as I know, Arginn doesn't," Kraes told me, sitting on a log on the other side of the device. "Helps the heat be more efficient, warming us and any food we're cooking instead of getting lost into the air. And it cuts down on the smoke ... it still comes out, but not as much, and it takes longer to get above the treeline. We're not interested in attracting any more attention than we need to."

"Apparently," I said, sipping water from a plain wooden cup. The night's temperature had dropped a fair bit since we had left

Elskeg earlier that evening, so the heat was more pleasant than I might have expected ... and the quiet, even with a few soldiers still milling about the smaller clearing where Kraes had led us, was welcome. Most of the others had melted into the woods of the Greenmark around us on our return journey—"to maintain the watch," Kraes said. Ress, munching away on a cooked piece of pheasant, seemed considerably more relaxed than when we first entered the Greenmark. But not everyone approved. I could see Fen, arms folded, glaring at me as she leaned against a tree at the edge of the clearing. I couldn't blame her; I had challenged her in front of the others, and even if she had threatened me first, my response hadn't helped. I had heard much worse. But I was an assassin, not a diplomat, and something about the situation had pushed me. Someone else might well have pushed back ... but not this captain.

"All right," Kraes said after a few more moments. "So here we are, and without an audience."

"Are you leaving her out?" I asked, nodding in the direction of Fen, whose scowl deepened.

Kraes chuckled. "No, and I won't. Fen's a good soldier, and she's been my lieutenant for a long time ... long enough for me to know I can trust her with secrets as much as my life. You can speak freely in front of her."

"All right," I replied, "then I will. What's your cause, captain?"

"Here, between us, it's Venner," Kraes replied. "Venner Kraes, Captain of the Calarginn Third Company."

"Grayshade," I answered simply, "of Cohrelle."

"Cohrelle?" Kraes said with a hint of surprise. "You're a good ways from home, Grayshade. All I've ever heard about Cohrelle is that people generally stay there. I'm a Calarginnian born and bred, but Cohrelle's probably got a lot more to offer than any of Silarein's cities do, except maybe Tellisar."

"Tellisar was my next destination before I ran into Ress," I said, as Ress grinned through a mouthful of pheasant. "But he suggested you might have the answers I was seeking before I continued my journey there."

Kraes shrugged. "As I said, I can't promise anything but my word to try and do what I can. But if it helps, I can tell you that you won't find a person from here to the Glacalta to claim I don't keep my word once given."

"Words aren't much to me, Venner. But I see how the others follow you, and that convinces me you command some loyalty. I'll accept that until I hear more."

"All right," Kraes replied. "Then I'll tell you our story, you do the same, and we'll see where we are. Fair?" She settled back a bit on the log and took a deep breath. "How much do you know about politics in Silarein?"

"If they're anything like politics in Cohrelle, enough to know I want nothing to do with them."

Kraes barked a laugh. "You're an honorary citizen, then. People in Silarein are born knowing to stay as far away as they can from anything to do with politics. Lot more blood found in a council chamber after a session than any battlefield I've ever been on, from what I've seen of it." Her expression turned serious. "The problem is that when councils make decisions, people have to go fight for them . . . and it's not the councilors who die."

Ress's smile dropped away, and he leaned forward, listening intently.

"Silarein's not a country as much as it's an area, drawn in by the land itself. Out past the basin, there's not much worth anything beyond an occasional raid. The real power lies in the cities, and there are four major ones in Silarein, all near the Glacalta," Kraes continued. "Really, it's more like Tellisar and everyone else. Calarginn, Arginn—which broke from Calarginn decades ago— and Sullbris are the other three. Sullbris is so far west that no one much bothers with them, but Calarginn and Arginn have been fighting for the scraps Tellisar leaves them for a long time now."

It struck me that this was exactly how the Arginnian soldier Rannik had described Tellisar, but I decided to keep the similarity to myself. "Sounds like the fight's gotten more serious recently," I said.

"Aye," Kraes said with a sigh, "that it has. Last couple of years the city leaders have been spitting at each other, and six months ago it got nasty. Patrol from Arginn got ambushed and slaughtered; they found a Calarginnian soldier among the dead, and a couple of Calarginnian swords to boot. Didn't take much to do the math from there, and soon enough Arginn declared war on Calarginn."

"Was it Calarginn who attacked the patrol?"

Fen snorted, shifting her stance against the tree. "Like the Hells it was. Why give Arginn the chance to get ready for an attack if we was planning something? Probably set up by Arginn to give them cover to attack *us*."

"Eh, no way to know," Kraes said. "There's some who think Arginn couldn't plan a parade, let alone something to get us into a war. But that's where we ended up anyway, Fen; no matter who started it, we're all in the middle of it now." Fen shook her head but made no reply, and after a moment the captain continued. "So we're in a war, and that means we need recruits."

"And you're getting them from here?" I asked, a little incredulous. "You're pretty far afield for a civil war between two cities on the Glacalta."

"Won't stay on the Glacalta," Fen growled.

Kraes casually waved in apparent acknowledgement. "True enough. And eventually Tellisar will get twitchy, and that's going to cause its own problems." She sighed again. "Either way, my job is to follow orders, not come up with them myself. My superiors say they need recruits to fight Arginn, I try to find them recruits to fight Arginn."

"Like they ain't got enough already," Ress said with sudden vehemence, and I looked at him in surprise. His usually placid face was intense, eyes narrow, and he was glaring at Kraes.

"All right, then," I said after a moment, looking back at Kraes. "You need recruits to fight. What's that got to do with me? I'm not a soldier, and I don't care about your local conflicts."

"Nothing local about it," Kraes said. "You said it yourself: we're far from the Glacalta now, and both Arginn and us have gotten every farmer and petty laborer we can find from the basin, at least in the main places. The ones left are either too much trouble to persuade, or so much better at milking a cow than swinging a blade that there isn't much point in recruiting them. Best we can tell, Arginn's in the same boat."

"And that means?"

"Impasse. On each side, the same number of simple fighters who can barely swing a sword without cutting off their own legs. The same number of people who care more about surviving than fighting for a cause that matters. So the war drags on, and no one wins."

"And Tellisar gets fat on all our corpses," Fen said, pushing herself off of the tree and walking to one side of the clearing, where she stared into the undergrowth beyond as if she could cut through it with her gaze.

Kraes nodded. "Aye, true enough. Unless," she said, leaning forward, "we get some more who really know how to handle themselves ... even when the odds are against them. People who've been trained to fight, and not just for a few weeks by me. Now I saw how you acted back there in the grove, when we had you surrounded and dead to rights. You didn't have the look of a man who was trying to get himself killed, or afraid if he was. You looked like someone who could take care of himself. And that's what I need—what we all need, unless we want to see Silarein rip itself apart, and probably take everything else around it, including Cohrelle, with it."

I put my cup on the ground and narrowed my eyes. Kraes was clever, all right, and probably sincere—in fact, I would have been surprised if she was lying about what she'd said so far. But I had known others like this, people who pushed me to fight for a cause, who spoke words of belonging and truth and faith, and in the end Esper and Caoesthenes and Jant had all been actors in the same fiction ... and all now dead. I held Kraes's gaze for a moment, then looked at Ress, who was watching me eagerly. "What's your angle on this, then, Ress?" I asked. "What did the good captain here promise you?"

"Nothing," Kraes said before Ress could reply. "He's got his own reasons."

Ress stared at her silently for a moment, then nodded and looked at me. "Aye, I do." He stood and took a few steps away from the center of the clearing, his back to us. "My son," he said after a long pause. "My son, Carner. My wife Alera died in childbirth, and he's all I have left of her, or any of my old life before I came to Elskeg. I was born and bred in Calarginn . . . blacksmith by trade. Used to make some of the finest weapons south of the Waves, I did. I used to supply the captains of Calarginn with their blades—even this captain's father." He glanced at Kraes, who regarded him steadily.

I nodded. "What drove you to Elskeg?"

Ress sighed. "Foolishness. When Arginn and Calarginn first started to fight—they're always at each other here and there, even when they're not at war like now—I was young and stupid, and I signed on with the Calarginn army. Alera was with child, and begged me not to go, but I was from Calarginn, and I wanted to help make it safe for her . . . and the little one to come." He looked at me for a moment. "And they told me it'd be over quick, especially with good men like me. Good men, they said." He laughed bitterly. "Not so good in the end."

"What happened?" I asked.

He smiled grimly and held up his hands. I had noticed his trembling before, but had put it up to nervousness or being overeager; now I saw his hands were trembling badly, almost uncontrollably, though his expression was steady. "Small fight between patrols from the two cities, about two days north of the Glacalta. One of the Arginnians hit me from behind. Must have been their shield, or I'd have been a dead man. I was out before I hit the ground, and when I woke up, I was in our own camp. We had won." His grin turned into a sneer. "That's what they said. But I was never able to get the shakes out of my hands, and so they sent me home. Funny, though—turns out you ain't much use as a blacksmith when you hit yourself as much as the metal when you're trying to shape it."

He lowered his hands and turned away. Behind Ress, I saw Fen watching us, her watchful expression softer.

"Alera gave birth two months later, but lost too much blood and died." Ress closed his eyes and took a long breath before continuing. "And I couldn't fight anymore, couldn't shape metal. The army was already looking for its next recruit, said it couldn't help. I used most of my savings paying for wet nurses to feed Carner . . . just until he was about a year old, eating solid food. Then I took Carner and everything I had, left the city and set off east. I ran out of money when I reached Elskeg . . . but turned out I could still swing a pickaxe, and there were enough people out here who didn't mind looking after Carner while I was working in the Depths, long as I paid for the food."

He opened his eyes and smiled. "He grew real strong and tall. Reminded me of myself, from before. Spent every second I wasn't in the Depths with him, taught him everything I could about blacksmithing . . . not weapons out here, but shovels, pickaxes, things like that. And he got to be pretty good at it. Told me he wanted to make enough money so I could get out of the Depths, buy a house we could both live in." Ress's expression darkened. "And then this war started. After a few months soldiers from both cities started passing through . . . not many at first, but a few. One day he comes in all excited, tells me he's met someone who wants him to join up with the war back in Calarginn. Says he can make three times there what he does here; he's a strong boy, could be real useful. Could be in for half a year, maybe less, then come back and get us the house he'd always said he would."

Ress turned away. "Wasn't nothing I could say to change his mind. That was five months ago . . . ain't heard nothing from him since." He fell silent, and for a long time the only sound was the quiet crackling of the flames inside the eldur. Finally he sighed and looked at me. "So that's my angle, sir, such as it is. I ain't got any idea where Carner is. He's a smart boy, got a good head on his shoulders, so I figure he's fine. If he ain't, I . . ." He trailed off and shook his head.

"Your boy went off to fight for his native city," Kraes said. "That's an act to make a parent proud."

"I don't give a damn about Calarginn," Ress snarled, turning on Kraes so quickly that Fen took a step forward, hand on her sword hilt. "Calarginn can go straight to the Hells, and Arginn with it." Then his brow unfurrowed, and his trembling hands relaxed. "But until we get this war finished, Carner ain't coming back one way or the other." He turned to me. "Now I seen lots of men fight in my time. I seen 'em look bigger, speak louder than you. But I ain't seen anyone take down two soldiers fast as you did, then leave without asking for payment, or stealing something on the way out. People who can do what you do . . . they expect to get something for it. That makes you different. I ain't been able to find anyone in Elskeg since the captain talked to me about recruiting a couple of weeks ago . . . but you're the kind that can help. I know it."

I took another sip of water from my cup and put it down. "I told you before, Ress—and you, captain—that I'm not a soldier. I'm used to doing my work in the shadows, not the sunlight."

Kraes nodded, her eyes searching mine. "It's shadows I need right now."

Hells.

I stood, Fen watching me warily with her hand still near her sword. "Captain, I don't think you're hearing me. I'm not a peddler, wandering around the uplands looking to sell my skills to the highest bidder. I came here because Ress said you could help find some answers."

Kraes nodded again. "I didn't expect this to go only one way, but you wanted our stories, and we gave them. So, Grayshade of Cohrelle. What are you looking for?"

I paused for a moment, trying to read the intensity in her eyes. "Argoth," I said at last. "I'm looking for information about a religious sect called the Order of Argoth."

Kraes glanced at Fen, who remained silent. "We've got our share of churches in Calarginn, but I don't know about any Order of Argoth," the captain said. "It's a small religion, then?"

I smiled grimly. The idea that anyone could think of the Order as "small" wouldn't have seemed possible a few months ago. Then again, many things wouldn't have seemed possible then, and I wasn't in Cohrelle anymore. "It wasn't small to me, or Cohrelle. But things might be different elsewhere ... I don't know. That's one of the things I need to find out. And I've got my own problems to solve, Kraes, without getting tied up in a civil war. Ress, I'm sorry about your son," I said, turning to him. His expression seemed almost hungry in its desperation, and I dropped my eyes from his gaze. "I can't get sidetracked now." For a moment a thought of Caron and Rillia passed through my mind, but I dismissed it. "I wish you the best of luck, but I'm not your man." I turned, but before I could take a step I heard Fen's harsh voice.

"Tellisar," she said.

I turned back.

"They're in Tellisar," Fen went on, folding her arms. "It's where I was born—came to Calarginn when I was ten, after Ma died. But I remember Da telling me stories of some of the people he knew down at Tellisar's docks. Worked from the shadows, they did. There was a merchant, once, sold goods for shipbuilding. Everyone called him Flask ... he was good at his job, but he got drunk too much, and he spent a lot of time laughing at the "churchfolk," he called 'em. One day Da saw a couple of men in cloaks talking with Flask at the door of his shop, and it looked like trouble. Finally Flask yelled at 'em, said folks who cared more about gods than men should go to their own Hells, and slammed the door in their faces. Two nights later Da came home early from the docks, said everyone had been told to leave by the Watch, that something bad had happened. But he'd seen what they was looking at when he was going past the shop ... bunch of them clustered around something on the ground. One of them moved enough for him to see, and ..." Fen swallowed. "Flask, dead on the ground, with a bunch of metal darts in his neck."

Kushuri darts. In spite of myself I found my hand drifting toward the pouch in my cloak where I kept mine. I silently commanded it to stop.

"Now look," Fen went on. "I ain't much for sellswords or thieves, and I ain't much for people who kill so much they get used to doing it. I ain't much for *you*, come to that. But if the captain says she can use you, I trust her; and if you can help us, we'll help you. Still got friends in Tellisar ... so does she. And we'll help you find what you need to know. Maybe give Flask some justice by the way." Suddenly she seemed to notice Kraes looking at her with apparent curiosity, and her expression hardened. "It's getting late," she said, no warmth in the statement. "I've said what I will."

Kraes turned directly toward me. "Told you, Fen means what she says ... and so do I."

I pursed my lips and looked from Kraes to Fen to Ress. Of the three, Ress now held the most tension, as Fen had dropped her ready posture. Kraes sat proudly upright, like a statue in Cohrelle's Government District, but a slight shaking in her legs betrayed her fatigue. Yes, Gods knew I'd been betrayed before, by those I'd actually trusted, and my instincts told me to walk away, now, without doubt or hesitation. But there was another voice with me now as well ... a younger one.

Just because one is false doesn't mean all of them are, Caron had said before I left Cohrelle. And even as I remembered their words, I thought I saw a movement in the woods beyond the edge of the clearing—a glint, perhaps, from reflected eyes, near the ground. I blinked, and it was gone. I looked back at Ress and the two soldiers, all now watching me intently.

Swim with the flow.

I nodded. "You've got three days, captain."

Kraes took a deep breath and smiled. "I've got a war, Grayshade. If three days will help turn the tide, I'll take them, and you, gladly."

CHAPTER THREE

A floorboard creaked just inside the door, and I silently drew my cucuri. I had been standing in the shadows near the house's entrance, waiting for the last evening bell when—as he always did—the first of the guards would emerge to check the outside of the building before locking and shutting the door for the night.

I had considered using a different route to get in, but as I'd learned over the six days since receiving the target, Sharlan's counting house was no typical building. There was only one entrance, and no windows at all on the first floor; the sharply slanting roof was made of light but polished stone, making a top down entry with fly hooks difficult, and its treeless plot was set well away from other houses in the surrounding streets to prevent access from neighboring buildings. No, Sharlan was no fool; he'd made his share of enemies, and knew enough to understand that some of them would want to settle their scores with him violently and permanently. This building was designed to prevent that kind of settlement, though, unfortunately for Sharlan, not designed to prevent me. *The larger the giant, the greater the weakness.* Not Caoesthenes's most subtle advice, but I returned to it often over the years.

The doorknob turned, and the heavy wooden door opened outward, bright light from inside spilling out onto the darkened street. The guard, shortest of the four who covered the building, emerged holding a lantern in his left hand with his right hand free; after a moment he looked to his right, away from the shadows where I stood. I stepped close and raked the cucuri's hilt across the guard's skull, and without a cry he crumpled into my arms. *One down, three remaining.* Resheathing my cucuri with my free hand I shifted him to the left side of my body and crouched down, laying him carefully in the shadows before extinguishing his lantern and placing it by his motionless form. I whispered a few words into his ear, listening with satisfaction as his breathing deepened and slowed.

Jant never approved when I used this soundshifting technique, but I was pleased to have mastered it, as it was one of the most difficult to learn. The method synchronized the heartbeat and breathing at a low level, stabilizing and extending the unconscious state for several hours. Inefficient, from a certain point of view. But dead bodies were messy, and I had no need for this nondescript guard to become one. No one else would dare to approach the counting house this late at night, and it would be at least three hours before the new shift of guards arrived.

A single large key hung from his belt; probably the outer door key, which meant that one of the other guards had the keys for the upper floor. I was in no mood for complications, but I had already eliminated one guard, so the plan was in motion regardless of my mood. Undoing the key, I slipped it into the pocket on the inside of my cloak. The door was open, and all was quiet within. I slipped inside, closing the door behind me.

Sharlan wasn't known for being flamboyant, and the inside of his counting house proved the point. I'd seen more elaborate entrance halls in upscale taverns. *What's the purpose of grinding out your life for some extra coin if you don't plan to spend what you earn?* I thought, though I couldn't pretend to understand the mindset of a merchant. The space was functional, at least: two doors flanked the entrance on the inside of the building, both made of the same heavy wood as the outside portal, and one wooden hallway, covered by a long red carpet, extended perhaps fifty feet before turning to the right. There were probably hundreds of gold coins in the two showrooms, along with some of the particularly rare spices for which Sharlan, one of the most successful traders in the business, was best known, but I had no interest in money. My goal, the single name on the rolled piece of vellum in my cloak, was on the second floor, and so my path was straight down the hallway.

Well, not entirely straight. I walked slowly, scanning from floor to ceiling. Nothing seemed obviously wrong, but leaving a hallway entirely open seemed unlikely for anyone with something to protect, particularly a cautious one like Sharlan. Sensing variation, I crouched and looked down at the carpet. It was a perfect red, each thread carefully interwoven; a material this fine was probably at least a hundred gold coins a foot. "So this is where he spends the extra coin," I murmured. But then I spotted what had caught my eye: a thin white thread running horizontally across the carpet—either an odd artistic decision, or something much more practical. I assumed Sharlan would prefer the practical course, and drawing my cucuri I took several steps back, lay down flat and placed the flat of the blade on the thread. I heard two quiet whooshes of air and two nearly imperceptible *thunks* above me, and looking up I saw a small dart embedded in each wall. *Poisoned darts*, I thought while sheathing my weapon. *I'd have expected something a bit more elegant.*

The good news about deadly traps was a person usually limited them to one. With that trap now sprung and my odds back to the normal mortal peril of an unknown guarded space, I again stood, and moved steadily down the hall.

At the bend in the corridor I stopped and peered around the edge. Guard number two stood next to a wooden door at the far end of the hallway, perhaps about thirty feet away. Her arms were folded, sword hanging from her belt, and she was gazing off into space, whistling softly . . . and badly. But what mattered was her posture—unless she was much more subtle than she looked, it was obvious that she had no idea that the dart trap had been triggered. Another cheap mistake by Sharlan, who for another couple of coins could have linked the thread to an alarm bell. Instead he had spent his money on a warm body to block a door entrance . . . not a bad obstacle, if it was permanently fixed in place. But all bodies must move eventually, and none of them are any better than the minds that control them. I cleared my mind for a moment, then focused my attention on the door behind the guard and knocked on the wooden wall next to me with my right hand.

The guard started and turned to look at the door behind her, and I knocked again. She fumbled for a set of keys at her belt, picked one and opened the door inward. "Gennel? Did—" she started to say, but before she could say more I was on her with the hilt of my cucuri, and with a slight groan she slumped to the ground. *Two down, but that was careless*, I thought as I whispered into the guard's ear, waiting to hear her breath slow before pulling her body back out of the door opening; a groan like that could have gotten me killed if the odds were worse.

Caoesthenes often said I was too enamored with my sound-shifting tricks and not in tune enough with my basic skills, and it was true . . . I tend to think creatively. I could have probably done the job with a simple bait and hit, but I didn't want to take the chance of warning anyone else nearby—though that was almost what happened anyway.

I slipped inside the door and closed it silently, leaving the guard's unconscious body on the other side. I made my way up the stairs, moving diagonally from one step's side to the next to avoid any traps (and noise) in the middle, and paused at the top. To my left was a wooden door much like the one at the foot of the stairs; to my right, a hallway extended out a few feet and then turned left, probably leading to the main counting room. As it seemed a logical place to look and did not require the potential warning of opening a door, I turned right. I backed against the wall just before the turn and risked a glance around the corner to see guard number three walking down the hallway, lantern in hand and sword at his belt. I ducked back and quickly moved to the staircase, descending a few steps and flattening myself against the wall in the shadows.

A few seconds later the guard appeared at the top of the stairs. He tried the door, nodded when he was sure it was locked and then checked the darkened staircase. After a moment he frowned. "Now why . . ." he muttered, but his voice trailed off and he shook his head. He stepped onto the first stair and raised his lantern high, and as he saw me his eyes widened—but my reshtar had already hit him, and I caught his lantern as he slid onto the steps unconscious. I pulled him onto the landing and waited as my whisper slowed his breath.

Three down, I thought as I retrieved and replaced the reshtar inside my cloak. *Too easy*. And it was too easy . . . something was wrong. I plan every job down to the smallest detail, but everyone in my line of work knows that something always happens that you hadn't anticipated . . . and if it hasn't, it will. Here everything had gone off exactly as planned, without a whisper of trouble, excluding one small groan that my own error had caused. I extinguished the lantern and set it carefully next to the guard's motionless form, then took two keys from the ring at his belt and stepped over him as I moved back down the hallway.

The door at the end was made of metal, not wood, and had two locks—very showy, but not particularly useful, especially when one guard carries both keys. I slid both in and turned them at the same time, and with a slight creak the door swung inward. It was indeed the master counting room, fairly large though not well furnished; a large desk stood near the back wall, a large wooden chest to its side. And standing next to the bed, crossbow drawn and pointed directly at my chest, was the fourth and final guard—his mask, as it had been for the past few days while I had reconnoitered, was down, covering his face.

"That's pretty good," the guard's muffled voice said after what seemed like an eternity of strained silence. "It's been a while since anyone's gotten in here." He shifted his weight and gave a short chuckle. "But I've been telling the boss to shore things up anyway. He should've had a couple more guards posted . . . but he's kinda cheap, you know?" I remained silent, looking at him steadily, and he laughed again. "Guess you finished off Gennel and the rest of 'em, huh? That's a shame . . . but hey, leastways now I won't have to pay him the money I owed him."

"I didn't kill them," I said, never taking my eyes from the mask.

"No?" the guard said, sounding a little uncertain. "Sounds kinda sloppy. What if they got away and raised the alarm?"

"They won't," I replied.

The guard tilted his head a bit. "Pretty sure of yourself, ain't you?" he asked, and I shrugged.

"Sometimes."

He sighed. "Eh, makes no difference anyways. Saves me some cleanup if they're not really dead, so I guess I should thank you. Too bad I'll have to pay Gennel after all, but maybe the bonus for gettin' rid of you right here'll make up for it."

Something clicked inside my head at that. "No . . . no, I don't think it will."

"Why not?" he replied. The finger on the trigger tightened almost imperceptibly.

I smiled. "One, because you won't be getting rid of me tonight. Or any other time, for that matter. My fate is in the hands of the gods." And I kneeled, clasping my hands together.

He laughed again. "I don't think a prayer's gettin' you out of here, friend."

I looked up. "I wasn't praying for me," I said, and whipped my palms up and outward.

Nothing happened. I stared for a moment, jaw open; I had thrown all my kushuri darts . . . or thought I had. But nothing emerged from my hands.

Grayshade.

I jerked my head to the right, but the whisper hadn't come from there. It was inside my mind, somewhere.

Grayshade. Beware the hunter.

The guard chuckled and pushed back his mask. Sharlan himself, of course. "Well, you should have been praying for yourself, thief. You won't get the chance now." He raised his crossbow slightly higher.

But—but this isn't how it—

The hunter in the shadows, Grayshade. Watch the shadows!

I looked around wildly as Sharlan's laugh grew louder and louder, suddenly so loud it felt like I was standing next to a waterfall. And from behind Sharlan, I suddenly saw fierce yellow eyes, racing toward me—so fast I couldn't—

The shadows!

I heard the crossbow twang.

———————◆———————

I sat up suddenly, heart pounding, ready to spring ... and saw there was nothing there. It was dim inside the tent, the tent where I had been led last night after agreeing to help Kraes and the Calarginnians, and I could just see the sliver of morning light through the unsealed flaps.

A dream. Sharlan was still dead, and I was still alive.

But that dream wasn't the way things had happened. Making my way into the counting house, yes; eliminating the guards one by one, yes. But in the end I had killed Sharlan, who had indeed been posing as one of his guards in his typically paranoid way. In fact, it was the ease of that mission which had triggered my questions, questions about the Service, the Order ... and eventually, Argoth himself. It was that mission which had begun the chain of events leading me into Silarein in the first place. And the yellow eyes—what were those?

Nightmares are nightmares, I reminded myself, wiping my damp forehead and looking briefly at the sweat on my fingertips, glistening in the sliver of light coming from the tent flap; *they have no dominion over the land of the living.* But I was lying to myself. I had seen what was—or what wasn't—in the Repository below the Cathedral, and I knew well enough that nightmares never stayed in the land of dreams. The only permanent answer was to escape the worlds of sleep and waking altogether ... and I had sworn I would never sink again to that level of despair.

For a moment I thought of Rillia, her face gazing at mine as I lay on my back, bleeding, in the Repository.

No. No, I won't give up.

I crawled out of the tent, eyes blinking as the bright morning light hit them, and made my way through the trees, to the clearing where we had met last night. The circle was empty, with only the now dark and silent eldur as a sign of the gathering. But without the sounds of the evening and the eldur, I now heard something new—trickling, gurgling water, and not far off. Getting to my feet, I followed the sound past the edge of the clearing and down a shallow slope, lightly wooded, to a small brook. It was narrow but fast moving, and as I bent down and scooped up a handful of water I was surprised how cold it was; too far from the Glacalta to come from there, so perhaps from the southern mountains— or maybe through underground passages and concealed natural aqueducts. Who can say how long a path can stretch? I splashed some on my face, skin tingling from the cold, and drank several handfuls, gazing into the whirls and eddies of the stream.

"You won't get better water this side of Calarginn," a voice said not far away, and I looked up in mid-drink to see Captain Venner Kraes sitting easily on the far bank of the brook, sword and scabbard leaning on a tree root next to her, her hair pulled down from the knot. She regarded me steadily.

"I'm glad to hear it," I replied, straightening up. "Fresh water isn't one of Elskeg's virtues."

Kraes snorted. "Not many virtues to be found in Elskeg, period."

"Yet for some reason," I said, settling back into a seated position, "you seem to think this is an important enough place to be doing secret recruiting missions here."

The captain nodded. "Aye. But that's more about the war than about a group of huts they've got the stones to call a town." She looked off to her left, down where the flowing brook disappeared again among the trees, and was silent for a time. "The truth is," she finally said as she looked back at me, "things haven't been going our way for several months now. I don't talk about it in front of the others—and if you tell them I said so later, I'll deny it and settle up with you personally—but this isn't just about recruiting soldiers. It's about resources."

I nodded slowly.

"Can't fight a war without weapons," she went on. "You need swords, and more: axes, armor, shoes for the horses, nails for the wagons and carts . . . it goes on. You need material, and you need metal."

"And Calarginn doesn't have any?"

"Not enough," Kraes responded grimly. "Our leverage was the basin, the farmland; northerners have to eat like anyone else. But farmland doesn't hold up against steel, when someone's priorities change. It's one of the reasons the city hasn't gotten into a fight with Arginn before. They're on the northern side of the Glacalta, not far from the southern edge of the Scales ... plenty of metal and raw ore to be found there, even if it's a bit dangerous to get at. And what they don't get they can buy from Tellisar, which is happy to sell it at a profit."

"I thought Tellisar was neutral. Wouldn't they be just as happy to sell things to Calarginn?"

"Met a few weapon dealers, have you?" Kraes chuckled darkly. "Fen'll tell you that Tellisar's wanted Arginn to win since the beginning. 'Course Fen's the most suspicious bastard I've ever met, and she's as loyal to Calarginn as they come. But there's something to what she says, all the same ... since Arginn and Sullbris are on the northern side of the Glacalta with Tellisar, it can keep an eye on them. Calarginn's the only city on the southern side, and Tellisar doesn't like the view. If Calarginn loses the war—not just signs a treaty and pays a tribute and stops fighting, but really loses, so Arginn takes over with Tellisar running the game—then Tellisar not only gets control of both sides of the Glacalta, it gets the basin, along with a free path to the mountains south and east. Hells, maybe it builds a road straight to Cohrelle."

"So it's up to Calarginn," I said.

Kraes sighed and looked away again. "Aye, that's about the shape of it. Arginn's got more money, more ore ... more of everything than we do. They've taken over the shipping routes, destroyed most of our ships. Only thing we've been able to count on is the material coming from the south, from the mines here . . . especially the Depths. There's your Elskeg virtue." She laughed unhappily, then was silent for a time before continuing. "A couple of months ago we got word that Arginnian soldiers had been seen out east—patrolling the mountains, showing up in Elskeg. We haven't been able to keep them on their side of the Glacalta for months, but this was a lot further than they'd ever gone before, and it didn't take long for us to put two and two together." She looked back at me. "They're after the Depths. If they get control of it, and we're cut off . . ." She shook her head. "Then we might as well start calling ourselves Arginnians. So my commander sent me here—not just to recruit, and keep as many as we can from joining the other side, but to figure out a way to keep the Depths in our hands, any way we can. Whatever it takes."

I nodded. *By any means necessary* was a concept I understood all too well. "Why not tell your people?"

Kraes shook her head again, leaning forward and idly flicking at the flowing water with a stick. "No reason for them to know how badly things are going. Some of them suspect anyway . . . Fen most of all, but she doesn't say anything. It doesn't make a difference to what they need to do, anyway: disrupt the Arginnians as much as possible."

I frowned. "Then you don't need me as a recruit."

Kraes looked at me seriously, running a hand through her brown hair and rubbing the back of her neck. "Not to fight Arginnians, no, I don't. I need you to do something we can't." She paused and looked around for a second before returning her gaze to me. "Two weeks ago we heard rumors of an advance squadron somewhere nearby—not just a patrol, but a squadron. If I had to guess, that's where the two soldiers you taught a lesson came from; it would explain why we've seen so many of the Arginnians around Elskeg without an obvious flow coming from the south. But we haven't been able to find the camp, and I don't have the people to spare for reconnaissance. And even if I did, if those people got caught and had the information about where we are tortured out of them, well . . . that'd be the last chance for Calarginn gone."

"You need me to scout a camp?" I said, incredulous.

The captain's mouth twitched, then broke into a crooked grin. "Oh, I need you to do more than scout it. I need you to sabotage it."

My frown deepened. "What?"

"Well, or at least break it up as best you can. My guess is that if we wipe it out or put a serious dent in it, we'll throw off the Arginnians' plans for this area enough to keep them out of commission here for months. If all I can buy here is time, then I'll do it. Maybe by then the war will have changed in our favor."

I shook my head. "Kraes, I don't think you understand what I do—what I did. My job was to deal with individual targets, not large groups. I'm no saboteur . . . certainly not of military camps."

"You weren't one before," Kraes replied. "But if what Ress says is right, and my own guess about you is true, you can easily be one now."

I stood and set my mouth in a firm line. "No. I didn't sign up to risk my life on things I have no expertise in doing."

Kraes reknotted her hair with a quick motion, then got to her feet slowly, her eyes fixed on mine. "You signed up to do whatever

I needed you to do, for three days, in exchange for information. If you still want that information, you'll honor our agreement."

Hells.

"Why me?"

The captain maintained her gaze for a while before replying. "First, because my people aren't trackers. Second ... because you're not us. You're an outsider—not from Calarginn, or Arginn, or even Tellisar. You're an unknown, and that's just what I need."

Ideals matter. But ideals are realized through practical actions. Forget the second, and you'll never get the first. It was a line of Father Jant's, from one of his lectures many years ago, but I hadn't thought about it for a long time—until now, when the sentiment seemed most clear. I nodded slowly. "It's not finding them you need. It's disposability. If I'm caught, you can deny I had anything to do with you. And if I'm killed, you don't have to care."

Kraes nodded. "Nothing personal."

"It never is."

"I'm not asking for miracles, Grayshade," Kraes said, picking up her scabbard from the tree against which it was leaning and buckling it around her waist. "I just need you to find that camp— if it even exists—do what you can to shut it down, and report back as soon as you can."

"And that's all?"

"I think that's enough."

But it wasn't—not quite. "Kraes," I said as she turned her attention back to me. "I know why Ress wanted me involved. But why are you doing this? What's driving you?"

Kraes looked puzzled. "The same thing as you. I'm trying to help the people I care about. Calarginn isn't much, but it's ours, and I'll be damned if I'll let Arginn take it over, or let Tellisar pick up what's left when we're done cutting each other to pieces." She sighed and looked up the brook, toward the spot where it first curved into view. "I don't have much beyond my city and my people to fight for, Grayshade. Never had a spouse or child . . . never had many friends to speak of either, and not much chance to find any, always on patrol or out beyond the city borders." She looked back at me, her expression suddenly fierce. "But I've got my soldiers, and they've got their love for Calarginn . . . and me, because I love it, and them. That's what drives me, and always will." She placed her hand on the hilt of her sword, not a threat but a promise of will put into action, and lifted her chin proudly.

Devotion. How many times had I seen it on the faces of Acolytes . . . or those which Acolytes were asked to kill? How many times had I felt it myself, now replaced with only the empty, aching near-certainty of nothingness?

Near-certainty. That was the problem, and the grace: that I wasn't wholly sure of anything anymore . . . even my own doubts. I bent down to the brook and lowered my hand into the flowing water one last time, then stood and faced Captain Kraes.

"Tell me what you know."

CHAPTER FOUR

I hadn't expected to have much of a lead on the Arginnian camp, and in that regard I wasn't disappointed. Kraes wasn't able to add much more to what she'd already told me; at first I couldn't understand how an entire Arginnian squadron could go unnoticed by the residents of Elskeg, but then it occurred to me that Kraes's company had also been largely unnoticed for weeks. And it made some sense: most people in Elskeg were either too busy trying to survive, or spending their off-hours trying to forget they were, to notice an uptick in the number of soldiers from one city or another, or wonder much about it if they did. What lone miner or innkeeper would go tracking down soldiers who weren't already part of Kraes's group?

Still, a squadron is a squadron, and the Greenmark was already occupied. There weren't any other forested areas nearby large enough to conceal a military group of any real size, so that meant they were either in the mountains near the Depths—unlikely, given the difficulty of keeping a supply line open—or . . . where? Concealed in the barns and haystacks of the farms in the uplands? There was only one way to know for certain . . . and at least this was something I *had* been trained to do.

That's how I found myself back outside The Mountain's Heart less than two days after I had . . . disrupted it, concealed in the shadows next to the closed town hall across the street as the hours crept toward midnight. As far as I could tell the incident from several nights before hadn't attracted undue attention; no doubt Rannik and Kester were none too happy at the humiliation they'd received, but I'd dealt with enough soldiers in the past to know that the only thing most of them liked less than being humiliated was letting others know about it. They'd find a way to make life miserable for Ress eventually, but not in the time I would need. In the meantime, there were other Arginnians in need of a drink.

Several hours had passed already—I was just starting to wonder if I might have misjudged the soldiers' thirst—when the tavern's front door creaked open, and a man wearing leather armor and an Arginnian tunic of green and gold exited a little unsteadily, humming something to himself. *Good: drunk but not utterly soused.* Now the critical question ... would he wander down to The Fan and Feather, or head home to sleep off the ale? I drew further back into the shadows as the man looked around, adjusting the scabbard at his waist, before moving off down the street. Allowing for a bit of distance, I left my hiding place and began following, slipping from shadow to shadow. I began to worry as he approached the end of the street, heading more or less straight for The Fan and Feather, but before he reached the building he veered off to the left and out of sight down the small street. I picked up my pace and arrived at the corner just in time to see the soldier vanishing at the end of the side street ... a direction which would lead him out of Elskeg. With a quick check to make sure I had not been noticed, I drew my hood further up and followed.

The soldier took an uneven but relatively straight course to the west, passing through the moonlit, rocky land surrounding Elskeg to the grass and scrub brush beyond, as Ress had when taking us to the Greenmark. But this path bent steadily further to the south until we were heading more toward the mountains than the forest, and soon enough I could tell that our destination was going to be some distance from where Kraes's people were stationed.

The soldier's pace was slow but steady, and as bits of his humming and singing continued to drift back to me he seemed in no particular distress ... he obviously wasn't concerned about the possibility of being followed. Was Arginn so confident of its own position in the war that it wasn't concerned about discovery? Then again, maybe they had their own protocols I didn't yet fully understand. But as my mark stumbled, sending a spray of pebbles into the surrounding bushes, I thought of a much simpler answer: *Ale has a way of reducing proper caution no matter what the circumstances.*

We continued in this way for a half hour or so, the evening sounds of clicking insects and the occasional distant howl of a wolf interspersed with the soldier's relentlessly upbeat singing, which grew louder as we continued. The land grew even drier and more barren, the scrub brush gradually disappearing, and soon we were heading for a kind of rocky outcropping—not high enough to be a mountain or even a hill, but isolated enough to stand out from the rest of the landscape. The path we were following began to descend, so that we would shortly be passing below the outcropping. I grew so intent in peering at the overhanging rock that I almost didn't see my mark stopping; when I did realize, I quickly stopped and lowered to the ground, letting my cloak cover me. He seemed to be talking to someone I hadn't seen, and I was confused for a moment before understanding that the other person was below him, presumably on the descending path. As the conversation continued I crawled forward and to the left, making my way to a spot behind a large rock which likely rolled down from the nearby outcropping.

" . . . not much of one, anyway," a rough voice was saying as the conversation became clearer. I leaned around the left side of the rock and saw a man in leather helm, with shield on his back and sword at his belt, talking to the one I had followed, who was swaying unsteadily from side to side. "You heard the captain, same as I did."

"Come on, Sharrik," my mark said. "Who's to know? It's a bell before midnight . . . whole camp's asleep . . ."

"I'm not."

"Might as well be," the Arginnian replied. "What in the Hells are we guarding here, Sharrik? Rocks? Ain't seen anything larger than a rabbit outside'a that dungheap. And what about them? You scared of a few dirt-eaters?"

"There's more around here than Elskeg, Kelless," Sharrik said with a scowl. "You heard the rumors about the Calarginnians, same as I did."

Kelless laughed harshly. "Aye, phantoms and shadows. All we been hearing for the last six weeks is be ready to move, orders could come any time, no telling when the attack's going to begin . . . pheh." He spat and shook his head. "Just stuff to keep us wound up, Sharrik."

Sharrik grunted. "You saw Kester and Rannik. Bruises seemed real enough to me."

"Sure, from a 'man in a gray cloak,'" Kelless said, tone mocking. "A man in a gray cloak no one's ever seen, no one's ever heard of, but somehow took down two men, trained and armed and ready. I've heard better stories between the sheets. Truth is they lost a fight with that old dirt-eater, or maybe the barkeep, and don't want to admit it . . . and so they make up children's tales instead."

Sharrik shrugged. "Either way it's got the captain on edge, and I'm with her about that. Don't need any more distractions until we get this thing started, and you'll need your energy then—we won't get a break until it's done."

"And so we sit here and rot until she gives the word."

"That's what you do." He waved an arm in Kelless' direction. "What you smell like, too. And you better go sleep it off. Word is we'll be moving soon . . . maybe by the morning."

"Oh?" Kelless said, sounding surprised. "That's more than I've heard."

"Too busy listening to the barkeep tell you what a fine soldier you are, then. Stay out against orders and you miss things."

"Come on, Sharrik, I—"

Sharrik shook his head and raised a hand for silence. "No, Kelless. I looked the other way last week when you stumbled in past time, and I ain't doing it again. This is your last. Now come on; the captain finds you here, she'll set you to breaking rocks for the next week, and you'll miss our little jaunt to Greenmark. Now, go on." He ushered Kelless along, who continued his string of pleas and complaints as they went. As they descended out of sight, I could see dim lights twinkling in the distance beyond them—torches or lanterns, probably, and more than a few.

I leaned back behind the rock and took a deep breath. *The*

Greenmark. Hells. Kraes's existence hadn't been as secret as she thought it was, then, and Arginn's game wasn't as subtle as she believed either; they were going to strike Kraes's company directly, and with a full division of their own . . . well, it wouldn't be much of a fight.

All right, then: what are the options? I could get back to warn Kraes if I went now. But if the division was that close to moving out, the camp would be a hive of activity within a few hours, perhaps four at the most, and any hope I'd have of infiltrating it unnoticed would be not just gone, but irrelevant. Kraes could move her people, perhaps . . . but where? And even if she could find a new base of operations, Arginn would have seized control of the Depths.

Damn it all to the lowest Hells. This was exactly why I shouldn't have gotten involved in a situation the details of which I didn't know beforehand. Had I just left Ress behind that night, I could have made my way to Tellisar on my own. But of course, I wouldn't have known I was going to the right place, or had access to Fen's contacts.

Suddenly I remembered Caron's face, expression serious. *"My teachers say that two things define a person: who they think they are, and who they want to be,"* they had said, gazing at me calmly while I lay in bed recovering from injuries both physical and spiritual. *"A few people understand both things. They accept who they are and imagine who they want to be."*

Then I pictured Ress's face. The haunted, hungry expression in Ress's eyes when he begged for my help was an expression I had seen too many times in my life.

An expression I had caused, more often than not.

I unclenched my hand from my hilt, and sat back, breathing against the boulder's side. The best option I could see involved disrupting any attack before it began . . . and that meant doing it now, before the camp was roused. I was working in the dark, but I was used to that. *Reconnaissance first, then . . . probably from the top of that bluff.* I shook my head, then turned.

Fiercely yellow-green eyes—animal eyes—greeted me. Only a few feet away, regarding me calmly as it stood on four paws, was a sleek, lithe panther, its black fur blending into the deep shadow of the rock.

For a long moment I did nothing, letting my hand drift back to my cucuri. I didn't know how prevalent panthers were in this part of Silarein; I had only seen one in person once . . . many years before, during a festival celebrating the founding of Cohrelle. But that one had been half-starved and small, still some years from adulthood, and it had been caged. This one was a full-size adult, and it was very much free . . . and, as I took in the rippling muscles along its side as it stretched its front paws, very healthy. I had never killed a panther, and animals generally weren't in my line. But if I had intended to fight one, I would have taken more time to search for weaknesses, consider the best possible approach . . . not taken it on in the wilderness, my back to a large rock, my escape routes a steep bluff above and an enemy camp below. Yet here I was. I had fought larger, more deadly beasts before, but not ones I couldn't outrun. Here, I could either stand my ground and fight, or try to run and brace for the feeling of the creature dragging me down from behind as I tried to flee.

"All right, then," I said quietly, keeping my eyes fixed on the panther, which had neither moved nor shifted its gaze—which, despite my situation, I found fascinating. The yellow outer rims of its unblinking eyes set off the green irises within, surrounding the deep, almost fathomless blackness of its pupils. *Animals are animals*, I reminded myself; *don't assign them human motivations and instincts.* Yet I felt ... an intelligence, somehow, a regard beyond simple hunger or fear or a play for dominance. The panther was watching me. Waiting for a reaction.

"So ... who moves first?" I said, keeping my voice low, shifting my weight to the balls of my feet in preparation for a spring. "You pounce and I defend? Or am I supposed to attack first?" The panther tilted its head slightly, as if it was listening, but otherwise remained motionless. After a long moment I shook my head, swallowing despite my dry throat. "Whatever you're planning, I can't wait for it to happen. Jump now and get it over with, if you're going to." But the panther still did nothing, continuing to gaze at me in motionless silence.

I should have been annoyed by the delay, but something about the panther's calmness kept my reaction muted. For many years I too had made a living out of steady, unbroken patience. Would I have answered a mark's request for action any more than the panther was answering mine?

We stayed that way for at least a minute, gazing at each other. Finally I sighed. "You win; I'll move first. If that gives you the advantage, so be it." I slid to my right slowly, then gradually stood, my hand still on the hilt of my cucuri. The panther remained stationary, tilting its head upward to keep its eyes firmly on mine. After another moment I took another step to my right, then another, and then turned so I could keep the path rising toward the bluff behind me, with the panther in front. I took several careful steps backward, feeling the rising ground beneath my feet, while the panther stayed where it was. But as I turned again and began to ascend, still watching the panther over my shoulder, I saw it pad forward a few steps. I stopped immediately—and, as if it were tied to me like a string to a puppet, it stopped as well. I stepped forward again; it followed at the same distance, then stopped as I did. And we continued this dance for a minute or more as I tried to make my way up the hill.

Finally I halted and turned to face the panther. "This is an odd way to hunt," I said. "But I can't have you follow me everywhere, whether you intend to attack me or not." The panther, predictably, said nothing, and as I looked at its impassive face I smiled in spite of myself. Six months ago, had someone told me I would soon be in Silarein, trying to win a bizarre dance with a panther so I could return to scouting enemy camps on behalf of a foreign city, I would have laughed and left them to their ale. Yet here I was, trying to do just that. To swim with the flow.

I waited for a moment . . . and then, letting impulse drive me, turned and sprinted up the hill. My pursuer hadn't been dissuaded by caution, after all; perhaps surprise and speed might cause it to hesitate. Yet even as I ran I knew how foolish I was being; how often would a predatory animal be taken off guard by its prey suddenly bolting? And what if I ran straight into an Arginnian guard at the top of the bluff? Still, I continued my run for a minute or more without looking back, tracing my way through low grass and rocks, until I had almost reached the summit of the hill. Slowing to a jog, then a fast walk, I walked the last hundred steps or so to the top of the bluff and stopped to catch my breath, turning to look behind me.

There, padding calmly to within about twenty feet of me before stopping, was the panther.

I smiled again. I could hardly have expected anything different, but I still found myself admiring the persistence of the creature, its calm eyes still set on mine. "So, I have a shadow," I said, lowering myself to one knee. "Where did you spring from, then? And what exactly do you find so interesting about me?"

The panther lowered its rear haunches into a sitting position and, looking away from me for the first time since I had seen it, began to lick its wide paw almost casually, carefully combing its tongue in a pattern along the sleek fur. By its build, it was probably a male, and obviously a particularly unflappable one. I watched it for a time as it groomed itself, then shook my head and turned back to the business at hand; if it wasn't interested in attacking me, it didn't seem particularly interested in leaving me behind either, at least at the moment. Over time it would, presumably, lose interest. In the meantime I had work to do.

I turned away, lowered myself to a prone position, and crawled forward to the edge of the bluff. In my experience even veteran guards seldom looked above them—threats, they incorrectly believed, always came from ground level—but I didn't want to take any chances, especially in an open environment where I had much less practice. After a few seconds I reached the edge and cautiously peered over.

Over a hundred feet below me lay most of the Arginnian camp, lit partially by the rising moon and partially by lanterns hanging from poles set at regular intervals on paths snaking among perhaps a hundred tents. Here and there a guard holding a lantern wandered, and in several spots two guards spoke quietly to each other. The order to pack up and move had obviously not been given yet, but as I took in the scene my heart sank just the same. Even though the camp wasn't massive, there wasn't any obvious entry point clear of the guards ... and no obvious way of taking down most of the soldiers at once. Judging by the size of each tent, I assumed two people could sleep in each one, which meant I was probably dealing with much more than the squadron Kraes had suspected—more like a division, probably close to two hundred soldiers. I could fight three, five, maybe ten at once ... but I wasn't a god, and taking on hundreds was certain suicide. Perhaps disruption? But there, too, I was at a loss. What rapid, undetected act would disrupt a group of this size? Seal up the openings to each tent and hope no one slept with their knives?

Hells, I cursed under my breath. What I needed most was what I couldn't have: time, at least a few days to create a plan of action. *Some well-placed explosives in particular spots could have an effect; they must have supplies down there, and oil for their lanterns which would light up nicely. If I could observe the shift changes with the guards, map their patrol patterns, follow one or two of them who might get too far from the rest of the camp and force them to give me more information ...* I sighed. I had no time for any of this; I had to come up with something within the next few hours. My only chance was—

And then I felt a tickling sensation on my throat, something cold and sharp barely brushing the surface of the skin.

"On your feet, spy," a rough voice said.

I slowly shifted my body and turned my head to look over my shoulder, my chin tilted upward to accommodate the edge of the blade held right below my neck. There, standing slightly behind me and to my left, was an Arginnian soldier, slightly bent over as she held her long sword at my throat; the panther was gone. There was a lantern on the ground some distance away, but with the moonlight the soldier hardly needed it—and the bobbing light of a lantern would have warned me. Assuming I had noticed anything at all, given my stupid focus on the camp without any care for my surroundings.

"Stand up, I said," she repeated in her gravelly voice, lifting the blade slightly to force my chin higher. I slowly, carefully got to my feet and turned to face her as the soldier, cloaked and armored in leather but with neither helmet nor hood, watched me warily. She was a bit shorter and probably younger than me, but the way she held her sword and the appearance of her sheared hair, flecked, like mine, with spots of gray, indicated this was not her first campaign. For a moment we regarded each other steadily.

"Looks like a bit of sleeplessness from time to time isn't all bad," she said finally. "Thought I'd give the overlook a sweep, and I'm glad I did. And as for you … you don't have the air of Calarginn, but the Gods only know where they're finding their spies these days. Speak; it's the last chance you'll get."

"What would you have me say?" I replied, noting the slight tension in her right hand as she held the sword firmly.

The soldier chuckled. "You can start with your name—and then, who sent you here. We'll get to why you're here in a moment."

"The name is Grayshade," I said. "As for who sent me here—no one. I work for myself."

The soldier laughed again. "So you just found our camp on your own, decided to watch it for a while, and then … what? Paint a picture?"

I smiled thinly. "Something like that."

Her smile faded quickly. "You lie poorly for a spy. Someone sent you here, and it wasn't by accident. You're going to tell me who it was." She lifted her blade slightly, forcing me to raise my chin in response, and I became uncomfortably aware of the nearness of the cliff's edge behind me.

Hells, I thought. *She knows I'm in no position to negotiate.* And it was my doing; Caoesthenes had taught me long ago that one mistake leads to many, and my survey of the camp and the encounter with the panther had caused me to let down my guard. Now I was going to pay the price. "From where do you get your authority?" I asked, trying to buy some time while I thought of a plan. "This isn't Arginnian territory."

"It will be soon enough," she replied with a smirk. "Until then, it isn't anyone else's territory either, and with all of this space, there's plenty of room for all."

"Unless they're from Calarginn, I suppose."

The soldier scowled and took a step forward, still holding her blade at my throat, making me take a step back in response. I was probably only three or four paces from the cliff's edge now. "Sounds like someone working for Calarginn . . . or paid by them," she said, eyes narrowed. "Unless you're planning on learning to fly in the next sixty seconds, I'd think about coming clean. Who sent you? What were you doing here? Who else was with you?"

I tried to chuckle to throw her off, but the steadily rising blade and the angle of my chin made any acting difficult. "You're not making this much of a conversation, friend," I said, stepping back again. I could feel the empty space behind me, the slight breeze coming from below swirling my cloak around my ankles, anticipating the imminent fall.

"It's not a conversation," the soldier said grimly.

"Do you always do interrogations on the top of cliffs?" I asked, trying to maintain my balance at the bluff's edge. "Shouldn't you be bringing me to your captain?"

She chuckled. "I will when we're done here. But she's sleeping right now, and might prefer you dead anyway. Last chance: who sent you, and what were you doing here?" She took another step forward, and I slid back, feeling my right heel extend over the cliff's edge. I had no room to maneuver; leap backward, left, or right to certain death, or forward onto a blade.

Then I saw, out of the corner of my eye, a dark blur on the edge of the cliff to my right, closing fast.

"You're out of chances," the Arginnian said, drawing herself up and beginning to move her blade back for a strike.

"So are you," I said, unsmiling.

I only had time to see her eyes widen slightly before the black blur collided with her left side, knocking her from her feet and the blade from her hand. My cucuri was already out as she hit the ground, and in a second I was on her. Reversing the cucuri I raked the hilt across her head, and her eyes rolled back as she fell back and lay motionless.

With my whisper complete, I lifted my head to see the panther silently regarding me, its impassive demeanor seemingly undisturbed.

Signs are found in the deepest shadows, Caoesthenes had once told me, *and lessons from the most inscrutable texts.* Deep shadows, inscrutable texts, and a mysterious panther as my teacher: no doubt the old man would have been amused. And pleased.

"Caoesthenes," I said to the panther as a thought suddenly came to me. "Caoes. You're trying to teach me something, and you're choosing to enter the chaos of my world; you better have a name that fits."

Caoes said nothing, lowering himself onto his haunches and licking along his shoulder; and so it was settled.

CHAPTER FIVE

I didn't know the exact paths or frequency of the Arginnian patrols, but I was fortunate that the guard had said she wasn't on duty when she found me up on the bluff; if patrols weren't scheduled, one probably wouldn't be back tonight. This made some sense; the narrowness of the single path to the spot where I lay watching the camp below would make any group larger than perhaps five or six people impossible to conceal. And a group that size, even one with the full resources of the Service of Argoth, would have a hard time inflicting damage on a military camp from this distance, even with explosives. So the primary reason to send guards would be to assess the camp's layout, or sweep for the occasional anomaly.

Of course, this was precisely my advantage and my problem; I had a comprehensive view of the site, but couldn't do any damage from this distance either. I could lie here, watching the guards with their lights circle around the camp until the order came to pack up and they noticed one of their people was missing, or I could enter the camp and do something to disrupt it. I still had no idea what that "something" was, but I wasn't going to get any further up here. The only chance was to hope something presented itself when I got into the camp. I'd have to improvise, with no script and no instructions, just whatever I could pick up on the ground.

I sighed, pushing myself up and shifting into a sitting position. "This isn't how I do things," I said to Caoes, who was stretched out with his head between his paws, next to the unconscious, bound soldier. The panther merely blinked his yellow eyes at me, and I shook my head in a mixture of mild irritation and amusement. "I suppose you think I owe you some thanks for your help with her," I said, nodding toward the woman. "You have it, even if I don't understand why you've decided to throw your lot in with me. Believe me, I'm not worth the risk." It struck me again how quiet Caoes was . . . panthers weren't mute, as far as I knew, but this one seemed abnormally silent. Yet in some ways it fit the scene; the wind blowing and the occasional distant cry of a wolf was not silence, but I still felt surrounded by a calming peace.

I was also, unfortunately, surrounded by light . . . specifically moonlight, from yet another cloudless sky. This area of Silarein seldom seemed to have any clouds at all, at least at night . . . good for the beauty of the country, not so good for the actions of an assassin. The moon had been full several days before, and was now in its two week journey to darkness . . . but that still meant plenty of illumination, even without the torches in the camp below. Still, the moon was now past the midway point of the sky. Dawn was probably four or five hours away, and with it preparations to move the camp; the moon would probably dip below the horizon within two hours. That gave me around two hours, more or less, to maneuver with some cover. It was still a fool's errand . . . but if I was a fool, I preferred to be a living one by the end of the night.

I rose and placed a few chikchaks in a wide circle around us, placing their partner stones on the ground closer to where I would rest. Between them and the panther, I would have enough warning even if I was wrong about the frequency of the patrols. "So we wait," I said to Caoes as I sat back down. "You're determined to stay with me in the meantime, I suppose?" Caoes yawned in reply, unmoving, and I gazed at his face. He couldn't be particularly old . . . there was no gray around his muzzle, and his muscle tone was firm. But there was something more mature about him too, a kind of steadiness of demeanor which comes from experience. How many winters could he have seen? And what had led him to me?

I pulled a small pouch from an inner pocket of my cloak and opened it, pulling forth several strips of cured beef. I tossed one to Caoes, whose head snapped up at the last possible moment, mouth open, and almost casually snatched the meat from the air. He chewed it quickly and swallowed before slowly lowering his head to the ground again, and I chuckled. "Perhaps you do come from the shadows, but you eat like anybody else," I said, taking a bite from my strip. I chewed, then swallowed quickly and spoke as a thought occurred to me: "You won't be able to come with me into the camp, you know. I'll have a difficult enough time on my own without having to worry about an animal."

Caoes did not stir, and as I took another bite of jerky and studied his stolid expression I wondered again what instinct was driving him to befriend me, at least for the moment. What I knew of panthers made them out to be solitary creatures, even when it came to being with their own kind; other than in traveling circuses which were as cruel to their animal inhabitants as the Order had been to me, panthers didn't associate with humans at all. Yet here a panther had not only stayed with me, he had quite probably saved my life. Why any animal would do that, without outside guidance . . .

I stopped mid-chew. *Guidance*. Was this creature actually serving someone else? In Cohrelle there had been rumors of rituals allowing one to bond with an animal, to connect with it so completely that the person could see and feel what the animal saw and did. It would explain his odd fascination with me, to be sure, and I had seen enough strange things in my time not to dismiss this as a possibility. But still, it wasn't likely; I had never actually confirmed this animal bond, and there were enough charlatans and con men operating in Cohrelle that truth was at a premium. And Caoes didn't seem obviously under the influence of anything else. "As if I'd know," I muttered before continuing to chew half-heartedly, watching as Caoes's eyes slowly drooped and closed. I considered: perhaps I could take the chance to knock him out now, but I didn't know how my soundshifting techniques would work on an animal, and … I couldn't do it to a creature who had just saved me. That left me with more variables I couldn't control or explain … an uncertain situation becoming worse.

Perhaps that had been the problem all along, though: desiring control over situations I couldn't possibly plan out in their entirety. In a way, the Service's greatest weakness had always been its predictability, its obsession with rules and procedures and structure, that damnable structure which had defined every part of my life for over a decade. The Order had given me purpose, and the Service process, a method of arranging my whirling life into something I could understand. But the cost …

Suddenly I saw the painted face of the Chief of the Sewer Rats in Cohrelle rise unbidden into my consciousness, the expression of accusation mixed with terrible, annihilating grief, and I closed my eyes. Yes, the cost had been great … and I was still paying it. I leaned over and checked the unconscious soldier—still out cold, and would remain so for a while. I lay back, giving myself enough margin from the edge of the cliff, and looked up into the pale white light of the moon, serene and calm. Not far away in Elskeg, Ress might be watching the night sky, thinking about his son. Somewhere a hundred miles from here, Rillia could well be looking up at that same moon. Perhaps Caron would be sitting next to her, the usual quiet smile on their face as they talked about—what? Religion? Politics? The Order? Me?

I grunted in annoyance. Like as not they were asleep, as I should be, and if they weren't, like as not they would be talking about their own lives, not someone far away with no reason to be on their minds. But the image stayed with me as I set my mind to sleep. Even at this distance, I could feel my body almost shivering with longing for the calm of that scene.

———————✦———————

I was standing behind a set of crates on the street opposite the Ashenzas' house, just past the intersection of Velman and Commerce Streets in the Merchant District, gazing at the front of their home. There were the four wooden columns, the two rows of four windows each, the two guards standing watch outside the front door, all symbols of Ashenza's dedication to order and symmetry ... and me, the one who was sent to kill his wife. Lady Ashenza: beautiful socialite, publicity-seeker par excellence, and apparently the local head of the sect of Rael. I didn't fully understand the Order's interest in her, but mine was to do, not to question, and in that belief I rested my conscience and care.

Suddenly I saw both the guards turn to face in my direction, staring into the darkness. Reflexively I drew back a step, though I knew there was no way they could have seen or heard me. They stood for a moment, silently watchful—and then, as if they had been marionettes on a string suddenly released by the puppeteer, they collapsed to the ground in a heap as the front doors swung open.

I stared for a long time, trying to reconcile what I was seeing with the reality of my experience. Doors didn't open by themselves, and guards didn't just fall down like this for no reason, as if they had been stabbed in the back by an invisible assailant, or hit with a kushuri dart from a distance. I looked at the roof extending from the second floor of the Ashenzas' home, but saw nothing; a quick glance at the building behind me and up and down both ends of the street on which I stood also revealed no hidden attacker. Finally I risked stepping forward, and with one last look around I crossed the street swiftly. Nothing stirred inside the building's open door that I could see, and I quickly kneeled next to one of the prone guards. His smooth, pale face was ashen, but more disturbingly, his eyes were open, staring sightlessly upward. Both he and his companion were unconscious, yet both still gripped their weapons tightly, as if they were more manne-quins than men.

Still, I didn't intend to miss my chance when I had it, and after another quick scan of my surroundings I passed into the home. The front door led into a large, empty hall, with a narrow staircase near the back leading to an open landing surrounding the room, and I marveled at the opulent decor of the interior as I moved into the center of the room . . . and stopped. On the landing were guards—twenty at least, all with loaded crossbows pointed directly at me. There was a long silence as my mind raced, thinking of possibilities . . . but before I could do anything, even turn and dash for the door, all of the guards silently and simultaneously fell to the floor of the landing and lay still.

I crept forward, feeling somewhat dazed. What in the Hells was going on? What kind of a trap was this? Yet if the intention had been to trap me, I had been in one already . . . why not spring it then? I reached the bottom step in the staircase at the back of the room and, after a quick check of the steps' surfaces for hidden wires or loose boards, slowly began my ascent. Nothing stirred; the house was utterly silent, save for the creaking underneath my feet as I climbed. But my moves were sluggish; my body felt heavy, my head in a fog.

I reached the apex of the stairs and followed the landing to the hallway on the neighboring wall, stepping carefully over the fallen guards as I did so. Like the ones outside, these were clutching their weapons, their eyes open and staring. But after a quick glance I ignored them, just as I ignored my own slow, uncertain doubts. *You're almost there*, I told myself. *Just a few more steps.*

I moved cautiously down the hallway, past two closed doors, then another two, barely noticing the prone, motionless guards I had to step over as I went; the world had seemed to go dim, all except for the door at the hallway's end, where I knew Lady Ashenza resided. Reaching the door, I gave it a cursory glance— somehow I knew it would be neither trapped nor locked—and opened it.

There stood Lady Ashenza, dressed in her black and purple robe. But as she saw me enter, her expression was not sad, but triumphant. "I expected you," she said with a high, trilling laugh. "I knew you would come." Something seemed odd about her appearance, but I couldn't quite place what. I drew my cucuri slowly, feeling as if I were pulling it through mud, and she laughed again.

"Toys," Lady Ashenza said. "Always playing with toys. You're not old enough to play with that one, though. You could hurt someone with it." She stepped forward and suddenly I noticed that what I had thought was purple in her robe was actually some kind of dark red, and to my horror I saw drops of liquid on the floor behind her. "You thought you could kill me, Grayshade," she said with a grin, bleeding from wounds which she could not possibly have survived. "But you're the one who's already dead." She took another step as I stared at her; I tried to lift my cucuri to deliver the killing strike, but it was so heavy, my muscles so weak, that I felt paralyzed. And I was tired, perhaps more tired than I had ever been. I dropped to my knees, my vision swimming as she closed in.

Suddenly I heard a voice inside my head—a familiar one. *Grayshade*, it said, as I swayed back and forth, barely able to keep myself upright. I mustered enough strength to look around me, but saw nothing but the walls of the room, growing ever fainter as I watched.

The hunter pursues you, Grayshade. Beware the hunter.

Lady Ashenza was now right next to me, and from somewhere inside her robe she pulled forth a dagger, sporting a viciously jagged edge.

This isn't how it happened. None of this is how it happened.
In the shadows, Grayshade. It comes from the shadows.

Lady Ashenza laughed again, and raised her dagger high above me. A drop of blood landed on the floor. And there, from behind her, as I raised my weary head for the last time, I again saw yellow eyes in the darkness, growing larger by the second.

Watch, the voice said urgently. *You must watch!*

The dagger fell.

My body jerked as I rolled left to avoid—nothing. There was nothing at all above me but the now moonless night sky, though starlight still filtered down to provide very dim illumination. I blinked as reality reasserted itself, then looked around to see the guard squirming slowly on the ground a short distance away, mumbling something; awake, then, but still groggy. As I sat up slowly, I saw we were alone on top of the bluff. Caoes was gone.

"Perhaps just as well," I muttered, though a part of me felt oddly sad. Even an animal companion could be a sort of comfort. But work remained for me to do, and I looked back over the cliff's edge at the camp below. It looked much the same as it had before, the same small lights twinkling as the guards moved back and forth on their rounds; as I had thought, the order to move hadn't yet come through. After a moment I turned away and went to check on the guard. She was indeed conscious, though her eyes blinked slowly and drifted slightly from left to right as I watched.

Eventually they refocused on me, and then widened slightly

in apparent recognition. I drew my cucuri and held it close. Her eyes widened, perhaps in fear from misunderstanding my gesture, and I shook my head.

"Insurance," I said quietly, shifting the cucuri from hand to hand. "Any shout you try to make will sound like a bird call when I cut it off. Any answer you don't want to give me will end up the same way. Understand?" She nodded slowly and blinked a few more times, breathing somewhat more deeply than normal, but stayed quiet. "All right, friend," I said. "Now that you've had the chance for a bit of a nap, perhaps we can try this conversation again . . . but this time I'll ask the questions. I'll start with an easy one: when were you supposed to report back to your captain?"

The response was slow and halting. "Dawn."

I glanced at the sky; the faintest gray was beginning to tinge the darkness, but dawn was still a good two hours away. "Dawn. When the camp is going to move out?"

Her eyes widened slightly, and given her earlier suspicions about me, it wasn't difficult to guess what she was thinking. I glanced meaningfully at my cucuri, then back to her, and she pursed her lips. "Around then," she finally said slowly, speech a bit slurred. "Didn't get the order yet, but pretty much everyone knows it's coming."

Good . . . at least what Sharrik had told Kelless was right, then. "And what's your target?"

Again the eyes widened, and she licked her lips. "Hells take you, Calarginnian filth," she said at last, stuttering through the words. "You'll know our target when we've wiped your sorry lot from Silarein."

Brave, but also tediously predictable. But I knew the look on the Arginnian's face, one which indicated feelings of defiance from imminent martyrdom had set in. I wasn't going to get more information out of her now, and in truth I now knew enough. I could knock her back out again, but even using soundshifting, two blows like that within a couple of hours of each other were as likely to kill as render her unconscious, and I didn't need her dead.

I shrugged. "As you wish. But until you get around to doing that, I can't have you calling out while I'm not here." With a scrap sliced from her pants with my cucuri, I fashioned a gag around her mouth, then moved her back a good distance from the cliff. She wouldn't find it easy to move while she was still groggy, but the last thing I needed was for her to struggle over and—intentionally or not—roll over and fall into the path below where a guard would find her body and raise the alarm. She glared at me as I stood over her, mumbling something through her gag, and I shook my head. "Nothing personal," I said, then turned and walked back to the cliff's edge to consider my approach.

There were a few possible ways to enter the camp: the first option was the main path down which I had watched Sharrik and Kelless make their way, but I had already rejected that idea. Too many guards, too much light, and few if any places to escape if things went sideways. The second possibility was to circle around to the far side of the camp, opposite where I was currently stationed, but that too was an uncertain course; it would take a while to get there, for one thing, and the longer it took to get into the camp the less time I would have to figure out . . . whatever in the Hells I was going to do to disrupt the Arginnians when I got there. Besides, I didn't know, and couldn't see, where the guards were on that side. I could try an aerial approach; it would certainly help avoid problems with guards used to ground-level threats. But I was much too far above the camp to try fly hooks, and even if I were closer, fly hooks were intended to attach to wood and tile roofs, not tent canvas. I couldn't resist a wry smile as I imagined what Caoesthenes would have said about leaping into a camp of hostile soldiers: "Death from above, lad? You've been spending too much time listening to drunkards' stories again, I see."

If only, old man. I might have wasted less time.

I sighed. No, none of the obvious options were viable. My only chance was to go for something in between the clear choices. Middle ground, then: head up the northern edge of the camp toward the far side, opposite the bluff, but cut into the camp about halfway down, between tents. It was far from an ideal arrangement; I still wouldn't know what guards were likely to be there, nor how to orient myself within the camp once I entered it. And with my luck of late, I was as likely to walk right into the captain's personal guards as to find anything constructive to do. But it minimized the possibility of traps and lessened the chances of detection, and it was a faster method of entry then heading all the way to the other side of the camp. And as I looked up at the sky, where the blackness was ever so slowly beginning to lessen in intensity, I knew I would need all the time I could get.

My mind made up, I turned back to see the guard now lying silent and motionless in the starlight. As I kneeled down next to her, I saw her eyes were still open, shifting slightly to left and right as I watched. With the certainty of a defiant death now stolen from her, she seemed to have resigned herself to whatever was to come ... which was fine with me, as passive resignation was always easier to manage than active resistance. "Someone will find you, or you'll make your way out of those bonds eventually," I said quietly, "though well after I'm gone, fortunately. Until then, stay well." Her gaze briefly flickered up to mine before moving away again. Suddenly her eyes grew wide, as if she had caught sight of something behind me, and I rose and turned quickly.

Out of the darkness padded Caoes, yellow eyes unblinking.

Instinctively my hand went back to the hilt of my cucuri, but as the panther drew near he slowed to a stop, holding my gaze with his own. For a long while neither of us moved as my thoughts raced. *It comes from the shadows*, the voice in my dream had said, the "hunter" which pursued me. The yellow eyes peering from the shadows. Yet dreams were treacherous, uncertain and ambiguous things, half prophecy and half childish fantasy. To trust my life to them—when I didn't even really know what they meant—was folly. And Caoes had saved me once already, for reasons I couldn't fathom, even if trusting him on that basis alone seemed equally reckless.

Folly and madness, Caoesthenes would have said. And he would have been right, as usual. All of it was folly and madness, either way.

"All right," I said at last. "I have to choose someone or something to trust, and it's going to be you. We're going into that camp, and I expect you're going to want to come with me." Caoes remained motionless, and with a nod I turned and started down the path; looking over my shoulder a few moments later, I saw the panther padding softly behind me.

Folly and madness, I thought, and smiled.

CHAPTER SIX

IT took us more time than I had hoped to make our way down to the camp site; it had taken me half as long to ascend to the cliff above, but then I had been leaving the source of danger, not heading toward it . . . and I had been trying to lose a panther on the way up, while I had gained one on the way down. Beyond that, I needed to be careful; I doubted either Caoes or I were visible in the dim illumination of the starlight, but anyone looking directly at the cliff might, if they were lucky, notice us . . . and that would be the end of any chance for either us or Kraes's company. Still, within twenty minutes we were back down on the path. There was no guard within obvious view, but I still moved as quietly as I could into the bushes on the other side.

After a moment, Caoes slunk across the path and into an open space near where I kneeled in the undergrowth, making barely a whisper of noise as he entered the outer edge of the bushes. I could just make out the pale gleam of his yellow eyes as he gazed at me silently. Despite my decision to allow him to follow, I had wondered how well Caoes would understand the situation when we got to the camp. Yet he seemed to instinctively know what to do to avoid detection without instructions from me . . . not that I would have known how to give him instructions in any case. I nodded at him, turned and stayed low as I began to head north, keeping the camp on my left as I went.

"*Settle into the ground, lad . . . don't try to float on top of it. Regular, quiet sounds are a part of nature; sudden tearing and breaking noises are not.*"

"*But I'm not going to be doing missions in the forest,*" I said in frustration as a stick snapped beneath my feet.

"*If you don't learn to do this, you won't be doing missions at all,*" came the stern reply.

I smiled at the memory as I carefully pulled a tough, wiry branch out of my way and slid past it, waiting for the panther to crawl through before carefully guiding it back into place behind him.

The Order of Argoth was a city organization, and the Service operated in and around buildings of stone, wood, and metal; we were used to avoiding detection in streets, alleys, rooms, and hallways, and moving silently through parts of the natural world was a much different matter. Yet not long after I had begun my work as an Apprentice, Caoesthenes had taken me to the large grassy rectangle in the center of the Church District, working on my ability to stay quiet on grass and leaves, dirt and rocks. I had always assumed he was just testing my obedience, an area in which I had never excelled. But as I made my way now from bush to bush, sometimes crawling, sometimes sliding, sometimes moving from place to place with my head low and body squatted almost to the ground, I saw he had more in mind than breaking his younger charge. It had been many years since I had been an Apprentice, and many years since learning how to avoid detection in a natural environment. Still, the lessons had not left me; and I was hardly any louder than Caoes as we made our slow but steady way up the camp's edge.

The further we went, the more relieved I was that I had chosen this route. The camp was better lit than I had observed from the top of the cliff, both from the patrolling guards and from lanterns hanging on poles at regular intervals, and trying to make my way from shadow to shadow would have been difficult. The tents had a decent amount of space between them, too, and concealment would have been a problem . . . and might still be when it came time to enter the camp, as far as that was concerned. But for the moment we progressed with relative ease, and it was only perhaps a quarter of an hour later that I saw we were approaching the spot I had chosen for our entry.

I stopped and turned to look at Caoes, currently lying on his belly and peering out of the bush with his piercing yellow eyes. "All right," I whispered. "Now's the tough part. Follow me when I leave, and—"

"I hear you," a gruff voice said, perhaps ten feet away, and I froze. I could barely hear myself—how could anyone else—

"But it don't matter," the voice continued. "Whatever we say about it, it's going to be the captain's call in the end."

"Aye," a thinner, reedy voice replied. "The order should be given. We're bound to miss something if we rush." I turned my head slowly, and looking out of a few breaks in the tangled branches of the bushes I saw the voices' owners—two Arginnian soldiers standing at ease, lanterns at their feet. One, a shorter woman standing with her arms folded, seemed to have just spoken.

The other woman, taller and thinner than her companion, shrugged. "Maybe. I got word this was coming a couple of days ago . . . I've had my crew gathering stuff together ever since. When she finally gives the order, we'll be ready."

"Maybe you. Not the others, until we're already miles from here," her companion said, rubbing the back of her neck absently. "That's when we'll realize we've left behind a couple of the swords ... someone left behind the hardtack ... can't find the extra lanterns ..."

"Pfft, when did you become quartermaster?" The taller woman crossed her arms. "Your job's to get your people ready to fight, not worry about carting supplies. Leave that to Jergen."

"I'd take Jergen's job any day of the week," the other Arginnian replied gloomily. "Ain't got anything against fighting, but sitting here for weeks with no order to move ain't what I signed up for. My crew will barely remember how to swing swords by the time we finally let them do it."

"They don't forget that," the other guard said with a laugh. "It's all they know how to do."

"I'll remember that when one of yours accidentally takes your head off when they meant to hit the one you're fighting. Or when they hit one of the barrels instead and send you and everyone within fifty feet to meet the Gods a lot earlier than you'd planned."

My ears pricked up.

"Come on, Braela," said the taller soldier with a slight shiver. "The barrels would take more than that to go up, and we ain't going to be carrying them on our backs."

"Not as far as you know," Braela said. "But if we need to move quick—and we might—captain's not going to want us pulling carts and whipping the few horses we've got in camp. Maybe the oil won't go up from a sword stroke that goes wide ... but if they crash into each other, or they get hit by a flaming arrow ... you know the rest. Anyway, the point is sitting around here rusting our blades is as much of a liability as whatever she's waiting for."

The Arginnian guard looked at Braela, lips pursed. After a moment she shook her head. "The captain's no fool." She picked up her lantern.

"Glad for your faith," Braela responded, reaching for her own. "Mine's set on a firm prayer that Calarginn will have surrendered by dawn." The guards laughed roughly as they headed toward the center of the camp. I waited until their figures had vanished behind the tents, then looked down at Caoes, who gazed at me steadily.

Oil barrels—not just for the lanterns, but stockpiles for battle. Lantern oil wasn't usually that explosive . . . but there was a type of oil we had used in the Service, quickburn, which ignited fast and burned slow, even with limited air to maintain the flame—useful for the longer missions where we wouldn't have much of a chance to resupply. If this oil was anything like that . . . and if it could be ignited in a similar way . . .

"It's possible," I whispered to Caoes, who tilted his head as I spoke. "Not much of a chance, but more than we had before." I felt within the pouch inside my cloak, running my fingers over the hexagonal edges of the small metal objects I found there . . . at least eight laquevoxes, part of the kit I always carried with me, along with the chikchaks and fly hooks. The laquevoxes, triggered through the use of soundshifting, were a mainstay of the Service, and I was loath to part with them . . . but I couldn't think of a more effective use for them than this, either. Certainly not enough for every barrel in the camp, but distribute them in a reasonably central location, and it could create a nice diversion. Once the last one was placed, I would need only to speak the trigger word in reverse, within range of one of the laquevoxes, and both it and the other seven would explode simultaneously in a shower of fire and sparks . . . enough to set off the barrels they were attached to. And if we had a bit of a breeze, to send sparks from tent to tent . . .

Yes . . . a chance, anyway. Looking left and right first to make sure the space beyond was still clear, I crept out of the bush and made my way into the camp.

I had been a bit concerned about finding the oil barrels without a long search—and how I was going to move them even if I found them quickly—but I quickly realized I had one less reason for worry, a bit of luck I was happy to take. In addition to a few narrow paths, the interior of the camp had one main route running north and south, long and fairly wide, with tents in rows of three on either side of the path; the barrels were placed at relatively regular spots along the same route, easily identifiable with an arc of short banners placed around each one. Despite Braela's worry, the Arginnians obviously didn't view the barrels as a liability. Most of the time, they might have been right.

So finding the barrels wasn't a problem . . . but placing the laquevoxes properly was another story. Whether it was standard Arginnian protocol or just a particularly clever arrangement by the captain, using a central path was a smart choice: anything on it could be easily seen by guards in either direction during the day, and even at night the lantern light would make a good portion of the camp visible. There wasn't an overwhelming amount of guards, but enough of them were wandering up and down the camp's center to make getting to the barrels a challenge. Here, though, two things aided me. First, some of the barrels were near tents closest to the path, giving me the chance to approach them from in between the tents rather than along the main route; and second—as important as it was inexplicable—was Caoes. He had an uncanny ability to both keep out of sight and attract enough attention to turn the nearby soldier away, sometimes with a low growl, sometimes with the sound of slight scratching, sometimes with a swift, subtle movement just enough to move the side of a nearby tent. It was as if he had been trained for exactly this kind of work.

And what if he has been?

I pushed the thought firmly away as I crept next to another barrel and pulled out the next to last laquevox. Even if he had been trained, that meant nothing for my current circumstances . . . I wasn't familiar with the mountains and surrounding environment here, and knew little about what animals might be taught to do. If he had been sent as part of an elaborate plan to eliminate me, he had much better opportunities to do so in the past few hours. In any case, I couldn't change the plan now, and as I placed the laquevox on the barrel's side, I saw Caoes's yellow eyes blinking from next to the tent on the other side of the path. *Folly and madness*, I thought, and leaning next to the laquevox I whispered the trigger word: "Paratur," listening with satisfaction as the soft *thunk* of the metal indicated the laquevox's legs had embedded themselves into the wood of the barrel, holding it in place. Eight oil barrels exploding at once would attract a great deal of attention … and with any luck, would disrupt the Arginnians enough to make it easier for Kraes's soldiers to attack them before they could regroup and continue with their plan.

I leaned out into the main path as far as I dared and looked both north and south. The guard on the northern end, some distance away, still had his back to me; the one to the south was facing in my direction at first, but turned after just a few seconds and began to walk toward the camp's southern edge. There, only a few rows of tents away, was the final barrel I had marked for destruction. I had avoided the main path so far, but the sky was growing lighter by the second, and I was anxious to avoid further delay. Besides, the shadows between the lantern poles were deep here, and I would only be exposed for a few moments. I nodded to Caoes, whose yellow eyes blinked again and then vanished. With one more glance left and right, I entered the main path and turned south, keeping low to the ground and to the shadows.

I passed two tents, three, five … and then arrived at the barrel itself, ducking out of the path and into the space next to the nearby tent. As I reached into my pouch for the final laquevox, I allowed myself a small smile. Infiltration with the intent of sabotage had never been my line, but there was always satisfaction in executing a plan well, and I had to admit I got a certain enjoyment from the feeling of beating the odds, even outside the boundaries of my training. I pulled out the laquevox and placed it on the barrel, looking up just before I could whisper the trigger word. But no yellow eyes greeted me this time, and I hesitated. With each of the previous barrels Caoes had waited across the path. But why should that matter? Caoes was a panther, not a human being, and obviously we didn't have an extensive plan.

Still, it broke a pattern, and I knew enough to worry when patterns were disrupted.

I waited for a few moments more, but seeing and hearing nothing else unusual I shook my head and frowned. *Caution and paranoia aren't the same things*, Father Esper had told me many years ago when I had first joined the Order and the Service, and it was a good bet I was confusing the two now. I leaned forward and whispered "Paratur," listening as the last laquevox locked into place.

Suddenly, a low growl rolled out of the darkness behind me.

I turned to see the looming shape of an Arginnian soldier exiting one of the tents, lantern held high. His eyes widened as he saw me, but I had my cucuri out already, driving the hilt into his midsection. He let out a loud grunt and doubled over, dropping his lantern, and in a moment I was up above him. I raked the cucuri's hilt across the back of his neck, and with a sigh he slumped to the ground. Immediately I crouched down and extinguished the lantern, but as I heard footsteps rapidly approaching I knew it was already too late ... one of the guards, probably the one to the south, must have heard us. With a silent curse I ducked into the tent from which the Arginnian had emerged, hoping it was unoccupied by a second soldier ... to no avail. Two bedrolls lay spread out on the ground, on one of which lay a man in tunic and pants, leather armor and sword next to him—he was asleep, but the unevenness of his breathing told me the encounter outside had disturbed him.

"Oy, Sarner!" a voice outside the tent said, and I stilled my breathing even further as I gripped the hilt of my cucuri. The voice had been a few feet away, and I closed my eyes as I pictured the scene: the guard standing on the path, seeing the fallen body of his comrade; calling to him with no response; walking to his side ...

Wait.

He looks around him for signs of the assailant, and sees nothing. After a moment he crouches down, holding his lantern high ...

Wait.

He puts his lantern on the ground next to him, leans in ...

Now.

I plunged out of the tent and planted my shoulder right in the chest of the Arginnian soldier, kneeling right where I had imagined him to be. He went over on his back and hit the ground with a quiet thud; his eyes were still struggling to focus as I knocked him unconscious. I extinguished his lantern and looked around quickly, holding my breath as I listened intently. A bit of a breeze, perhaps the slight movement of the nearby tent flap ... but otherwise silence. After a few moments I exhaled. I had never relied on fortune either good or ill, but I was forced to admit I had gotten a generous portion of luck here; I had avoided disaster by the narrowest of margins. As I dragged the unconscious bodies of the two guards outside the camp and into the bushes as quickly as I could, I kept watch for Caoes, but saw no sign. Could he have been spooked and fled the scene? Yet that seemed wrong, somehow ... he had seemed more ...

Enough. I had no time to worry when my job was not yet done.

I turned and re-entered the camp, keeping low to the ground as before. Nothing left now but to speak the trigger word in reverse, as soon as I got close enough, and I would have the diversion I needed—and without much time to spare, as I saw the ground starting to become dimly visible in the rapidly lightening camp. Just a bit further, and—

Suddenly I stopped and blinked several times to make sure I was seeing properly before redoubling my pace. *No*, I thought, but a moment later I slowed to a halt as I was close enough to confirm what I had seen. It wasn't possible—and yet . . .

The barrel where I had placed the final laquevox was gone.

I looked around for several moments in bewilderment. Then, a fiery pain exploded in my brain as something impacted heavily on the back of my skull, and I fell into a deep and silent darkness.

———————————✦———————————

". . . the search, and I don't think there's anyone else."

"Maybe. But I don't want . . . one of Calarginn's plans . . . move quickly."

". . . lads have been on edge . . . running off now before we know what's waiting for us, I don't know . . . got a surprise ready."

The voices were faint at first, floating in and out of my hearing as I drifted in blackness.

". . . not interested in what everyone thinks. If I say he . . ."

". . . see it differently. Maybe . . ."

". . . won't convince me . . ."

Then the voices became louder, stronger, and I saw the blackness beginning to lighten. And I was beginning to notice something else, too . . . a repeated sound, a kind of rhythmic hammering.

"I'm not trying to argue, captain. I know this isn't an easy decision to make."

"You're wrong, Sharrik . . . it's actually very easy. What's hard is ignoring people acting like they ought to have a say in my decisions."

Sharrik . . . Sharrik. I had heard that before. The blackness lightened further, and the hammering more pronounced. It was starting to get painful, in fact, and I began to wonder whether I had somehow stumbled my way into a forge. But Cohrelle had few forges, and certainly no places to rest inside one . . . why was I . . .

"Starting to stir, captain," a rough, familiar voice said.

"Good. We'll have the chance to get some answers," came the reply. The pain from the insistent hammering now throbbed, and suddenly I remembered I was not in Cohrelle . . . nor, I guessed, in a forge. I opened my eyes, wincing as the action set the hammer to work even more strongly on my skull. Lantern light flickered, and as I lifted my head slowly, wincing again as the blood flowing to my head pulsed painfully, I saw I was seated on a chair within a large tent, my cloak gone. My hands were bound behind the chair's back, ankles tied to the chair's legs—and, as the voices had indicated, I was not alone. Sharrik, the guard I had seen talking to Kelless when I had first arrived at the camp, stood next to the closed flap which granted entrance to the tent with his arms folded, a sour expression on his face. Standing in front of me, hands on hips, was a woman of medium height, dressed in the same leather armor as the others. Her straight black hair, accenting her pale face, was drawn back and tied, and her brown eyes stared down at me.

After a moment she nodded curtly. "Welcome back to consciousness. It might have done you some good to experience for yourself what you've put some of my people through this evening." Her voice was clipped and angular, but not low and rough like Sharrik's.

"I've been knocked out before," I replied as the hammer continued to pound on the inside of my head.

She raised an eyebrow. "It doesn't seem to have knocked much sense into you. Perhaps you consider it a kindness to lay out a target instead of killing them? Avoids problems of disposal, perhaps."

I smiled without mirth. "Perhaps."

The woman returned the smile. "I would hope you had a reason other than whimsy. We found two of my people knocked out already; another one's missing, and assuming you haven't killed her, I imagine I'll find her the same way."

"Probably."

"We would appreciate it if you'd save us the trouble of a search."

I smiled again, trying not to wince as I moved my arms experimentally against their bonds. "I can't seem to remember. Maybe the knock on the head had something to do with it."

"We can give you another, if the first one didn't work," growled Sharrik from behind the captain.

"Never mind, Sharrik," she said, holding up a hand. "A man like this isn't going to be frightened into talking." She leaned down, head tilted slightly. "But I don't have time to spend hours convincing you to tell me what I want to know . . . and you can stop testing the strength of those ropes," she said, nodding toward the back of the chair. "I assure you they're strong enough to hold you for a good while. So we'll have to speed up the pleasantries."

I nodded, almost immediately regretting it as another sharp pain shot through my skull. "That usually begins with an exchange of names," I said, resisting the urge to grit my teeth.

She stood straight and pursed her lips. After a moment, she nodded. "My name is Merynne, captain of this division from Arginn."

"I see."

"And you?" she said after a few moments of silence.

"Grayshade," I said after a brief pause.

"That's all?" Sharrik said from behind Merynne. "No title, no place of residence? Other than Calarginn, of course."

"I'm not from Calarginn."

Sharrik's eyes widened as he took a step away from the entrance. "You just happened to stumble on our camp, then. Just happened to find this location, then started knocking us out for the fun of it."

"I don't do my work for fun," I replied drily.

"Money, then," Sharrik said with a sneer. "One of these filthy sellswords, captain, and—"

"Enough," Merynne said, a tinge of annoyance in her voice. "Getting paid doesn't make him a sellsword, Sharrik. He'd have to be getting an awful lot to agree to take on an Arginnian division by himself." She paused, her expression turning thoughtful. "And most sellswords wouldn't be well trained enough to get into our camp without being detected or challenged."

"Luck," Sharrik said with a shrug.

"I doubt it," Merynne said. "And when's the last time you saw a Calarginnian using weapons like his?"

Coming to now, I glanced around the tent for the positioning of my gear, but saw nothing but Sharrik and his glare.

"In fact," the captain continued, "this looks like the man Kester and Rannik were crying about—the ghost from the tavern." She leaned down again, staring at me. "No, I don't think this one's from Calarginn, though they're probably involved somehow. But if you're not a Calarginnian—who are you?"

"You seem to be answering your own questions fine, captain," I said.

"I'm speculating," she replied. "You're going to tell me how right I am with my speculations. And you're going to start by explaining these." Standing up again, she tossed a few objects onto the thin wooden floor of the tent, where they landed with metallic thuds.

Hells, I cursed silently; now I knew why the last barrel was missing. They had found the laquevoxes.

CHAPTER SEVEN

FOR a long time there was silence in the tent as I stared blankly at the laquevoxes. Finally Captain Merynne cleared her throat meaningfully. "I see you're familiar with these." She waited until it became clear no reply was forthcoming. "We've found three of them so far, and I have to assume there are more. And all positioned quite nicely, to—what? Explode? Send out a shower of sparks? Set the oil on fire? Let me first assure you, we are in the back of the camp, with a stack of barrels right there." She pointed through the canvas wall. "If they're on a fuse or trigger, you'd best tell me now, or we'll all go up in flames together."

I looked up at her searching eyes, keeping my expression level, but internally I was gripped by doubt. The laquevox was an invention of the Service of Argoth—of Caoesthenes himself, in fact, despite his ambivalence toward the soundshifting used to trigger them—and not used or, as far as I understood, even known about by anyone else but the Service. They weren't designed to be easily found, especially once set. Yet somehow Merynne and her troops had tracked down three of them in short order, with some reasonable idea how they worked. What in the Hells was going on?

"Just a bit of disruption," I said. "Nothing Arginn's many enemies wouldn't welcome if the chance arose."

Merynne snorted. "As if Arginn's enemies could stop beating each other up long enough to focus on anything else. Whoever hired you might have had delusions of grandeur, but the truth is that Arginn is too knuckled under with orders from the higher-ups and the populace wanting information about the political situation to be a legitimate threat to the rest of the cities outside of it. In time, this squabble will be squashed, and people will come to their senses."

"That assumes you're still around when they do," I pointed out. "In the meantime, they don't seem to share your opinion. They seem to think you're the aggressor here."

"By 'they' you mean Calarginn, I assume. And that city has its own crimes to answer for."

"Crimes?" I said, raising an eyebrow and wincing as the hammering in my head briefly increased its tempo. "That's awfully honest of you, captain. Most soldiers don't like to acknowledge the impact of what they're doing."

Merynne shrugged. "War is war, and bad things happen. But Calarginn is just as guilty as Arginn ... something you should keep in mind as you're deciding whether or not to die for them." Something struck me as odd about that, but I didn't have time to consider why before she leaned in again. "And make no mistake, Grayshade ... I'm not in a mood for pleasant chatter. Even without your 'disruption,' you've set the camp on edge, and got my people anxious, right when I needed them steady. I want to know why."

I smiled thinly. "You act like we're in Arginn, captain. The real question is what you're doing around Elskeg at all, and it's a question everyone wants to know the answer to."

"Not in Elskeg, they don't. I've been around that glorified patch of dirt and rock long enough to know that no one in Elskeg cares about anything other than ale and surviving another day . . . until they get rock-lung, or something else to make their trips under the earth permanent." She chuckled, and I felt something familiar about the bitter edge to her voice . . . a kind of faint reminder of my own emptiness. "No, what we're doing here is our business," she went on, her expression growing serious. "And I've known for a while that Calarginn has got its own rabble nearby. I just didn't expect they'd be finding others to do their dirty work."

"I said I'm not from Calarginn."

Merynne stood straight and folded her arms. "I didn't say you were. You're a lot better trained than most of them, for one thing. And as I said, unlike Sharrik here," she said as she jerked her head over her shoulder at the scowling soldier by the tent entrance, "I don't think you're a sellsword. But you don't strike me as a fool either, and thieves don't blow up the target they want to rob. So someone asked you to disrupt our operations here, and that tells me Calarginn. Something convinced you to work for them, and I want to know what it was."

"You're making a lot of assumptions, captain," I said.

"And you're wasting time," Sharrik growled. "Why are we playing games with this filth? While he's sitting here doing this little dance, Calarginn could have a division closing in on us."

"I don't think so," Merynne said, her eyes flickering to Sharrik for a moment before returning to me. "They would need to give him enough time to finish whatever he was trying to start. But it's true that he found us, and if he found us, they could know where we are. This site isn't safe anymore." She turned to Sharrik. "See whether the lads have woken up from their naps yet, and tell Tannek to get them conscious if they haven't. If they complain," she said, glancing briefly at me, "tell them they'll get their chance to go after the one who put them to sleep soon enough. Make sure all the barrels have been checked for more of these things," she went on, pointing at the laquevoxes on the ground. "Three times each, by three different soldiers to confirm. Then get the camp rousted; we move out in a half hour. I'll join you in a minute."

Sharrik scowled, but nodded. "Aye, captain." He shot a murderous glance in my direction before leaving the tent, starting to bark orders before the flap had even finished closing again.

Merynne looked back at me. "Even with the preparation, I wasn't sure whether or not to move this morning ... but your little game has forced my hand. And although I don't think you're going to care that much about saving your friends, or whatever these people are to you, I'm pretty sure you'll have an interest in saving your own skin, Grayshade." She leaned down to me, very close this time, and I could smell the faint odor of sweat mingled with a kind of musky incense. Outside, I heard the sound of barked orders and running feet. "They can get ready pretty fast when they want to," she said, noticing my listening expression. "They'll be ready to move within half an hour. The question is whether you'll be moving by then."

I smiled, trying to project a sense of calm I didn't feel. "Not sure why you're wasting your time, if you've already made up your mind what to do."

"Because I haven't made up my mind on what to do with *you* yet. I'll find out who sent you here and why ... but I'd rather find out from you, especially if you don't want me to wipe out the Calarginn cretins just in case they're behind this." She shrugged. "I've known where they are for a while, of course. Hiding a company of soldiers in the one patch of bushes Elskeg's residents call a forest isn't the smartest choice. But even if you don't give a damn about them, you should still tell me what you know if you want me to be more favorably inclined toward *you*. It'll save me time, for one thing . . . and it'll prove something to me."

"Which is?"

Merynne chuckled. "That you're a reasonable man, not a fool or a fanatic with a misguided sense of loyalty." She turned, gathered up the laquevoxes lying on the ground, rose and walked toward the tent entrance. As she lifted the flap to exit, letting the pale gray light of pre-dawn filter into the tent, she stopped. "Something about you strikes me as sensible. We leave in a half hour; I'll give you twenty minutes to choose whether to fill me in about your friends, or leave your noble corpse here for their mourners to find. I trust you'll make the right decision." And without looking back, she exited the tent, leaving me alone with my thoughts.

They were not happy ones. I had tried to be cautious, plan for most eventualities, but somehow I had still managed to under-estimate the situation. If I had botched things this badly when I was still in the Service, Father Jant—Hells, even Father Esper— would have had my head. But part of that wasn't my fault; I was rushed, and working in an unfamiliar environment, with sabotage instead of assassination as the goal. And Captain Merynne . . .

Merynne. I had certainly not planned on anyone like her— someone who would know to check for the laquevoxes, or to recognize them as the threats they were even if they were spotted by accident. And to be able to so quickly judge a part of my own nature—to guess whom I was working with, and that there was another reason why—was something well beyond the abilities of any Arginnian or Calarginnian I had met out here, even Kraes, who was no fool. She was . . . different, for certain, yet at the same time oddly familiar in a way I couldn't quite explain.

But solving her mystery was secondary to my two main problems: first, I had to get back to the Greenmark to warn the Calarginnians. Any chance I had of disrupting the camp's activities was long gone, and with the amount of noise I could hear outside, it was obvious that the captain's assurance was true; the Arginnians were working quickly. Assuming they had been preparing for this for a while, and were willing to leave a few things behind, they could be on the move well within the hour . . . and if they marched straight there, they could be at the Greenmark within less than two. And given the Greenmark's relatively compact size, there was only so far out that Kraes could set the watch; by the time the lookouts saw the Arginnians, there wouldn't be much time for anything other than a full-scale, disorganized retreat, or a fight against a division with far more people and better weapons. I needed to get there first.

That led to the second problem: getting out of the tent while still breathing. I tested the ropes binding my wrists and ankles, and my heart sank . . . they were like iron. Perhaps rocking back and forth to knock the chair over, freeing the ropes from the legs . . . but no, they were also looped around the seat of the chair itself. Falling over would just leave me on the ground, as helpless as before. Whoever tied these had known their business. Given time, I could work my way out of most ropes and cuffs . . . yet time was something I didn't have. I looked around the tent hoping something might have escaped my notice the first time, but no—there was nothing else in the tent besides myself and the chair, unless something was placed directly behind me. I half jumped, half dragged the chair to turn its angle, gritting my teeth against the pain the movement was causing, but when I finally had it around far enough to see behind me, nothing was there. Like the rest of the camp, the tent had been prepared for travel.

I lowered my head and closed my eyes. Perhaps I shouldn't have expected anything different, but still ... dying here, bound and helpless in a foreign camp, had not been how I imagined my final end. Again my thoughts shifted to Rillia and Caron. When word of my demise reached the Order of Argoth, it might convince them to call off the Service. But even as I thought this, I knew it to be untrue. If anything, not having to worry about me would free the Order from having to divide its attention; now it could focus on getting the others who had helped kill Jant and the Prelate, and wiping out Governor Jarrett's influence in Cohrelle in the bargain. I hadn't been able to discover what the Order's plans were beyond Cohrelle, but whatever they were, there wouldn't be anyone or anything to stop those either.

Suddenly I heard a strange, muffled sound from outside the tent—something like a cry, cut short. A few moments later a rustling sound told me someone had entered the tent, but as I lifted my head and opened my eyes I saw I was partly wrong. What had entered my tent was not someone ... or at least, not a human someone.

It was Caoes.

The panther padded over to me and leaned his head against my right leg for a moment before baring his fangs. I didn't have time to wonder before he began, almost delicately, to chew at the rope holding my ankle to the chair. As well tied as it was, it was a fiber rope, and soon I felt it slacken and then release as Caoes bit through it completely. He repeated the process with the rope on my other leg, then set to work on the rope around my hands, and a minute later I was free and standing, rubbing my wrists and shaking my ankles as the blood rushed in its painful way to the newly opened areas.

"Thanks," I whispered to Caoes, who was now regarding me with his usual implacable stare. "I owe you twice. But we still have to deal with the guards outside—" Paying no attention, Caoes turned and padded to the entrance of the tent and nudged it with his head, and as a shaft of dim morning light shot though the opening, I caught sight of something lying on the ground outside. I walked to the entrance and lifted the flap to see what it was— the body of an Arginnian guard, face down. The camp beyond was a whirl of activity, many of the tents already down and folded, several wooden carts already loaded with material while some of the soldiers were lining up to leave. Yet no one was looking in this direction; the tent where I had been kept had already been emptied, which, as it was the captain's, made some sense. But with Merynne herself out and supervising preparations for departure, and surely having ordered the tent to be undisturbed, I didn't think I'd get a visit from anyone else—until she returned herself, and that would be soon.

I dragged the body of the guard inside the now empty tent, and peeking out, saw the attention of the Arginnians was still focused on their tasks. I nodded at Caoes and exited, and as I turned to leave the camp, saw my luck had been even better than I first thought. Sitting next to the entrance of the tent was a worn canvas sheet, with my cloak, cucuri, and my other weapons—including, blessedly, the niscur, the last and most powerful weapon Caoesthenes had made for me, tossed into a pile. My kit, along with my ferrin cloth to protect against noxious fumes, was gone, but only fools complain about a few missing coins when they've stumbled onto an unguarded pile of gold. I equipped myself hurriedly, took a quick look behind me to see Caoes waiting patiently, and glanced for one last time at the rapidly disappearing Arginnian camp before heading silently away and into the rocky wilderness beyond.

———————◆———————

It had taken me nearly an hour to travel from Elskeg to the Arginnian camp, but that had been following a half-drunken man in no particular hurry. I could cover that same ground in less than fifteen minutes when moving with purpose, especially now that daylight had fully banished the darkness. On the other hand, now I was going to the Greenmark, itself some distance from the town, and I couldn't rule out the possibility that there were already Arginnian scouts posted. I still had to use a bit of caution. Moreover, the Arginnians were going to be close on my heels, as my escape had certainly been discovered: only about five minutes outside of the camp, I heard shouts and yells in the distance. I had no choice given the alternative, but if Merynne had been motivated to get to the Calarginnians before, she was going to be absolutely determined now. Glad to know that at least her horses were needed for the carts, I picked up my pace. "I hope

Kraes figured out a way to use more advance scouts," I muttered to Caoes loping easily beside me. As ever, he remained unmoved.

Kraes. She had acted like the Arginnian presence was just a rumor—a dangerous one if true, but still unconfirmed. But I had found the camp by following a drunk soldier, and had dispatched two Arginnians myself with ease. Something about the older woman's gruff ease had lulled me into believing her lack of knowledge, but I found it hard to believe Venner Kraes, an experienced captain, here for weeks with the express orders to track and disrupt Arginnian operations, wouldn't have already found this camp herself, or at least confirmed that it existed. And Merynne . . . had Kraes heard of her? How much had she known about the whole business before sending me into the middle of it?

"No way to know until I talk to her," I growled, jumping lightly over a low-lying bush in my path as we ran. *But I am going to know*, I promised myself. *Before I'm done with all of this, I'll know about both of these captains . . . and I'll know what to do with both of them.*

Despite my fears, we didn't encounter any Arginnian soldiers on our return to the Greenmark. The day had dawned clear, dry, and noticeably chillier, presaging the colder months to come, but we saw nothing more ominous than a startled rabbit jumping out of our way as we hurried along. Sound carried well in these conditions, though, and occasionally I thought I heard a faint shout behind us . . . but at such a distance, it was as likely to be a farmer yelling at a dog as a soldier urging his compatriots to greater speed. Yet I had to assume Merynne had chosen to pursue immediately, and I found myself increasing my pace further, almost to a sprint, using my training to fully deny both exhaustion and pounding head. Soon I could see the green line in the distance heralding the outer edge of the Greenmark, but despite our increased speed the shouts and yells behind us had reached a clamor, and it was now obvious they weren't coming from farmers. Evidently Merynne had dismissed the idea of stealth entirely, reasoning that getting us before we got to the camp—or at least falling upon the Calarginnians so quickly they wouldn't have time to react—was worth any attention she might attract with moving even a small force that quickly.

It wasn't bad logic, all in all. The Greenmark rapidly grew darker and more solid on the horizon as we approached, and without even a word of challenge from a Calarginnian guard thus far, it was clear to me that Merynne's troops would be awfully close before I could warn anyone of their existence. Looking over my shoulder, I still didn't see the Arginnians, but the sounds were clear; I could now hear an occasional curse cutting through the cool morning air, and once in a while a rough laugh from a number of people. "Glad you're enjoying the hunt," I muttered; it was a feeling I did not share, and the dull throb in my head, a reminder of my recent captivity, wasn't helping. But how? A group of soldiers, even lightly armored ones, could not easily gain on a lone runner—they must have had energy to spare after waiting for action for weeks, and the distance wasn't great, but still . . . this wasn't normal.

"More mysteries," I said to Caoes as we ran along. The panther had maintained our increased pace with no difficulty, silently bounding over rocks in our path as he went, and again I wondered what was passing through his mind. What did he think we were doing, infiltrating camps and then escaping from them, running over rocks and toward forests? I still didn't know where he had gone right before my capture, except to avoid discovery himself, nor how he had managed to find me afterward ... but without him, I wouldn't be alive now to wonder about it. Once my training was complete I always worked alone, as all Acolytes in the Service did. Solitude was both a benefit to my profession and a state with which I was comfortable. But the last few months had begun to teach me the benefits of thinking differently about a number of things, and I was starting to realize that an intelligent animal capable of being as stealthy as me could be a valuable asset. As for genuine companionship ...

Well. One change in outlook at a time.

Within a few minutes we were nearing the edge of the Greenmark, and as we slowed to a stop I listened intently. Behind us were the noises of our pursuers, growing louder by the minute. But in front of us I heard nothing other than a few birds twitter-ing in the trees. "I don't like it," I said to Caoes, whose yellow-eyed gaze swept to mine and then back to the forest as if in agree-ment. "Where in the Hells are Kraes's people?" I knew she didn't have many to spare, but when Ress and I had first come to the Greenmark we hadn't gone all that far in before being confronted; surely at this point Kraes should have had a few patrols or at least a lookout or two on the edge of the trees, waiting for my return. Yet silence and stillness reigned, and my annoyance at Kraes began to shift to worry. Something was certainly wrong, and I wondered if she was already in trouble. Had someone attacked the Calarginnians while I was away? It seemed impossible—so many things would have to have been concealed to set up a double-cross like that—but very little about this experience had worked out as

I had anticipated. Another shout in the distance shook me free of my thoughts. "We'll never know until we find her," I said to Caoes. "Let's go." With another glance at the landscape behind me, I turned and plunged into the forest.

Despite our need to move quickly, I knew we would be of no use to anyone if we were heard by any Arginnians . . . if they were even here. So our pace was reduced as we made our way through the bushes and undergrowth of the Greenmark, trying to avoid loose branches and dry leaves as we went, and for the most part I was pleased with how quietly we were moving. A few minutes later we had reached the edge of the first clearing, and I stopped; it looked empty, but it had looked just as empty then, before I was surrounded by forty Calarginnian soldiers. "All right," I whispered, "we'll chance it. The camp is past the tree line on the other side of this clearing; we'll stick to the edge, but—" Suddenly I stopped, for I had looked over at Caoes. He was gone again.

I was beginning to wonder whether I was imagining Caoes— who seemed to drift in and out of reality as much as he drifted in and out of my thoughts. But before I could consider the possibility, I saw I was not alone: Captain Kraes and Fen, swords drawn, had just entered the clearing. Kraes's face was tense, and Fen's usually sour expression was equally strained; both women were looking about as if searching for something. Leaping out of the forest to greet them probably wasn't going to endear me to either of them, but I didn't have time to play games.

Hands down and away from my sides, I entered the clearing. "Captain," I said as I nodded to her in acknowledgement. Kraes and Fen started as I spoke . . . then relaxed, ever so slightly, upon seeing me.

"About time you got back," Fen growled, sword still held in a ready position. "You should have reported hours ago."

"You're right," I responded. "And the reason I was late is the same reason we need to talk immediately, captain."

Kraes scowled. "Indeed we do, Grayshade. I told you time was of the essence, and you told me you were willing to help . . . and here you are, hours after your time. What in the Hells happened?"

"Complications," I said, a bit surprised by Kraes's strident tone. "Enough complications that I'm lucky to be here at all. Enough complications that I need some answers from you. And quickly."

"What do you mean?"

"You need to tell me what you know about the Arginnians, Kraes. Specifically, you need to tell me about Merynne."

Kraes's expression hovered between bemusement and anger. "Who?"

"Their captain," I said impatiently. "The captain of a division much larger than you gave me reason to believe it was."

"What are you talking about? You found the Arginnians?"

"You mean to tell me you didn't?" I said, growing angrier. "Somehow you overlooked an entire division no further than a two hours' march from here? You didn't know anything about Merynne?"

Kraes's eyes flashed. "Who in the Hells is Merynne? And what do they have to do with Arginn?"

"She," I shot back. "If you're not being straight with me, Kraes, I'll know about it soon enough. But this isn't a discussion to have here. We need to get back to the camp, and fast."

"Not before we confirm what's happened to my people," Kraes responded angrily.

"But I—" I stopped as a thought struck me. "Wait ... your people? Are you out on a patrol ... yourselves?"

Kraes nodded. "Couldn't spare any others."

"Others?"

"Last two patrols haven't reported back, and we can't find them," Fen put in. "The captain and I went to see what we could."

My heart sank. "How long have they been missing?"

"Four hours at least ... we've been out searching for the better part of an hour," Kraes replied, suspicion beginning to mingle with the anger in her tone. "Why? What—"

"Never mind," I said, words beginning to race as fast as my thoughts. "Captain, we need to get back to the camp right now. You and all of your people—"

Suddenly a bowstring twanged, and an arrow struck Fen in the shoulder, sending her reeling back several steps as she roared in pain. There was a brief, eerie silence.

Then all the Hells broke loose.

Arginnian soldiers flooded into the clearing, and arrows flew as Fen and Kraes backed up several paces. "There's too many of them, Kraes," I yelled as I drew my cucuri and parried a sword strike from an Arginnian, ramming my shoulder into his shield to drive him back. "Get out of here and warn your people!" Kraes glared at me in obvious anger, but before she could respond the Arginnians were upon her, and with Fen she fell back step by step toward the edge of the clearing, then turned and fled. Most of the Arginnians pursued them, but three remained with me. I threw a spray of kushuri darts toward the one I had stunned briefly, and he went down clutching uselessly at his throat even as I ducked under a vicious slash from another Arginnian and kicked out at his leg. He jumped back just in time, and I let the momentum of my kick carry me into a roll as a sword thrust from the third soldier came down on the dirt where I had been a moment before.

I came up from the roll with cucuri held high just as the second soldier was bringing his sword down and parried again, then reversed my blade and drove the hilt into his exposed midsection. He doubled over, gasping for breath, and a second later I hammered the cucuri's hilt into the back of his skull, sending him crashing to the ground unconscious. Only one remained, but I knew I had taken too long; the third soldier would already be beginning his strike, and I wouldn't be turned in time to block it. Yet as I spun, I saw the sword fall from the soldier's hand as he screamed in pain. Hanging from his wrist, jaws locked in place, was Caoes. A second later my blade's hilt struck the Arginnian, and he fell to the ground to join his companions as Caoes released his grip and leapt away gracefully before impact.

I didn't take time to ask any of the hundred questions whirling in my mind, instead retrieving the kushuri darts from the now dead soldier who had first attacked me—a death I regretted, though I hadn't had time to do anything else if I were to survive myself—and then standing and listening. The clearing was empty for the moment, but combat was clearly raging all through the Greenmark now, and I hesitated. I could go and try to help, but I doubted even Caoes and I together could fight off an entire division of soldiers here, any more than we could have at their own camp. If Kraes still trusted me enough to listen to my advice, she might be able to escape with at least some of her people remaining . . . and if I was indeed one of Merynne's targets, I could help draw off some of the pursuit. So, shutting out the screams and shouts of clashing steel as best I could, I turned and ran, Caoes bounding after me.

Wanted in Cohrelle, enemies in Arginn and Calarginn, and no real hope now of finding allies in Tellisar. I was on the run again, with only a panther for company, and only the Gods knew if I'd stay clear of the blade long enough to regret my failures.

PART TWO
DEFIANCE

The smith shapes the metal to his will as the Just God shapes the Acolyte to His Service. Both metal and Acolyte will bend or be broken.

—The Fifth Rite of Devotion

CHAPTER EIGHT

"I'LL admit it's pretty," I said, "but it's still too warm for late autumn." Caoes, eyes closed as he lay stretched out on the grass near me, gave no sign of having heard what I said, and I couldn't blame him. Given what we'd been through, a bit of warmth and quiet was not easily interrupted. A good distance away, the sunlight glittered off swords and shields of the small encampment . . . the ones still left.

It had been a week since the attack on the Calarginn camp in the Greenmark, and five days since I had picked up the trail of the Calarginnian survivors. There weren't many. Of the nearly fifty originally in Captain Kraes's company, only fifteen had made it out alive . . . though from what I could tell, they had inflicted more than their fair share of casualties on the Arginnian division. I hadn't been able to get close enough to see how healthy the survivors were; for several days Kraes had kept her people tightly clustered on the journey out of the Greenmark, no doubt expecting pursuit, but none had come so far, and so the camp now was spread a bit more widely. Even so, there was little cover here; we had entered the basin proper, traveling mostly west. The placid land was striped by streams and bridged rivers flowing from the River Glacal to the north, and now sheds and barns were more common sights than hills or forest groves. So Caoes and I had to keep our distance, especially since the company made its camp during midday and traveled at night … a sensible precaution, against either the Arginnians or me.

"Not that they need to worry about me," I growled, and Caoes lazily opened an eye for a moment before closing it again and rolling onto his other side. Probably the right response to a childish plea for fairness, but it annoyed me all the same. It was clear now that Merynne and the Arginnians had played Kraes and the Calarginnians for weeks; they certainly hadn't anticipated *me*, but they had been preparing to move against Kraes's company for some time. The attack had been too well coordinated and too large to just be coming from the one division; there had obviously been other Arginnians already in wait near the Greenmark, waiting for the signal to strike, and when it came they overwhelmed the Calarginnians. Without me, and my warning, the attack would have been even more devastating than it was.

But despite my annoyance, I couldn't really expect Kraes to understand what had happened. From her point of view, I had agreed to help them, was late getting back, appeared just as she was searching for her missing patrols, then vanished again after a warning of an attack I could have brought on myself. And of course, I was a stranger to begin with; why she had decided to trust that stranger with this sort of task was another question, but I certainly knew what desperation felt like, and Kraes was desperate when I met her. I had managed to at least distract the Arginnians when fleeing the Greenmark, and staying to fight alongside the Calarginnians when the attack began would have been suicide, perhaps … but I had traded trust for survival, and it would take a major shift in fortune to get Kraes back on my side.

I was invoking fortune far too often these days.

For the first day or so after the attack, Caoes and I had laid low an hour away from the Greenmark, waiting in a deserted, broken-down house on an abandoned farm, its walls barely secure enough to hold up a roof rotting from neglect and long years of exposure to the elements. A patch of gourds had grown wild, and, my own supplies scant, I dried a pile of seeds out on an old board in the still-warm sun while Caoes and I sat, mostly silent in the shadows. It wasn't much of a base of operations, but I needed time to think and plan, and at least this wouldn't be an obvious place for pursuers to search first. For, like Kraes, I assumed further pursuit was inevitable. I was a wild card for Merynne, and I doubted very much she would let that random element remain outside her control. But when no one appeared that evening, much of my thinking revolved around the primary question: where to go next? Returning to Elskeg was as impossible as it was pointless now; without the Calarginnian company, the Depths were certainly lost, and in short order the area would be crawling with Arginnians. I could return to Cohrelle, without having found the answers I sought and without having dealt with the fundamental threat, to certain eventual discovery and death ... not a particularly attractive prospect. That meant I had to keep going, perhaps directly to Tellisar. If Fen had been correct—and despite her dislike of me, her story had the ring of truth—the Order at least had a presence there, and it was becoming clear that Tellisar had an interest in things well beyond its own borders. Arginn was out of the question now. But so long as Tellisar remained at least theoretically neutral in the conflict between the two other cities, I could probably operate with a bit more freedom.

Then what of Calarginn? I hadn't intended to get involved

in the affairs of another city; I had my own problems. But I had given my word, and whatever other sacrifices I had made, keeping faith with those I had pledged still mattered to me. I didn't know if Ress had survived the attack on the company, or if he was even there when it happened. But my implicit promise, to try to help his son if I could, remained. To reach Tellisar, I had to cross the Glacalta. And if I were fortunate, staying unnoticed on a standard ferry from Calarginn would be much easier than finding my own passage elsewhere.

On the evening of the second day after the attack and my hesitation getting me nowhere, I let the river's flow make the decision for me. Caoes alerted me with a low growl, and crawling to the window of the ruined farmhouse where the panther stood, I peered out to see Captain Kraes and the remainder of the Calarginnian company, not far from where we lay and clearly visible in the bright moonlight, marching at a steady pace into the grassy fields of the basin uplands—toward the Glacalta, and Calarginn. Caoes seemed to be urging me to go, and as soon as it was safe we slipped out to follow. We would have to be careful . . . but at least now we had a more reliable path, rather than just heading for the Glacalta and hoping for the best.

The Calarginnians traveled at a steady but not particularly fast pace, and at first I reasoned that the survivors might have injuries slowing them down. As I thought more about it, though, it struck me that the last thing Kraes would want to do is call attention to what was left of her company by moving them too quickly . . . especially if Arginnian spies had been placed in strategic spots along the route back to Calarginn. It seemed unlikely that Arginn would have either the cleverness or the resources to maintain such a network—it wasn't Tellisar or Cohrelle, and I knew that even the wealth of those cities would not be able to sustain outposts like that for long. But then Arginn had already surprised me, and no doubt Kraes, with this operation, far more sophisticated and involved than we had suspected it could be. And it had already surprised me with Captain Merynne.

Merynne again. Of all the oddities I had encountered since leaving Cohrelle, she was the one for which I still had no reasonable explanation. Being able to find the laquevoxes; the way my bonds were tied, making it impossible for me to escape without Caoes's help; her suspicion that I was not from Calarginn, and that my motivations were more complicated than money. All of those were things most soldiers wouldn't have considered, unless—

Hells. Unless the Order of Argoth got to her.

The more I thought about it, the more likely it seemed. Arginn was desperate for help in the war, and if the Order was now in the business of selling the Service to the highest bidder, a group of trained assassins would be an enormously valuable asset. With a little bit more luck, my own involvement would have disrupted an entire Arginnian division; if thirty or forty Acolytes were deployed to strategic positions, prepared to strike at military commanders or political leaders used to conventional threats, not sophisticated assassination plans driven by faith and unshakeable determination . . . yes. Such a group could easily turn the tide of the conflict.

Then it struck me. "Tellisar," I said as we walked, giving Kraes's company as much distance as we could while still keeping them in sight. Caoes looked at me. "What if Tellisar is behind all of this?" I went on. "Not the Order at all. Tellisar sees a chance to lock in a permanent supply line from the Depths, eliminates Calarginn as a potential threat, and keeps Arginn subservient..." I sighed. "But why now?" I went on, arguing with myself. "Why become interested in regional power now—"

Unless the Order has taken over. Maybe I have it backward. If the Order has taken over in Tellisar, the way it was trying to do in Cohrelle... then there's much more at stake than a civil war between two smaller cities and the larger city watching them fight. Suddenly I remembered the words of Lady Ashenza right before her death, right before I had finished my final successful mission for the Service: "The threat you face is your own—that of your Order, and your Service." At the time, I had dismissed her claims as manipulative attempts to distract me from my purpose. But of course, all she had said had been proven right so far, and now there was no telling how far the Order really wanted to go. If it was through Tellisar, it would benefit from a civil war between its two rivals... and if the winner owed Tellisar and the Order for the victory, so much the better.

"Dangerous," I said, again out loud. "Nothing for it, then, Caoes... we've got to get to Tellisar one way or the other, and figure out how to stay in one piece. So long as Kraes's company keeps this course, we follow them, all the way back to Calarginn if we have to." This time Caoes kept his yellow eyes focused on our marks in the distance, and for a few moments I turned my attention from the Calarginnians. I was surprised that Caoes had so easily settled into my life, how his presence had become both a familiar and unforgettable part of my world. In some ways I had begun to view him as a sort of extension of myself: the darker, silent portion of my inner thoughts. *A bridge to your soul*, Caron might have said, and there was a time I would have laughed at such notions. But now … now, I was not so sure. I had learned, after all, that faith, certainty, and arrogance were all inextricably linked conditions, and I had spent far too much time with them all.

And so we followed, traveling at night and stopping for rest during the day as Kraes's company did. For a time I spent as much time looking behind me as in front, waiting for Merynne's pursuit to arrive, but it never came. But I stayed suspicious, and even as the days passed with no sign of the Arginnians, I could never entirely dismiss the feeling that somehow, somewhere, Merynne was watching … waiting for a moment of weakness to strike.

In another day we began to encounter increasing signs of civilization; the farms were more closely clustered together here, and the livestock more numerous. Kraes now changed tactics; her company began to stay on farms themselves instead of out in the open, knocking on farmhouse doors in the evening hours and requesting—or perhaps demanding, since I was too far away to hear what was being said—shelter in the barn. I didn't know exactly what had prompted Kraes to alter her pattern of travel, but I had to assume we were entering territory friendlier to Calarginn, where the residents would be more willing to help the fleeing company and moving by day was safer than by night; besides, even a small group of fifteen armed soldiers would have stood out here if they tried to camp in the open. Caoes and I had no other option, of course, and so we were forced to make do with nearby fields lying fallow, or sometimes a partially vacant stable or even haystack, sleeping lightly and departing when the company did. At least I could vary my diet from handfuls of dried seeds, though probably more than one bleary-eyed farmer rising before the dawn scratched his head at a missing chicken or vanished carrot. And for a while, it seemed that we had escaped any real danger.

But then other things began to appear, not nearly as pleasant. Caoes noticed it first, two days after entering the farmland as we followed the Calarginnians at our usual distance. His nose wrinkled, and his tongue flicked out of his mouth a few times like a hopeful frog, his usual impassive face twisted in some vague approximation of disgust. A minute later, I too began to pick up the scent, acrid, slightly sulfurous, and all too familiar; and not long after that, I noticed that the company was picking up its pace, hustling over the fields faster than it had done for days. It wasn't the safest course of action, if what I suspected was true . . . but I had seen the look in the captain's eyes when she had told me why she was fighting for Calarginn, and I knew something about feeling a desperate desire to stop the inevitable. A flash of red crossed my vision: a bloody message on a wall, a motionless body . . .

No. Mourn the past after you've dealt with the present.

Within a few minutes we reached a gentle rise, and as the company went over it and disappeared from view on the other side, there was a momentary silence, a kind of stillness in the air. Then we heard a loud shout, and as Caoes and I reached the top of the slope, slowing down and dropping into a crawl as we approached, a few curses followed. We laid flat and peeked over the crest of the hill, and as the cool breeze reached us, the sulfurous stench of ash and dust it brought was almost overwhelming. Caoes snorted softly.

Hells. I had known, but, as usual, wished I was wrong.

Down below us was the remains of a farm—but this one had not fallen into disrepair from age or neglect. What was left of the farmhouse, ruined bits of darkened wood and scorched stone, smoldered on the ground, black ash drifting here and there in the wind. Nearby was the destroyed barn, three walls entirely collapsed and the other with one remaining broken and burned wooden post which might once have supported one of the large front doors. The fields had been burned to the dirt. And there, in front of the farmhouse—

I closed my eyes, the vision of Caoesthenes's dead body reasserting itself in my mind with a vengeance, then opened them again. A pile of burned, stinking corpses lay in front of the farmhouse … the remains of some large animals, perhaps horses or cows. But in front of that pile, bodies far too small to be livestock still smoldered, two larger ones and—

A small one. Probably younger than Caron.

Next to the pile kneeled Captain Kraes, the company clustered behind her at a respectful distance, swords drawn. From this distance I couldn't make out her expression, but her silence and stillness said more than outward demeanor could anyway. I lifted my gaze to the rest of the landscape.

"Hells," I whispered. "Who would do this?"

There were four other farms visible from our vantage point … or at least the remains of them. Each had been burned to the ground just as this closest farm had been, and in front of each was another pile of bodies; too far away for us to see details, but I could take a good guess as to what each would look like. A dark cloud wavered and drifted over the whole area, and the mingled stench of scorched flesh and wood hung upon the scene like a shroud. And as I looked further, the dark cloud seemed to extend miles into the distance, as if signaling further devastation on the path ahead.

I didn't have experience with farms; I had seen more of them in the last two days than I had in my entire life before. But I knew wooden buildings, and I knew that the danger of fire could be realized from many sources: a fallen lantern, a spark from a briefly unattended fireplace, the collapse of a wood stove grown brittle from age and misuse. Yet none of these things would cause a fire large enough to utterly annihilate a building as these had been ... certainly not more than one, along with the livestock and their owners. The only fires which could do that were manmade.

Someone burned down all of these buildings. Someone killed all of these animals, and people, on purpose.

I turned my head, eyes wide, to look at Caoes. His nose was wrinkled again, teeth silently bared as if warning off an unseen attacker, and as I looked back at the ruin below I heard him growling faintly. Captain Kraes and her company remained motionless.

Arginn, I thought numbly. *Arginn must have done this ... but why?* There was no military value in destroying places which could help maintain its army's supply line, especially given how far afield Arginn had decided to venture to press its advantage in the war. None of these farmers, even if they were friendly toward Calarginn, had any strategic value or presented any real threat to Arginn. Taking the time to do this to them would be a waste of time and precious resources. The only reason at all would be ... to send a message. To generate fear, to warn potential adversaries, to put everyone else on notice: Arginn, the little city of fishers and crafters, rutting with the Calarginns and Sullbrises of Silarein, had become a player, and no one would stand in its way. Delivered in the right fashion, a message like that could be worth almost any cost.

It was entirely logical, very sensible from a strategic point of view. Yet somehow it felt too neat, too obvious. *Take a step back from the statue: what else do you see?* Caoesthenes had told me, a warning not to get bogged down in details. But if I looked at the big picture . . .

An unintelligible shout echoed from the ruined farmhouse below, and startled, I refocused on the scene below. Kraes had one of her people, presumably the one who had shouted, by the shoulders, and was talking to him quietly but animatedly. After a minute or so, the soldier broke away, several of the others following and patting him on the back as he turned and stalked off into a nearby field. In the meantime Kraes spoke to the rest of the company, and soon thereafter the soldiers spread out among the ruined farms. "Investigating," I muttered to Caoes. It made sense; the fire was still smoldering, and this couldn't have happened much more than a day before we arrived. Now was the time to gather evidence, before wind and rain blew and washed it away. But if the people who did this were still nearby . . .

I shook my head. "Not much we can do but wait, then, Caoes," I said. "We move when they do." The panther rose as I did, and turning from the scent and horror, we slipped away from the crest of the hill to find a safer place to continue our vigil.

I stood outside the entrance to Caoesthenes's home in Open-Heart Alley, looking at the wide open door with a frown. It all seemed peaceful enough, but Caoesthenes was not the type to leave his home vulnerable at any time ... let alone now, when things in Cohrelle had become this dangerous. "Follow me and stay close," I said quietly to Caron, but as I turned to look at my young charge, I saw no one at all. That was odd ... they had been right behind me, hadn't they? I drew my cucuri and passed through the open door slowly, tense, ears straining for any unusual noise which might indicate an attack. Nothing. Inside, the kitchen was its usual orderly chaos, shelves crammed full of various teas, tinctures, foodstuff, and weapons in various states of repair ... still, the fire was dark, and no one stirred. Slow as death, I crept down the stairs to the basement and Caoesthenes's workshop; no one had challenged me yet, but I didn't see how that luck could continue. *What is the old man playing at?* I thought as I looked around, noting with surprise that the basement seemed clean and entirely devoid of the usual collection of gadgets and weapons Caoesthenes liked to make. *This isn't the time for a brush-up lesson—*

And then, against the far wall, I saw another body, staring up at the ceiling. But as I walked toward whomever it was, something flashed, and I blinked. When I opened my eyes again, I saw what had caused the disturbance: a short man, wearing a cloak with its hood up, was now kneeling by the body.

Where did he come from?

I opened my mouth to challenge the silent figure ... and then I saw the dead man's face, and I felt my stomach twist in horror. It was Caoesthenes, eyes staring sightlessly.

Hells.

The figure kneeling next to him had not moved—but now, as I stared at them, they seemed to suddenly notice my presence. And as they turned, I caught the flash of a sneer within the hood. They pushed it back.

Hells, it can't be . . . but no one else could . . .

It was Caron, their calm features now twisted and distorted with malice and rage. "You've come too late, Grayshade," they said, their normally gentle voice rough and low. "But you always come too late, don't you? Always one step behind; always figuring things out after everyone else has. Always following orders, no matter who dies, no reasons needed. Such a good little boy, to do what you're told, always." They grinned again, and now I could see their teeth were stained red. Suddenly it struck me: I was looking at Caron, but the voice wasn't theirs.

It was Father Jant's.

The hunter is there, Grayshade.

Another voice, this one strangely familiar, echoed through my mind as the Caron-figure rose and walked toward me slowly, drawing forth a long, curved dagger which glinted in the lantern light. I felt myself drop to my knees.

Careful.

"You've never learned," the Caron who wasn't said. "You've never learned to think for yourself, to reason for yourself."

Grayshade!

"You've never done anything but kill for others," the rough voice said. "You've never done anything but hit and stab and slash and kill, always when they tell you, always exactly what they tell you. Now they're telling you to stay right there. Stay right there and wait as we hit and stab and slash and kill you. Stay right there as you die."

False Caron grinned again, their mouth a smear of red, and raised the dagger.

The hunter, Grayshade!

Something about the desperation in the other voice pierced my stupor, and I lifted an arm as the dagger began to descend. Something flashed across my vision again—the briefest glimpse of yellow eyes.

CHAPTER NINE

I jerked awake, grabbing for my cucuri, but saw only Caoes watching me with an expression which might be mild surprise. There was no dagger, and no Caron, and no voice of Jant—just the panther and me, lying in the patch of long grass we had found in which to bed down for the evening. Kraes had spent the rest of the day here, either to gather more information about who or what had destroyed these farms, or to gather her wits and consider what to do next . . . or both, most likely. If Arginn could strike this close to Calarginn, any plan Kraes might have had to report back to her superiors would have to be reconsidered. And until Caoes and I knew more ourselves about what had happened—and we couldn't get close to the area to inspect it with the Calarginnians around—we didn't have many more options than they did. While some of the Calarginnians had stopped for a quick, unpleasant rest, I doubted they would stay here the full night, as even burying the dead had not erased the smell from the wafting ash. So we waited for them to move, and finally I allowed myself to drift off to sleep again as Caoes watched the company. Such a curious thing, to have such trust in a creature I had no connection to or knowledge of a fortnight ago . . . and yet, the feeling of trust, not simply blind devotion, was a welcome one.

"No movement yet?" I said to Caoes quietly as I rolled over on to my front and looked out of the grass at the farmhouse some distance away, illuminated by the campfire and flickering lantern light, the soft red glow of smoldering ruins around it still visible in patches. The guards Kraes had posted at the outskirts of the camp were still visible not far from where we were concealed, each standing silently with a lantern in one hand and the other hand on their sword hilt. I didn't know them, but then in the days following the Calarginnians I hadn't seen many I recognized besides Kraes—so, I surmised, Fen hadn't made it. Ress either, if he'd been in the Greenmark that night rather than in bed in Elskeg, as I continued to hope. Fen hadn't liked me, but I could hardly blame her for that, and I had appreciated her dedication to their cause. It was an echo of my own devotion in the past, and if the devotion had been misplaced, at least it had felt real.

Suddenly I saw movement and stiffened, and Caoes growled quietly. "Hells," I breathed. "I should have known." I stared intensely into the darkness; after a few seconds, something else stirred at the edge of the lantern light. But this was no cow or horse, or even a wolf. It was, though only visible for the briefest moment, the edge of a cloak.

A quick glance showed that the guards had not noticed the disturbance . . . and had I not been trained for years to detect slight changes in the environment, I wouldn't have seen the movement either. Arginnians, perhaps? Whoever they were, they weren't likely to be friendly. I opened my mouth to whisper to Caoes, but before I could say anything the first of the Calarginnian guards turned his head slightly, as if curious; then he slipped to the ground, lantern falling from his nerveless fingers. The second guard turned as he heard the sound of his companion's body hitting the ground, but almost immediately went rigid and collapsed himself. Both had fallen within ten seconds.

For a moment I was frozen, staring at the motionless bodies while trying to work through what I had just seen. Those men would never move again, and I knew why, for I had done the same thing countless times before; and suddenly I knew exactly who the attackers were.

Acolytes of Argoth.

"Caoes," I hissed, pointing to the right, beyond where I had seen the first sign of movement. "Head that way . . . work around behind them. And be careful; these people are dangerous." Caoes gave a slight growl, then slunk off, body low to the ground, in the direction I had pointed. I watched him vanish into the darkness, then pulled myself into a low crouch and set off in the opposite direction. These Acolytes might well be from the Service operating in Tellisar, if Fen's story about the Acolytes there was correct, but it was hard for me to imagine that they would be trained much differently from Acolytes in Cohrelle. So unless they were instructed to avoid other contacts for a given mission, Acolytes were trained to work from the outside in. Pick off guards on patrol on the outskirts of the environment, then move in to the more well-defended places. And whatever Kraes thought she knew about fighting soldiers from Arginn, she wouldn't have any answers for Acolytes of Argoth, especially when she wasn't expecting them.

But then, they weren't expecting me, either.

I skirted around the end of the burned field, heading for the back of the destroyed farmhouse. With only fifteen fighters left, Kraes had few options for protecting the area, so there were no guards here ... which almost certainly meant that any attack would come through this way. As I saw the light of the campfire flickering through the smoldering rubble of the farmhouse, I slowed my pace and lowered myself to the ground, covering the last few hundred feet at a crawl. Suddenly something blotted out the firelight, and I stopped dead. *Thought so.* There, only a few feet away, a cloaked figure was now crouching at the back of the house, peering around a pile of blackened stones toward the camp in front.

One step at a time, then. I drew my cucuri, crawled up behind the figure and, reversing my blade, raked the hilt across the back of his head. With a groan he slumped to the ground, and I took a moment to look at the face—clean-shaven, no scars, and young. For a moment I saw Ravel, my Apprentice of only a few days ... just as young, perhaps just as new to the cause ... though Ravel, of course, was dead. I closed my eyes and took a deep breath. *That was in Cohrelle, and you're not. Not anymore. Stay focused.* Opening my eyes again, I came to a crouch and quickly searched the motionless body. No cucuri, but a healthy amount of kushuri darts in a belt pouch, along with a collapsible quiver of some kind. Definitely Acolytes from somewhere, then, as I had feared.

I moved to the left, following the line of the farmhouse's stone foundation to the opposite corner, where part of a beam which had once supported the roof still stood. As I came to a stop and looked around the beam, I saw a second person creeping along that side of the house, low to the ground. I followed, still crouched, until we were both near the front of the house. The light from the campfire was brighter here, and as I paused to watch, I saw the figure pull something forth from within the folds of their cloak—the same item the other had carried, which they unfolded into a long, thin tube. They placed it to their lips, but before anything else could happen I was on them, wrapping my arm around their neck and pulling backward as I put my knee into their back. The figure reached back for my arm and pulled at it, scrabbling wildly but silently, and jerked around with surprising strength ... now I was ready, though, and held my grip as the motions grew more feeble and then ceased. As quietly as I could, I pulled the figure back a few feet from the front of the house, then lay it down just within range of the firelight to look at the face. The woman was young, with light, shoulder-length hair, lips twisted with her effort to escape, and as I looked down at her face I was again surprised by the age. Were Acolytes now being recruited this young, then? Or had I grown old in the meantime, old enough that the two I had rendered unconscious could easily have been my own children? I frowned. *It's only been weeks since you left Cohrelle.* And the young are the easiest to make into true believers; if the Order had decided to start recruiting them even younger than Ravel had been, defiantly declaring his allegiance to Jant and the Service as he stood in Caoesthenes's kitchen, hand clenched around the hilt of his cucuri ...

I dismissed the thought; there'd be time enough for worries later. Now, I had an unknown number of Acolytes to concern myself with. I heard a grunt from the other side of the firelight, and as I looked up I briefly saw something being dragged quickly out of sight—a body, but whose?

"Ernis!" a voice suddenly barked. It was Captain Kraes's for certain, and I crept up next to the front of the house again, still cloaked in shadows unpierced by the flickering firelight, to see more. Kraes was standing next to a rumpled bedroll near the fire, sword drawn, eyes wide as if she were trying to pierce the surrounding darkness with her gaze. "Ernis!" she said again. "Ernis, why aren't you at your post?" There was no reply. Suddenly I felt a presence nearby, and looking to my left I saw another cloaked figure crawling slowly along the ground, just about to enter the circle of light. They were moving in complete silence, and Kraes showed no sign that she had seen anything. I hesitated; I could take whoever this was out, but I would be exposing myself to any others who might be surrounding the clearing. Then I remembered what the other Acolytes had been carrying, and I quickly turned to the body behind me and took the tube from beside her. As I had suspected, a kushuri dart had been placed in the other end . . . and that gave me an idea. I turned back, placed the tube to my lips, and just as the cloaked figure's body was fully within the light, I blew. The dart flew, faster than I expected but on target, right into the hand of the would-be attacker. He gave a grunt of pain, quickly muffled, but Kraes had already heard the disturbance and whirled to see the Acolyte struggling to get to his feet, grasping at the dart. In two steps she was across the clearing, and with a vicious kick she knocked the Acolyte onto his back. I rolled away from my spot, and crouched to listen.

"I'd shut up and stop squirming if you'd like to be able to do either of those things five minutes from now," Kraes hissed as she kneeled down next to the Acolyte, whose movements immediately ceased. The captain quickly scanned the clearing. "I'm only going to ask these questions once," she went on, "so I'd recommend you answer them correctly the first time. How many are you?"

"Enough," came the curt answer.

Kraes smiled unpleasantly and lowered the blade of her sword to the Acolyte's neck. "Numbers, now." She pressed the blade, ever so slightly, into the Acolyte's skin.

"Eight," the Acolyte replied, his voice obviously strained. Eight, and I had taken out two; Kraes was interrogating the third, which meant five remained somewhere, if the Acolyte was being truthful. And no Acolyte I'd ever met knew how to lie worth a damn. We'd left that to our masters.

I had given Kraes the opportunity to ask, but now knowing the answer, I worried when to act. Five Acolytes could easily take the captain down while she was standing over the one. Kraes would never know what had happened.

"Better. Next: was your mission to kill, or capture? What have you done to my people?"

There was silence for a moment, then: "We did what were told to do. You'll see the rest for yourself." A second later he cried out; Kraes's blade had cut him, ever so slightly. "We—we were told to eliminate everyone here."

The blade pulled back. "Looks like you failed, then," Kraes said, nodding in the direction of the Acolyte's wounded hand. "In the future you might want to watch how you grab your darts."

"It's not mine," the Acolyte said, looking vaguely in my direction . . . a tinge of anger, and perhaps frustration, in his voice. I could have thrown the kushuri dart at him, but I had used the tube for just this reason: the way the dart had hit him made it seem like an Acolyte he knew had attacked him and prepared him for these questions, and I could imagine the mixture of confusion and suspicion he was now feeling. Yet I was still troubled . . . if there were still five others, what were they waiting for? At any moment, I expected Kraes to crumple over her target, but with five waiting Acolytes I could only watch, and assess.

Kraes saw the Acolyte's look and gazed into the shadows herself. "Double-crossed, were you?" she asked as she looked back down, as if she had picked up on the Acolyte's thoughts. "Then that's a good lead-in to my last questions. Who are you? And who sent you?"

The Acolyte opened his mouth as if to answer, then closed it and gave a small smile. "It doesn't matter. Very soon, none of it will make a difference to you."

"I thought we were done with being defiant," Kraes said as she lowered the blade of her sword again, but I was already looking around the edges of the circle of light. The Acolyte had noticed something. At first I saw nothing, but then something stirred; across the way, next to a burned fence post, something sliding into view . . . a glint of light reflecting off . . .

A metal tube.

No time to reload my own; grabbing a few of my kushuri darts from the pouch at my belt, I threw them in the direction of the glint. A second later I heard a shout of pain as the glint disappeared, and Kraes twisted in that direction.

Then everything happened at once. The Acolyte at her feet jerked his knee upward into Kraes's stomach, knocking the captain's sword from her hands and driving her backward. Roaring as he yanked the dart from his hand, he picked up Kraes's sword and rolled to his feet as two other cloaked figures charged into the light. Hoping Kraes was only staggered and not knocked out or worse, I drew my cucuri and leapt toward the Acolyte I had injured; at the last second he turned and brought his sword up to parry my descending blade. We stepped back from each other for a moment, giving me enough time to see that Kraes had recovered, though wincing a bit from pain, and had drawn a dagger from her belt as the two other Acolytes pressed in upon her. Kraes was obviously a competent fighter, but she had no hope of holding out against two people trained by the Service. I couldn't get to her in time.

And then a black blur shot from beyond the edge of the light and impacted the Acolyte furthest away, knocking him to the ground.

Caoes.

The panther was upon the downed Acolyte, who shouted in a mixture of anger and fear as he tried to ward the silent creature off; and Kraes, eyes wide, ran toward the other Acolyte, who just had time to block the captain's assault. Three on three for the moment, with the fourth one unaccounted for . . . more reasonable odds, if still weighted against us, and I turned my attention back to the Acolyte in front of me. He had light brown eyes over a neat goatee, his face covered in sweat. Younger than me by a good fifteen years, he held the captain's sword in his left hand with ease . . . so I probably hadn't hit his dominant hand with the dart, though Acolytes are usually trained to wield weapons with either hand anyway. I waited, watching him intently; he mirrored me, but I could tell it wasn't his preference. He wanted to strike, to dictate the terms of the fight, and when I was younger I had wanted to do the same. It was Father Esper who had taught me that the one who gathers the most information about his opponent almost always wins, and that means patience and time. As I had grown older, I had finally understood what he meant: it's always the young, with the most time, who act like they have the least of it.

The Acolyte stepped to his right several paces, then back a step, but I wasn't fooled; his weight was leaning forward even as he moved backward, and I was ready when he made a sudden lunge, thrusting forward with the sword. I dodged to the right and brought my cucuri down upon his blade, knocking it almost to the ground, and threw a punch to follow up. But he had already anticipated the attack, and jerked his head out of the way of my fist as he brought his blade back up toward my outstretched arm. I slid right again just in the nick of time, and the sword cut into the folds of my cloak, missing my arm by a few inches. I whirled in place, allowing the cloak to wrap the sword even further, and then pulled hard. As he stumbled forward, my knee came up into his stomach, and he doubled over in pain, gasping for breath. I reversed my cucuri, but before I could drive it down on his head he released the sword, dropped to the ground and rolled away as I tried to get the cloak free of his blade. I managed it just as he came to his feet not far away, still coughing, eyes narrowed as he prepared his next assault.

He was fast for certain, and his style of fighting, though familiar, was different enough from my own that I knew he was not from Cohrelle's Service. I wouldn't get the benefit of under-standing his pattern of attacks . . . but then, *surprises work in both directions, lad,* Caoesthenes always said, and I had already sur-prised him once. The second one would be the end of it. He drew forth a dagger—not a weapon I recognized as an Acolyte's, but deadly enough—and came charging in on me, gaze fixed on my face. Yet this was all too simple, for I knew he would not actually attack my head or torso with a dagger; and I leapt into the air just as he dropped down at the end of his charge, swinging his legs in an effort to undercut mine. I dropped directly onto one of his thighs, focusing all of my weight in that direction, and was rewarded with a satisfying crack and roar of pain as he reflexively grabbed for the leg, letting his dagger fall. One blow to the head later and he was on the ground, on his side, out cold.

As I turned to take in the rest of the battleground I saw that Caoes had eliminated his Acolyte, though there were some nasty-looking cuts parting his fur, and he was just turning toward the fight between Kraes and the remaining Acolyte. Both looked to have been injured; the Acolyte was favoring his left leg, and Kraes had a ragged cut on her face. But still, the fight looked like it had been fairly even, and as I charged toward the two, Kraes noticed my approach before her opponent. Dodging a slash from the Acolyte's cucuri, which despite the movement bit into Kraes's left arm, the Calarginnian captain managed to shove her opponent clear just as I reached them, and I drove an elbow into the man's chest, sending him backward and onto the ground. Then Caoes was on him, and there was only time for a cry, quickly cut short, before silence returned.

Kraes stared at me, holding her arm and wincing. "Grayshade! What devilry—"

"That'll be enough from you, captain," a voice said from behind us, and we turned to see a cloaked figure, sandy brown hair over eyes glittering in the firelight. It had to be the last of the Acolytes ... but he was not alone. His right hand held a dagger like the one his companion had wielded, but his left arm was wrapped around a young, raven-haired girl, eyes set and staring.

His hand was clamped on her mouth. "You call this ralaar waste and his pet off, or you can watch another Calarginnian die from your choice." Six more people, dressed in Calarginnian armor, ran into the firelight with swords drawn, but they skidded to a halt as Kraes raised her good arm.

"Never figured the Arginnians to be into killing children," Kraes said, breathing heavily. "Thought there was some honor left in your city."

"Tell them to drop their weapons," the man said, pulling back slightly on the girl's head as her eyes widened.

"We do that, you'll get the rest of your people to kill us anyway, and her. You already showed us how much you care about innocent life," Kraes replied, jerking her head toward the destroyed farmhouse.

"Innocent?" the Acolyte sneered. "I've seen enough from Calarginn to know about your brand of innocence. Would you be feeling the same way if this was a girl from Arginn?" He shot a quick glance down at the terrified child, whose breathing had intensified.

"I would," I said, taking a step forward. "So should you."

The Acolyte stared at me. "Who in the Hells are you?"

"Not a Calarginnian, or an Arginnian," I replied, ignoring Kraes's stare, "and neither are you."

His mouth worked for a moment. "You're in the Service. But you're not from here."

"No, I'm not. But I'm with these people for the moment, and I'm telling you you're not in a position to negotiate. Kill that child and you'll be dead with her, and you won't have done anything to fulfill your mission. And everything is about the mission."

I took another step forward, and the Acolyte's hand tightened around the girl's mouth as she gave a small, frightened cry. "Stop where you are," he hissed. "I don't know what kind of Acolyte you are, or were, but any real Acolyte would know not to interfere in the Order's business."

"Any real Acolyte would know when he was outnumbered and outflanked," I replied, taking another step. "Don't be a fool, and don't accept a meaningless death. The Service can't afford to waste Acolytes."

"What in the Hells are you talking about?" Kraes said at last, a mixture of surprise and anger in her voice. "You're telling me this man isn't Arginnian?"

"Not unless Arginn's been taken over by the Order of Argoth as well," I replied. "I don't know what this is all about . . . but these Acolytes are from the Service, though not from my city's."

The Acolyte glanced over his shoulder at several of the Calarginnian soldiers, eyeing him warily with swords still drawn. "I'm going to leave now, and this girl is coming with me," he said, looking back at the captain. "You want her alive, you'll tell them to drop their weapons and back off. And when I'm gone, if you want to keep her alive, you'll stay where you are and not try to follow."

"Because you won't kill her the minute you get out of earshot, when she starts slowing you down?" I asked, smiling grimly.

The Acolyte's eyes narrowed. "I've had about enough of you, stranger," he said, pulling the girl's head back further, so that she had to rise to her tiptoes to keep from wrenching her neck, wiggling unsteadily. "I won't ask again, captain. You get your band to stand down, or I'll take them down, and this girl with them. Up to you if you want to keep your hands clean."

"The last thing any Acolyte of Argoth should be talking about is keeping clean," I said. "Captain, this man is lying. He won't let the girl go, and he won't leave peacefully."

The Acolyte opened his mouth to reply, then hesitated. "Where the Hells is that filthy cat of yours?" he asked, suspicion creeping into his voice.

I was tempted to look down to see if Caoes was nearby, but I knew enough to keep my eyes level and expression clear. Finally I smiled. "Right where he needs to be," I said, as a low growl came from the shadows behind the Acolyte and the Calarginnian guards. His eyes widened, and I could see his hand release her mouth, letting her back onto her feet.

And . . . now.

"Duck, girl!" I shouted, throwing a spray of kushuri darts at the Acolyte's neck. The girl pulled down hard as the Acolyte brought his dagger up to deflect the darts, but something slammed into him from behind, jerking his head backward. The darts pierced his throat, and he fell back to the ground with a crash and lay still. Standing above him was not Caoes, but one of the Calarginnian guards, sword stained with blood, a savage grin on his face. As the panther emerged from the shadows, I looked over at Kraes, who looked first at the dead Acolyte, then the terrified girl, and finally at me.

"We have some talking to do, Grayshade," the captain said, taking a deep breath. "It's time we find out whose side you're really on."

CHAPTER TEN

DESPITE Kraes's urgency, it was actually almost an hour before we were seated around the campfire again and ready to talk. Of the fifteen fighters of the Calarginnian company we had been following, only ten had survived the Acolytes' attack; another was still alive when we found him, but died within minutes. A few of the others had various minor injuries, and Kraes's left arm, now in a makeshift sling, was probably sprained, if not broken. "It would have been far worse if you hadn't been there," the captain said, staring into the fire. Nearby stood several guards, staring into the darkness, while Caoes lay between me and the captain, head between paws, his left side to the firelight.

Not far away, seated on the ground, the Calarginnian girl had a blanket wrapped around her shoulders and was holding a metal mug with steaming hot water inside. She had said nothing since her rescue, but her clothes were coarse and simple, and her hands calloused . . . probably a worker on the farm, or the daughter of the farmer herself. Somehow she had survived the initial attack, perhaps by hiding in one of the few bales of hay which had escaped the first burning—and then, with the Acolytes around, and then the arrival of more armored soldiers, had been too frightened—or stunned—to attempt escape. Whatever the truth was, the expression on her face was haunted, the firelight reflected in her eyes an echo of the larger conflagration she had watched consume her world. I couldn't know for sure what she had seen, but I could well imagine what she felt. I had both caused, and felt myself, the horror of seeing a loved one who would never move or speak again . . . and there was no removing the mark from one's memory once it had been burned there, black and twisted.

I closed my eyes for several seconds, letting my feelings settle, before turning my attention to Kraes. "That was their intention," I said. "Wait until you were at your weakest point, when you were least ready to respond, and then attack without warning."

"But why?" Kraes asked. "If these people weren't Arginnians, why go after us at all?"

"I don't know yet. But that was obviously their plan: no one left alive to report on the attack, or who was behind it."

Kraes paused. I knew she wasn't thrilled that her soldiers had eliminated the rest of the Acolytes, the ones I'd left unconscious, before they could be questioned, but it wasn't a thought she was going to voice.

"You knew a lot about their tactics," Kraes replied. "So this organization you wanted to find—this Order of Argoth—you were part of it once, back in Cohrelle?"

"Yes. I was an Acolyte in the Service, which carries out the will of the Order."

"But this Acolyte didn't seem to know you."

I nodded. "He was certainly a member of the Service, but not from my city. If Fen was right, I'd guess he was from Tellisar." I stopped as I saw Kraes wincing. "The arm?"

Kraes grunted acknowledgement. "I've had worse; it'll heal. And I'm still here . . . unlike Fen," she said grimly.

"And Ress?" I asked.

"Sleeping in town." Kraes did not seem relieved at the idea, but then, they'd only recently met ... and there might still be a couple of Arginnians who would want to settle a score with the old miner, now that Elskeg was theirs.

I nodded slowly. "I'm sorry you lost Fen. She seemed like a loyal soldier."

"She was a good one, and we can't afford to lose those," Kraes replied. "She was as stubborn as a bull ... always thought she'd outlive me. Not having her around is—strange." She paused and shook her head, then looked at me. "So you've been following us since the Greenmark?"

"I picked up your trail the next day."

"Why stay in the shadows?"

I grunted. "Would you have welcomed me?"

Kraes raised an eyebrow and opened her mouth as if to reply, then closed it again and looked back into the fire. "I would have tried to kill you," she finally said. "But that doesn't mean it was right for you to follow us. If one of my people had found you out there, someone would have gotten hurt."

"Maybe. It wouldn't have been me."

Kraes shrugged and rubbed the back of her neck. "Well, Gods know we'd have been dead for certain if you hadn't stepped in. So unless you're playing the strangest game I've ever heard of, I'm going to guess you aren't planning to off us in our sleep. But it doesn't explain what happened back at the Greenmark, either."

"What happened is I was delayed leaving the Arginnian camp."

"You failed."

I hesitated, pushing down a long trained reaction to the

suggestion of failure, then nodded. "More or less. And I shouldn't have; if everything had gone according to plan, the camp would have been disrupted."

"What went wrong?"

"Captain Merynne." Next to me, Caoes lifted his head and looked at me, yellow eyes blinking.

Kraes shook her head. "That's the second time you've mentioned this woman, and I don't know anything more about her now than I did the first time. She captured you?"

"Yes ... and you might not have known about her, but she knew about you. She knew where your company was stationed for weeks."

Kraes stared at me, eyes widening. "That's not possible. We'd have picked up word—"

"You didn't. She knew about the Greenmark, and she'd been planning an attack on your position for weeks. You think your patrols vanished before the attack by chance?"

The captain's mouth worked, her free hand clenching. Then she winced and turned away again. "I knew it was too easy for them, but I just figured we'd gotten soft." She sighed. "Didn't think that we—that I—had been stupid to boot."

"You were doing the best you could, Kraes; she covered her tracks well. And if she figured out what *I* was doing, she was pretty insightful to begin with." I left out my theories of her working with the Order, for the present. I watched Caoes lower his head to the ground again, eyes open, before continuing. "You've really never heard of Merynne? Or any Arginnian Captain in the area?"

Kraes shook her head. "No. But it sounds like she wasn't very public about her identity . . . not soldiers as much as sellswords in the shadows." She glanced at me. "No offense."

"None taken. As I said, when I was in the Service, I wasn't killing for money."

Kraes nodded. "All right, then, let's hit it on the head. Why, then? Why did you serve this . . . Order?"

I hesitated again, mind whirling with a hundred possible answers. How to sum up a lifetime of doubt and uncertainty, comforted by a faith I eventually found was as much a lie as the promises made at The Fan and Feather? How to explain what the Order had done for me . . . and then to me? How to explain how . . . *infantile* I felt, to have gone so long not just following, but praying for a set of lies that seemed so obvious; a set of lies that I had heard called as such, in every alley and murmur.

I glanced at the Calarginnian girl, who was still staring into the fire, eyes glittering, and remembered when my world had first gone as dark as hers. The crawl back to the light had not been pleasant . . . nor was it over, yet. "I needed . . . a purpose," I said at last. "A goal, a reason to push forward. I took the one that was given."

"By killing?"

"By visiting justice on those who deserved it," I responded automatically before thinking twice. I blinked. "As my superiors perceived it, anyway. I did what I was told and I pushed it onto others. It took a while to realize the difference between their teachings and our reality. I can't fully explain why." Sickened by the softening in the soldier's eyes, I glanced away.

Her voice had softened also, and that I could not avoid. "When you're used to taking orders from others, you can lose sight of what reality is outside of what they tell you. Run into that myself more than once." She paused. "So that's why you killed for them. Why did you stop?"

I didn't reply for a while, possible responses competing in my mind. Finally I looked back at the captain as I settled on the simple truth: "They lied to me. Not structurally, but directly . . . and I found out."

"I see," Kraes replied. "Then you found your own path sooner than I did mine."

"Not sure about that. I just left *their* path."

"It's a start."

We were both silent for a while then, listening to the crackling of the slowly dying fire. Above us, the sky was beginning to lighten. As I looked over I saw the girl had placed her head between her arms, drawn up on her knees. Her breathing was regular and steady . . . asleep at last. "What's your plan for her?" I asked Kraes, who started slightly at the sound of my voice. "You can't just leave her here."

"No," she agreed. "She hasn't talked, but she's not Arginnian, that's certain. No idea if she's got family in Calarginn, but I can't leave a twelve-year-old out here to fend for herself, not with Arginnian soldiers wiping out anyone they find." She looked at the sleeping child, her expression softening again. "Poor girl. Wager she didn't plan on something like this."

"What if she doesn't want to go?"

"Would you want to stay around a place where something like this had happened?"

I thought about Caoesthenes's body in my arms, the blood on the walls, and closed my eyes for a moment. "No."

"Neither would I. We'll be gentle, but I'm not leaving her behind . . . I've had enough deaths on my watch."

Noting the watering in Kraes's eyes, I leaned back, looking at the rapidly brightening sky. "So you're still headed back to Calarginn?"

"Nowhere else to go," Kraes replied with a shrug of apparent resignation, her voice steady. "There's only ten of us left, and a few of those hurt beyond fighting for a bit." She nodded toward the sling on her arm. "Amazing the ones left haven't deserted by now. Better soldiers than I would be in their shoes."

"If not for you, the ones left wouldn't still be alive," I said, looking at the silent guards standing by the campfire. "They know that."

Kraes spat into the fire, listening to the water sizzle as it hit the flames. "They're bigger fools than I think if that's true. As far as I can see it, the only reason any of us are alive is you, and you're not their commander. I'll be lucky not to get knocked down to scullery maid when my superiors see what's left of the company. Assuming any of my superiors are left."

I raised an eyebrow. "You think Arginn has moved in?"

"Look around," the captain replied, voice irritated. "We're less than fifty miles from the city . . . if whoever ordered the burning of these farms and this attack could do this here, whether it's your Order or Arginn or someone else entirely, then we can't be certain of anything. Probably too soon for Calarginn to be overrun, but who knows?" She sighed. "Still, it's the safest possible place left for us now. If we can get back there and the city hasn't fallen, at least I'll be able to report what happened and get new orders."

"Orders to do what? Go back out and wait for the Service to finish the job? Let the Order take over Calarginn?"

"What would you have me do?" Kraes snapped, loudly enough that Caoes opened one eye. "I'm not even sure this Order of yours was involved. These people could have been waiting for anyone. You can buy a pack of darts in the alley." She kicked the log at her feet.

"Kraes, you're a smart enough soldier to read a sign when it's handed to you," I said, leaning forward. "This is the Order of Argoth's work; I don't know why, but it stinks of them. They won't stop until they've destroyed you and your people—and they'll take the fight to Calarginn one way or another."

"Which means what?"

I sat back as Caoes closed his eye again. "Which means our goals are linked. The only way to save your city is to stop the Order, and the only way for me to find the answers I seek, and stay clear of the blade myself, is via the same path . . . the path that leads all the way to Tellisar."

Kraes watched me for a moment, a searching expression on her face. "So you're still going there?"

I nodded. "I don't see any alternative. The Order is still active in Cohrelle, but all of this," I said, gesturing at the ruined buildings behind us, "didn't come from there. Tellisar's the only city in Silarein big enough to give the Order the base of operations it needs. That means I have to go there, as I'd thought. But I don't know the layout, the structure, anything about the environment I'm walking into. If I don't get help from someone who's been there, the chances of my getting where I need to aren't good. That's the help I need from you."

Kraes looked back into the fire and was silent for a long while. "As I said, I owe you, even if our original deal can't hold," she finally said. "But I don't know what help I can give you, when I've just lost a whole company myself. And I don't know about religions or groups of assassins. Seems to me the last thing you want is someone like me involved."

"I need help, not perfection," I replied.

Kraes sighed. "Well, if you're planning on getting into Tellisar, you won't be able to do it the easy way. In times past you could take a ferry to Tellisar from Calarginn, but the Arginnians took the channel in the first weeks. Tellisar gets through, but they control every passenger, every load. And Tellisar has actual ships, ships that can do damage . . . they've been keeping the Calarginnian boats Arginn didn't burn from traveling for months now. They say they're trying to protect their own citizens, but my guess is if you board one of their ships, you end up in an Arginnian net."

"I assume swimming isn't an option."

The captain chuckled. "You have any idea how wide the Glacalta is? Or how cold and deep, once you get out toward the center? And there are things in the water, they say . . . things you wouldn't like discovering on your own. No one crosses the Glacalta by swimming . . . even if you crafted a boat, you'd get spotted before you were halfway across. Wouldn't have anywhere to go then."

I nodded. "Not a pleasant prospect. And so?"

"So the best chance you've got is to get around the Glacalta, and that won't be quick or easy. You'll need to head northeast, toward the place where the Glacalta is fed by the two rivers, Glacal from the east and Carrtish from the north. Once you put the delta past you, crossing the Glacal shouldn't be terrible this time of year; get over that, head straight northwest and you'll reach the Carrtish." She hesitated. "That's a rough stretch, but keep on your way. Once past Carrtish, you can make for the Scales to the west. You'll have to go far enough to the north so you can avoid Arginn, but keeping to the southern edge of the Scales will ensure that. A few days travel to the southwest from there, and you'll be right in line with Tellisar to the south, on the shore of the Glacalta. That, you won't miss."

I thought for a minute, remembering the maps I'd found in Elskeg. "Isn't the marshland near the Carrtish impassable?"

"Not impassable," Kraes said grimly. "Just avoided. They call it the Bloodmarsh."

I grimaced. Whatever the soldier had intended by skipping this detail, I did need to know whether my hazards would be real or superstitions.

Kraes must have noticed my look, as she sighed, then continued. "Not the nicest place, for sure: slow travel, treacherous terrain, strange beasts. The worst land this side of the Silver Coast. And for a long time, there's been rumors of . . ." She hesitated. "Well. Stories about places no one goes tend to get built up a bit. But people live there for certain . . . not many, I'd wager, given what it's supposed to be like. But a few."

I thought about the Sewer Rats in Cohrelle . . . criminals, cutthroats, the desperate and lonely, all living hundreds of feet below the surface of the city, where at least they could be free to think for themselves.

Kraes glanced at me. "Not sure I'd want to run into anyone

or anything that could survive in the Bloodmarsh for months or years at a time. But that's in your favor, too—don't think your Order would want to waste people there, and I can promise you Tellisar and Arginn won't. With luck, you won't run into anything at all."

I smiled. "Luck's something I've had an odd relationship with over the last few months, captain."

"You're still breathing," Kraes pointed out. Her gaze fell on the lithe form of the panther. "Not sure how he'll do in the Bloodmarsh, though. Footing won't be good, and I hear the muck can get pretty deep." She shook her head. "Seems like these things are useful enough that they'd want to give all of your Acolytes one."

"He isn't from the Service," I replied, looking at Caoes. "He just . . . showed up back near Elskeg, when I was first scouting the Arginnian camp. He hasn't left, except for a couple of side trips here and there, ever since. He's adopted me, I suppose."

"He's not wild, that's certain," Kraes said, nodding. "Only animals I've seen in combat are horses and hawks, a trained dog or two. But a panther? Not usual for this area, and certainly not with humans. I'd make sure I took good care of him, if I were you. And maybe thank your luck a bit more than you have been."

I nodded, looking to change the subject. "All right; if all goes well, that gets me outside of Tellisar . . . what then?"

The captain shrugged. "Then it's in the hands of the Gods. The guards aren't likely to be spending much time looking for intruders or criminals coming from the north of the city; most trade to Tellisar comes from the east and west along the coast, and from the south by ship. They've had to deal with some refugees from the war, but shutting down the boats from Calarginn made that a pretty small problem, from what I hear. Anyway, the northern gate's bound to be the easiest way in. Get past that, and you'll have your wish . . . being in the middle of a big city crawling with people, only some of them wanting you dead."

"Then I should feel right at home," I said, watching the flickering shadows cast by the dying fire play across the crossed arms of the sleeping girl.

———————◆———————

It was only an hour or so before sunlight broke over the eastern horizon. The temperature was more seasonable now, the air crisp and cold, and sleep had been impossible, though I had given it a try. But it didn't really matter; unlike the girl, whose exhaustion had finally overcome her fear, I was still more curious than tired. If Kraes was right, all paths to Tellisar were bound to be dangerous . . . but only one of those paths would actually be viable. I wasn't looking forward to the prospect of difficult travel, particularly through a swamp with the reputation of the Bloodmarsh; I didn't want anything which could slow me down, not now, when my questions were continuing to multiply. And I wasn't at all sure how I, or Caoes, would fare against wild beasts in that environment. Since leaving Cohrelle, the worst creatures I'd encountered were a half-starved and not particularly brave coyote—and Caoes, who for some reason had decided to join my side. Encountering fiercer or stranger things, in slow and difficult conditions, was not an encouraging possibility.

But there was no better alternative, as Kraes reiterated while what was left of her company gathered their camp supplies in the early morning light. "If I were you, I'd head as straight northeast as I could from here. Keep the Scales to your left as you go, and soon enough you'll be able to spot the western edge of the Glacalta, narrowing as it reaches the delta. You'll enter the Bloodmarsh before you come to the Glacal itself; get across that and then cut northwest." She glanced behind her at the Calarginnian girl, who was standing not far away, and lowered her voice as she turned back to me. "And once you cross the river, keep your wits about you. Stories of the marsh tell of some of the creatures there, but it's more than that. Some say the place itself is alive … sending out things to draw people to it, and keeping them there when they come. I don't hold with superstition myself, but I'd hold my blade a bit tighter while I was there, all the same, and keep on my way until the Carrtish's at my back." She fell silent, then held out a hand. "Thanks for your help, Grayshade. Good luck on finding the answers you seek. Perhaps we'll meet again."

I nodded as I gripped her hand. "A safe return to Calarginn, captain."

Kraes nodded, then turned and strode off. I looked one last time at the girl, then turned away myself and crouched down by Caoes, who turned his yellow-eyed gaze to me. "Time for us to go, Caoes. Our path lies elsewhere." I checked northeast against the sun and season, then set off.

It looked to be a day of clear skies and sunshine, but the beauty of the waving grass and fields had little effect on me. I could already imagine the darkness of the Bloodmarsh, and the faint smell of burned wood and flesh seemed to linger in my mouth, no matter how far behind we left the devastation of the smoldering farms. Nor could I escape a sense of creeping dread starting to set over me; I was traveling to Tellisar for answers, but my nightmares were getting worse . . . and all the time, I was beginning to worry as much about what was behind me as in front. If the Order was operating in Tellisar, and Arginn had gotten word of my prior activities, there was little doubt they would want to stop me before I could disrupt them in Tellisar the way I had in Cohrelle. This whole journey was probably foolishness; any sensible person would gladly have gone to a cave and stayed there, rather than hope for the best and travel as the world fell apart around them. But here I was, a foreigner on distant soil, a stranger in a land with different customs and uncertain loyalties, desperately trying to seek out allies without committing myself to them for fear of betrayal, all the while trying to get to the only place I could think of to get answers.

And Caoes, padding silently beside me with his usual aplomb: what did he think about this? How would he handle the Bloodmarsh? Even if I was inclined to do it, I doubted I could convince him to stay behind . . . and given my very small list of advantages, I was in no rush to get rid of one of the best ones I had, as uncertain as I was about his motives. *Never turn down a sharp dagger because of the shape of its blade*, Caoesthenes had told me once. Turning away from his namesake would have seemed just as foolish.

We encountered no one else for the rest of that day, and kept a fast pace until dark was well set in. Despite the chill we lit only a small fire, in a spot low and flat somewhat below the level of the grassland. Caoes usually vanished at this time of night, but he always returned within an hour or so, usually carrying a rabbit or fox in his mouth, from which we were both able to make a decent meal; I never heard a sound from the things he was hunting, but clearly he was feeding well enough. I also had some provisions I had procured before leaving the camp along with the rest of my seeds; put together, I would have another few days of reasonable access to food, and then I would need to be careful. I had to assume that food and water in the Bloodmarsh would be scarce at best. But if all went well we wouldn't be there long.

Because all's gone well so far, I thought, and sighed.

The next day brought grayer skies and a faint impression of mist, and as we traveled on, the grass grew shorter and the ground more moist. Finally, around midday, we crested a gentle rise and saw, below a line of squat trees and bushes, the southern edge of the River Glacal, not far from where it fed into the eastern side of the Glacalta. On my first view of the legendary Glacalta, I could see why swimming here, as tempting as it might be to speed our journey, was impossible. Even here, at the delta, the distance was vast. Docks and what looked like small guard stations dotted every piece of shore, and a mix of boats teemed the water, reaching into the river itself. As I gazed at what must be the edge of Arginn on the northeastern bank of the Glacalta, I knew that taking a chance to cross here would be foolish in the extreme.

Cautiously we made our way down and east until our path merged with the river's edge, where Caoes drank as I knelt down and dipped my hand in the water. Clear and shockingly cold— but, as I found when I took a few long drinks myself, fresher than I might have imagined for a river that wound its way through swampland. Feeling the weight of the next stretch upon us, I washed and refilled my flask.

After a quick lunch we turned east and followed the bank of the Glacal, and as several hours passed, the river became narrower and shallower, the air warmer and more humid. Now clear of the line of trees and bushes, we could see to the other bank, but with boats still visible in the western distance, I decided to continue on, until a thick tangle of twisted trees and roots began to spread onto both banks. In front of us stood the heart of the Bloodmarsh; on the other side of it lay our answers.

"There it is, Caoes," I said with a sigh. "Take a good breath. It might be a while before you taste pure air again." Then, with one last look behind us at the open land, we turned and plunged into the Bloodmarsh.

CHAPTER ELEVEN

I kept to the surety of the river for a while longer, to obscure our point of crossing, and because an adjustment for the delta here would reduce our chances of encountering it further in. The travel was less difficult than I had feared. The ground was soft underfoot, and the air was close and damp . . . but we'd found no bogs or sinkholes, and the trees were not too close together to obstruct passage. With the riverbank as our guide, we continued forward, watching as the water grew narrower and narrower, the other side closer.

We saw few signs of living things besides ourselves, though there were clearly some small fish in the brackish water, and the occasional cry of a bird overhead proved we had not left the living world behind entirely. Still, for a while it felt as if we were largely alone, an odd and somewhat isolating feeling . . . and not wholly unwelcome. I could already see that Captain Kraes had been correct; our tracks vanished into the increasingly soft ground soon after we made them, water rushing into the spaces we left as we walked. The chances of anyone tracking us seemed unlikely, so that even if we had been followed, this would slow down our pursuers considerably. For his part, Caoes seemed untroubled by the footing, plodding along as usual, the soft squishes and plunks of his paws echoing my own louder steps. When and if the water got deeper, though . . . well, I saved that fear for the future.

The Glacal grew narrower every minute, and soon enough it was more like a large stream, though I knew the volume feeding the Glacalta was both seasonal and also spread around us. The river proper still wound back and forth, and I knew we had to cross it soon . . . and the sooner we did so, and set our path toward the Carrtish, the sooner we could turn our attention to getting to that river and out of the marsh.

"This is our best chance, Caoes," I said, watching the water as the panther looked at me. "No telling if this gets any deeper further in. I should cross first; you wait, then follow after." I removed my cloak, and wrapping my cucuri and belt pouches in it, held the bundle above my head as I gradually lowered myself down the short, steep bank into the river. It was slow-moving and quiet, and much warmer than near the Glacalta, but my concern was the riverbed itself; if it was too soft, I'd have trouble making it across safely, and swimming wasn't a pleasant prospect with my arms raised and without knowing what creatures I might be disturbing as I went. Still, my feet touched bottom with the water level still an inch or so below the middle of my chest, and I only needed a little more effort to keep my feet moving through the mud. Two thirds of the way across I felt better; perhaps it was indeed time to thank my luck.

Then my feet touched empty water, and I plunged downward.

I almost gasped in surprise before I caught myself and pulled my arms down, kicking my legs wildly. My body stopped its descent, and after a moment I began to rise toward the surface of the water. I surfaced, spluttering and twisting my body so I was on my back and could keep my possessions out of the water. I kicked and splashed my way to the riverbank on the other side, where I twisted again and pulled myself to land, tossing my bundle in front of me. "Hells," I gasped, pushing myself into a seated position. "Should have known I—" Then I thought of something, and looked back over my shoulder—just in time to see the silent figure of Caoes climb out of the water next to me, paws holding firmly to the slick, marshy surface as he ascended the bank.

"I thought I told you to wait for me to cross," I said with a touch of annoyance as I turned away to separate and inspect my waterlogged cloak and possessions—less damaged than I had feared, though I doubted the food was still edible. I draped the soaked cloak over a group of stalks; the fabric used for cloaks of the Order was designed for movement, lightness, and lack of sounds, but one downside to that was that when completely drenched, the fabric held its water. As I worked, Caoes lay on the ground nearby, head between paws though his eyes were still open; in truth, he had crossed the Glacal more easily than I had, though he was doing so without gear or clothing. I frowned. Of course he could think for himself, but right now I was considering the potential danger we had been in, especially him; if anyone or anything had ventured by right then, he would have been an easy target. And I still wasn't sure of our environment. "If some river-dwelling beast had decided to make an appearance—" I began . . . then stopped and turned. I thought I had heard a splashing sound, as if something had jumped in the water on the other bank; but I saw nothing, and heard only the same calm gurgling which was audible before I first entered the water. "Jumping at shadows," I muttered, but I was still ill at ease. The sense of dread I had started to feel yesterday had not lessened, and it had been joined with a desire to quicken our pace. But as I looked deeper into the marsh, watching as the trees grew denser, the darkness in the space beyond inscrutable and ominous, I saw that speed was unlikely at best. Our passage through the Bloodmarsh had only just begun.

As we traveled further into the swamp, finally leaving the river behind, the light grew dimmer as the leaf cover overhead closed in upon us. But we were still able to see even without the use of a torch, for there was a dim, blueish glow coming from a kind of iridescent moss growing on rocks and tree trunks all about us, not intense but bright enough to light our way. Still, there was little variety to be seen in that light, and not much visible distance; while the glowing scenery was fascinating, it provided little contrast, and as glimpses of the waning crescent moon grew less and less frequent I became uncertain of our path forward. Northwest was our course, but I no longer knew how well we were on it, or what would happen to us if we diverted too far from our path.

I knew we had margin for a little error, but dire consequences with more. Too far west would lead to the delta, and too far east could prevent us from hitting the northern river entirely, the implications of which I was uninterested to learn.

Our unrelenting march had not yet allowed for a rest; already Caoes seemed to be laboring just a bit as we went, pulling his paws up as they sank deeper and deeper into the marshy ground below, and I too felt the first inklings of fatigue starting to set in as I squished along. The temperature was continuing to rise, the air growing more oppressive; I was already covered in sweat, enough that I wondered if I would be able to grip the hilt of my cucuri cleanly if necessary.

Then there was the sound. A strange buzzing grew gradually

louder as we traveled deeper into the Bloodmarsh; at first I had assumed it was simply stinging or biting insects, but I could make out nothing in the muted blue light, and I couldn't feel anything biting the exposed skin on my face. Yet the buzzing became more prominent and less bearable by the minute, until it surrounded us; even Caoes seemed bothered, his head shifting from side to side as we went as if looking for something at which to snap. In the distance, several odd cries, sounding like the harsh, strangled calls of a large bird, were suddenly cut short, followed by the sound of muffled snorting and choking. Most unnerving, I could get no sense of their distance from us—they seemed both far away and right next to us at the same time. Part of the normal aural landscape in a swamp? Or a threat?

I choked down a handful of swamp-seasoned seeds as we walked, the fresher provisions having absorbed too much water to be safe, and worried where either of us would find more. Living things were clearly all around us, but making every effort to stay out of our sight and reach. Caoes caught a few small lizard-like creatures, thin and slimy, with small ridges on their dark green skin, but they were too small to really sustain him, and no help at all to me—the taste was revolting, and there was barely enough meat for more than a couple of bites, even had I dared to eat them raw instead of trying to cook them over the small campfire I had built for the evening when we finally found a patch of solid, if damp, ground.

Given the increasingly oppressive heat of our environment, a fire was less than appealing, but I did not relish the thought of sleeping in the blue-infused dimness with no better light to help in our defense. Gathering material for fuel had been difficult; the fallen tree branches were damp and took a while to light, and there was little in the way of kindling to be found. Even when the fire was lit, the flames were unsteady and small, and the smoke thick and unpleasant.

Neither Caoes nor I slept well in that weighty half-darkness, beset with mysterious sounds and, at least for me, troubled by unwelcome thoughts. We had been in the Bloodmarsh for over a day, and I didn't know how much longer to hold this course. Even if going back with essentially no provisions wasn't impossible now, doing so would leave us right where we started. Without food, we could lean west to shorten our path. But with my sense of direction waning to mearly "forward" and backward," if we overshot to the west, we'd be right up against the Glacalta's unstable delta, and if we were to slip into its grasp ... well, there wouldn't be much left for any pursuers to find.

For that was my other worry, as I stared at Caoes's supine form, twitching as he dreamed—of a place far away from here, I hoped. I hadn't seen anything but the small lizard-things for some time now, but the sounds of splashing in the River Glacal had unnerved me, and reminded me of my pursuers. If the Order could reach across the breadth of Silarein to strike at patrols from Calarginn, then its ambition and power was greater than I had imagined. And why? What was the endgame, especially when Argoth himself ...

I sighed, again remembering Caron's words cautioning me not to lose faith in all just because I had lost faith in one. Perhaps it was true, but I had grown tired of listening to lies disguised as truths, wrapped and sold by charlatans and tricksters to those desperate for light in the darkness. Did any other Acolyte know of the great void at the center of our faith? Could anyone continue to work for the Service, to kill for the Order, knowing what I did?

I doubted it. But then I had walked in darkness for so long, I was used to being adrift in it; how could I know what others would do when confronted with a failure as total as mine? Perhaps they would just ignore reality, bury themselves in the comfort of ritual and discipline which had defined my life for years, rather than strike out on their own in the search for a new path. At least that way led to a measure of peace, unlike mine . . . which led only to more questions, and doubts, and half-understood secrets. Yet doing anything else now seemed unthinkable. I needed to know, or lose myself entirely to doubt and despair.

On the third day, our food supply even lower than our morale, we came across a body of shallow, muddy water, extending well into the distance as far as we could see in the unceasing dimness. The ground had been softer, almost spongy, for at least a day now, and our pace had slowed to a tedious slog, putting one foot in front of the other with more weariness than purpose. But as Caoes trotted into the first part of the water and sank nearly to his chest, pushing himself back out again with difficulty, we saw that we could not walk across here in any fashion, though it looked too shallow for swimming. Anxious to avoid getting any closer to the Glacalta, we turned right and followed the edge of the water, but twenty minutes brought us no closer to the other side. The buzzing was becoming intolerable, and sweat was pouring down my face, my breathing heavy, as I held up a hand and stopped.

"This won't work, Caoes," I said, wiping my face uselessly

with the edge of my equally damp cloak as the panther shifted his paws to firmer ground. "I don't want us going any farther into the swamp. This water might mean that we're getting closer to the northern river. If we can cross it, we might finally get out of this Hells-cursed place." That sounded good enough ... but how? I looked above us, but the tree cover overhead had more thin, leafy branches and creeping vines than anything sturdy enough to hold our weight, even if I could fashion a form of fly hook. But we had to get across somehow.

Caoes peered across the water, then at me, then sniffed and padded slowly away from the water; a short distance away, he turned and lowered his head. Suddenly he sprang forward, loping to the very edge of the water before leaping out, into it. I waited for the splash—and then watched in astonishment as the panther landed lightly on top of the water, which rippled only slightly at the impact. I stared as he looked over his shoulder at me, his yellow-eyed expression strangely casual ... and then saw what had happened. He was standing on top of several mounds of what looked like grass—possibly the stumps of trees over which grass had grown years before—barely visible above the surface of the water. As I watched, he turned away and lightly jumped forward again, landing on two more hillocks of grass, and turned again to me.

I shook my head and smiled in spite of my discomfort and fatigue. "I didn't know that pathfinding and water-walking were among your skills, Caoes. I'll keep it in mind in future." I took several steps back, then ran forward and leapt to the first tuft of grass on which Caoes had landed, considerably less gracefully than he had—but the ground held below my feet, and I grinned. *Led across the expanse of a swamp by a panther. Not what Caoesthenes himself would have planned as a training exercise, maybe . . . but he would have approved of the improvisation.*

For the next ten minutes we crossed the water in this fashion, Caoes leaping to safe spots of ground at the surface of the water as I followed. Sometimes he warned me off with a growl, trying paths and retracing from dead-ends. The air had grown somehow more oppressive, making my breathing painfully labored, yet my heart felt lighter as we leapt from spot to spot. We were making good progress, and ahead of us I thought I could make out a sliver of brighter light in the distance. *Only a little further, and we can be clear.*

Caoes leapt onto a much wider piece of flat, dry ground, and padded to the other side of it as I stumbled forward to join him. But right before he was about to leap again, he stopped and sniffed. After a moment he lowered himself into a crouch, nearly to the ground, and gave a low, long growl. I saw nothing, but the buzzing grew suddenly louder—and then ceased. I turned slowly, scanning the water around me, but nothing stirred. And then I felt the ground below me shift ever so slightly, my legs vibrating as if I was riding on the back of a cart being driven through the streets of Cohrelle. "Caoes," I just had time to say—and then the surface of the water near the panther erupted.

Shooting upward from the mud was a massive shape, all scales and teeth, and Caoes barely had time to jump backward before it landed with a thud in the space he had just vacated. It looked like a cross between a lizard and a fish—perhaps it was the adult version of the lizards Caoes had tried to bring us to eat. But this one was at least fifteen feet long, body wide and low to the ground, skin covered with warts and scales, its long face topped with two fierce eyes which glowed bright green. And as it opened its mouth, revealing three rows of pointed teeth on top and bottom, wide enough to bite Caoes in two, I had yet another reason for the Bloodmarsh's evil reputation.

The beast struck, lunging at Caoes and snapping its great jaws shut . . . on air, as Caoes dodged backward, teeth bared. I drew my cucuri and brought it down on the back of the creature's neck as I ran up—a strong blow which would have ended the life of any human, and cut most animals deep. But the blade rebounded off the thing's hide as if it were made of granite, painful vibrations running up the blade into my arm as I drew it back, wincing. *Not getting into it that way*, I thought as I backed up a few steps, watching as it swung its huge head toward me, baleful eyes wide. It opened its mouth again and lunged, so swiftly I barely had time to sidestep the attack, stumbling slightly as I tried to keep from slipping off the edge of our little island. It was much quicker than its bulk would have suggested, and combined with the toughness of its skin . . . Yet we were in the middle of a wide expanse of water; escaping the way we had come, by leaping from tuft of grass to small hill of dirt, would be much too slow, and the beast would slaughter us in seconds if we landed in the water. It had to be dealt with here.

Caoes swiped at the side of the creature's head with his paw, having about the same effect as my cucuri had . . . but at least he distracted the thing back toward him. Given its strength and toughness, it would have been better served to focus on one of us at a time; we couldn't yet harm it. But it was driven by instinct, not tactical skill; a small comfort, but something to work with. It snapped at Caoes, who dodged again, landing right by the edge of the water, as I threw myself forward once more with my cucuri, this time aiming for its side. The tip of the blade hit the beast in the neck, and was again turned away as the vibrations from the recoil rippled up my arm. But this time the thing swiveled its head so quickly I wasn't able to back away fast enough, and the side of its mouth slammed into my hand, knocking my cucuri free. It flew into the air, rotating blade over hilt, until it fell with a splash into the dark water some distance away. My heart rose a bit as I saw the handle still visible—the blade must have landed in one of the tufts of grass right below the water's surface. The beast turned toward me. I had one reshtar while it had two eyes, but losing one would be painful and could buy time to retrieve my blade, I thought in knowing desperation. I tossed it with all my strength, and watched as the thing blinked, the reshtar bouncing like a pebble off its eyelid, and away into the water with a sickening plunk. I fell back as the beast turned its body in my direction as well, green eyes fixed on mine, and opened its jaws wide, revealing a wide tongue, dull white in the blue glow of the moss.

A wide tongue, inside a fleshy, unprotected mouth.

Automatically I went for my kushuri darts, pulling four of them free from the inside of my cloak. These were the only ones I had left, and I was loath to lose them . . . it would be some time before I could find or fashion more. Yet this was hardly the time to worry about future needs, and as I took another step back, fanning the darts in my hand, I got ready for the thing's attack. It drew itself up, jaws opening even wider, then suddenly charged forward with incredible speed. I waited for a beat, then threw my kushuri darts toward it. All four embedded themselves in the top of the beast's open mouth, and its head jerked back as the jaws closed, then opened again as it roared in pain, its tail flailing as its body thrashed. I felt a surge of triumph—but as the creature swung around wildly, I saw Caoes, with no room to move, get slammed in the side by its tail and flipped backward off the patch of ground on which we stood, landing in the water and disappearing below its surface. "Caoes!" I yelled as the reptile-thing turned its attention back to me. Blood was dripping from its mouth, but clearly not enough to slow it down, and the blaze in its eyes told me it was now worked into a fury ... and I with no effective weapons left but one.

The niscur.

I drew forth the crescent moon from its loop at my belt, holding it steady as the creature's mouth opened and closed in an apparent mixture of pain and rage. The niscur had saved my life twice before, driven by soundshifting magic and Caoesthenes's craftsmanship; use the trigger word and the weapon would seek out its target unerringly. But there was no steel blade to pierce this creature's hide, and even the revellit steel of which the niscur was made might not pierce this beast's skin. Even if it did, would it hurt the thing enough to stop it before it could kill me?

Only one way to find out.

The monstrous reptile drew itself up, its muscles tensing, and I drew my hand back as I stood at the edge of the dry ground. "Come on, then, vermin," I said, my voice harsh and angular. "Let me give you something tastier to eat."

There was a brief pause, during which I felt the air around us grow even more still, as if the Bloodmarsh itself was holding its breath. Then the creature leapt forward, its bloody mouth open, as I simultaneously threw the niscur at it. "Aven!" I shouted as the projectile whirled toward the monster, and the moon clicked open into its familiar s-shape, sparkling slightly even in the dull moss light. It embedded itself into the roof of the creature's mouth with a satisfying squishing sound, right alongside the broken shafts of the kushuri darts, and the beast roared in agony. But its speed did not slacken, and it slammed into me, sending me toppling backward into the water. My head landed painfully on one of the small tufts of ground, my body half submerged, and the beast's great weight landed on top of me, crushing me as its jaws opened wide. I felt no pain . . . just a quiet sadness, as I looked away and waited for the mouth to close on my neck and my life.

Then I heard the thing give a terrific roar, its body thrashing above me, and I looked up to see blood pouring from one of its green eyes as its head swung back and forth. Behind it, I caught sight of Caoes, stumbling backward and falling. But above me, I saw the glittering of the niscur's blade, sticking out of the roof of the creature's mouth, right below the top of its skull. And driven more by desperation than hope, I reached up, grabbed the top of its mouth, and yanked down with all of my strength. The jaws closed as its head slammed into mine, and my vision swam as I fought to remain conscious—but then the beast gave one final jerk and rolled away, into the water. I caught sight of the top of its head as it sank below the surface, imagining the shape of the niscur's curved blade where it must have penetrated the thing's brain. Then silence and darkness fell, and I knew no more.

When I stirred, head pounding and back hurting, it took me a moment to remember who and where I was. But when I saw the limp body of Caoes lying on the patch of ground where we had fought the reptilian monster, it all came back to me, and lurching up (and immediately regretting it as pain shot through my back and skull), I pulled myself with difficulty onto the land and over to the panther. At first I went cold as I saw his right front leg twisted below him, his body motionless—but then I saw his chest was still rising, and lowering my ear to his mouth I heard air moving in and out of his lungs, albeit shallowly. Still alive, but he wouldn't stay that way if he didn't get help soon . . . and I, though not fatally hurt, was in no great condition myself.

Standing slowly, every muscle in my body screaming its resistance, I looked around and saw the hilt of my cucuri still visible in the half-light, maybe twenty or thirty feet away. I stepped carefully to a nearby hillock, then lowered myself into the water, touching the soft bottom when I was waist-deep—with my kushuri darts and food gone, and my cloak already torn and soaked, there was nothing much left that water could damage—and waded out the last few steps until I could reach the blade and pull it free. I reversed the process to get back to land, and wiped the blade as dry as I could on the grass before resheathing it. Without any other weapon left, I would need my blade more than ever . . . especially without the niscur. I looked into the water where the beast's body had disappeared, but could not see below the surface, and with Caoes's condition, I had no time to seek out the creature, even if I had felt inclined to risk meeting anything that might be attracted to the blood. "Sorry, old man," I muttered. "Your little gadget saved my life three times . . . that's a pretty good payment on your investment, I'd say." Then I turned away and knelt down by Caoes's body. As I ran my fingers over his leg I felt no broken bones, though I was no healer. Still, he was unconscious and looked likely to stay that way for a while, and that meant dragging him behind me . . . or, of course, leaving him behind entirely.

I grunted in fatigue and frustration. In the old days, the Order's strictures would have given me the guidance I needed: *The blade which loses its edge must not be sharpened, but destroyed and remade*, Father Jant would have quoted from the Writ of Argoth . . . a writ of lies, as I had later discovered. But the meaning was clear regardless of its source: at a certain point, an Acolyte (or other asset) who could no longer help themselves was not worth saving. Caoes was a burden now, an impediment to my survival. Carrying him from this place was foolish, sentimental madness.

I frowned, my mouth tightening, and shook my head. Reaching down, I placed my hands underneath his motionless form, and with a strain which sent jolts of pain through my body, lifted him up. In the old days, I had woven the fabric of my reality with a network of half-truths and illusions, supported by a spiritually empty faith. But in my new world, adrift from my spiritual moorings, I could only count on what I knew. And I knew that Caoes had saved my life several times already. Foolish and sentimental or not, I'd be damned if I was going to let him rot here, breathing out the last of his life in the foul reek of this Hells-cursed swamp. "One step at a time, Grayshade. It's the only way to get anywhere," I said, and with a deep breath, I stepped onto the closest hillock of grass.

The first few hours of that weary trek were nightmarish. I had no broken bones or large wounds to speak of, yet my back

and neck were still throbbing with pain from where they had
struck the ground during the creature's attack, and my energy
had already been low. Caoes was no house cat, and eighty, maybe
ninety pounds was a lot to carry. At first I tried to stick to the
obvious mounds of dirt and grass I could make out in the dim
light, but I soon gave it up; I didn't have Caoes's nose, nor his
instinct for solid ground. So I waded instead, braving the possible
dangers of the watery bottom. It was soft and yielding, not easy
to push off against as I slogged forward, though at least it didn't
bottom out or drop further. Yet the progress was painful and
dreadfully slow, and I grew ever wearier as I went, Caoes's body
straining my arms to the breaking point as I forged on, my mind
a blank, my training the only thing left.

When the ground began to slope upward again, I was barely
conscious of the difference until I found myself stumbling forward on the bank, released from the weight of the water around
me. But the mosslight, the smell, the oppressiveness of the air
remained . . . and the buzzing, which had started again in earnest
not long after we had left the place of battle, was even louder. I
don't know how much longer I traveled in that almost lightless
gloom, putting one heavy foot in front of the other first from
training, then determination, then simple habit: an hour? Two?
Ten? On and on I went, listening to Caoes's labored breathing as I
plodded forward, until the world around us seemed to drop away,
and I lost all sense of past or future. Only the next step mattered,
and the next, and the next.

At some point, I heard Caoes's body hit the ground with a
loud thump, and before I could process the noise fully, another
followed it—the sound of my knees hitting the ground, then

my hands as I tried to hold my body upright. I struggled for a minute more, crawling forward as best I could, before pitching face first onto the ground. Darkness swam around the edges of my vision as the buzzing increased to an intolerable level. But as I felt consciousness slipping from me, I heard a strange voice, high and distant.

"A man in a shadowy cloak, a cat in a cloak of shadows," the voice mused. "Strange days, my loves. Most strange."

Then darkness embraced me, and I surrendered myself to its touch.

PART THREE
DESTINY

There is no fate, or chance, or coincidence.
There is Argoth's will, or darkness.

—The Sixth Rite of Devotion

CHAPTER TWELVE

THE first thing I felt was a vague irritation on my arm, like a cross between an itch and something scratching it. Then I noticed more sensations: the air was warm and damp, and the irritation was repetitive and thick, as if something was repeatedly brushing the same spot again and again. Next was the smell: a strange mix of smoky incense and something dark and woodsy ... mushrooms, perhaps? And then the sound: a rhythmic creaking, like wood on wood. For a time I just listened to that, enjoying the rounded quality of the creaks, but finally the other stimuli became impossible to ignore, and I gradually opened my eyes. It was still dark at first, and then I noticed bits of flickering orange at the edge of my vision. I turned my head to see the source: a small fire burning steadily inside a rough fireplace set into a wall, a pot of some kind hanging on a spit above the fire. Then I looked to my left, down to the place where I felt the irritation, and saw its cause: Caoes lay next to me, his right front leg bandaged, licking my arm patiently. As I saw him, his yellow eyes, only half-open, swiveled to take in my gaze.

"You're as much house cat as panther, Caoes," I said, my voice rough and slow. As usual, Caoes did not reply, content to simply stop licking and close his eyes as he lowered his head to the ground. But the ground was not dirt; it was a wooden floor, and we lay on a pile of soft furs upon it. Above us I could see a relatively low ceiling, made of some mix of straw and wood, and hanging from the crossbeams were herbs of all kinds and forms; some, like garlic and rosemary and calenna, were common even in Cohrelle, while others, white and rough, dark and smooth, fiery red and large, icy blue and tiny, were strange and unfamiliar. For a moment I took the scene in, and then I remembered the creaking, and turned my head again in the direction of the sound.

Past the fire, near a fairly low, sturdy looking wooden table, was a rocking chair. In the chair, rocking as she hummed tunelessly to herself, was the only other inhabitant of the room: a woman weaving what looked like reeds together into a large basket. It was impossible to tell her age; she had long streaks of gray running through her wild black hair which extended below her shoulders, and her face was lined and worn. But her eyes glittered in the firelight, not with rheum or the passing of years, but wit and mischief. Her calloused hands seemed twisted with age, but they moved as nimbly as a young thief on crowded city streets as she wove the reeds back and forth again, almost too quickly to be seen.

"There was a time," she said after a moment, "when people stared at me for longer than that, my love. Then I laughed at 'em, and off they'd go with red face and quick breath." Her voice was high and thin, almost flute-like, but steady and clear, and as she turned toward me I caught a glimpse of even, pale teeth as she gave a crooked smile. "Not so much now, though. A swamp's a poor place to find a friend, or a lover, unless you fancy scaly beasts in your home." She winked. "I don't."

I lay silent, trying to read the environment around me as I struggled to recall why I was here. I barely remembered my own name, much less what had happened to me, except in bits and pieces—there was water, for certain, and some ... attack? A ... creature?

"A krellic," she said suddenly, startling me. "He's a nasty one, my love, he is. All teeth and more temper, I always say, scales and sadness," she cackled. I looked at her suspiciously; there was no obvious malice behind her crooked smile, but she had reacted as if she had read my thoughts. Either startling insight or something more sinister, but either way I was inclined to be cautious. And yet she had triggered a memory: the splashing, the scales, the teeth ... and green eyes. Yes, we had fought a beast of some kind, large, fierce, and unrelenting. A ... krellic, she called it? I had never heard the term, but my thoughts were still halting and slow. But there was no pain ... the throbbing in my neck and back was gone, and as I looked down again, Caoes's breathing was deep and regular.

"You're—a healer?" I finally managed to say, searching for the words. "A mage?"

"A scavenger, love." She cackled. "A gatherer, a finder, a cutter and steamer and boiler. Lots to be found in the Bloodmarsh: rosemary, calenna, fireweed, saltpetal, marjoram. Dry roots upon the mounds. Lots to help those who know how to put them all together in the right ways." She smiled again and turned back to her weaving, hands moving swiftly among the reeds.

"Then ... I owe you my life. And Caoes's."

She glanced at the panther. "He's a strong one, he is. Strong and silent." She winked at me again. "The way I like 'em." She cackled again as she looked back at her weaving.

I opened my mouth to reply, then hesitated. I still didn't know what I was truly dealing with here. I had heard of witches before, of course, both tales to frighten innocent children and more believable stories of ones who worked in the shadows for their own dark purposes. Whatever this woman was, she had healed both of us, and managed it so well that the lingering effects were minimal. But I had no idea if it was magic or medicine, nor what I needed to be afraid of in either case. More and more was beginning to take shape in my memory, from the days in the Bloodmarsh to the weeks leading up to it, and my thoughts were growing less sluggish; but until everything was back, I needed to remain cautious. "How did you move us here?" I finally asked, deciding that questions about our immediate situation would be the safest course.

"One step at a time, love," she replied with another chuckle. "And not too fast. Weren't any way I could get the both of you back at once, and I didn't fancy running into anything else on the way. I got you hid away nice and safe, then took him back home to fix him up," she said as she nodded in the sleeping panther's direction. "Then I left him with his leg bandaged, peaceful as you please, and went back to get you. Thought I heard another krellic on the way back, but no problems in the end."

"Do krellics hunt in packs?"

"Not likely. One of 'em's as big as a pack as it is," she said, her laugh now a bit grating. "Found that out yourself, love, I think?" She pulled one of the reeds tight as she prepared to tie off the handle of the basket. "And so did your friend there. I've seen enough krellics to know when one of them caught you off guard. Not that I blame you. Been more than one venturing here who found themselves on the wrong end of a krellic bite. But still, you're lucky you made it here with everything still attached. Nothing untoward; simply for your health." She chuckled again as she started to wrap the basket's opposite side.

Suddenly conscious of my state of undress, I sat up more quickly than was perhaps wise—but I saw that I was clean, with slight bandaging, and a soft, thick cloth wrapped around my waist and legs. On my arm, where Caoes had been licking, a dark spot had been scratched into my skin. Taking in the implications of all this at once, I looked to see my shirt, undergarment, and pants, cleaned, stitched, and folded neatly beside me. My cloak, belt, and gloves were draped over some kind of stand, with my newly polished boots and unsheathed cucuri next to them. Beside me sat my flask. Picking it up and feeling the weight of liquid inside, I opened the top and raised it to my nose.

"Mmm," she said, as if sensing my doubt. "Rainwater. Well-filtered for safety."

The water tasted cool and clean, and I gratefully allowed myself several long gulps.

"Sorry you couldn't get everything back in the end, of course."

"What do you mean?" I set the flask back down.

The woman shook her head, eyes glittering in the flickering firelight, and resumed her weaving. "I mean you didn't kill a krel-lic with your damp blade and empty flask, love. Something else must have helped you."

I grunted. "You might be surprised what desperate people can do, damp blade or not."

She chuckled. "And I might at that, love." She pulled a reed tight as she rotated the basket in her hand, her lined face yellow-orange in the firelight. "What name do you go by, then? Be nice to know which desperate one I saved."

"I'd like to know the name of my rescuer, first," I replied. "Or at least the name she's willing to share."

Her face turned serious at that, and there was a long pause before she nodded. "Alarene," she said. "No risk in sharing a name . . . not here anyway."

I nodded. "Grayshade," I said.

She smiled. "And you called him?" she asked, looking again at Caoes, who was now deeply asleep on his side, his broad front paws crossed in front of him.

"Caoes," I said. "My name for him, although we've only been on the road together less than a month. But it seems to suit him, as far as I can tell."

She nodded. "If you feel so, love, who am I to say nay? He certainly seemed calm enough when he came back to himself."

"He's pretty tough," I replied.

"Mmm. Anything survives a krellic bite's more than that," she said, pushing an offending reed back into place.

"A bite?" I said, startled.

"Aye, love. You didn't notice how he was acting when you first woke up, did you?" I looked at Caoes and thought of his half-closed eyes when I had first seen him; he had been awfully subdued, even considering his usual state of calm. And this was as deep a sleep as I could remember seeing him in since we had begun traveling together.

Alarene nodded. "His leg. More of a scrape than a bite, but that's enough to do it. Most wouldn't make it more than a few minutes afterward. But him, now . . . he's a strong one. Still a close thing, but no need for him to visit the darkness just yet." She smiled and began humming to herself, rocking back and forth on the creaky wooden floor.

"He'll pull through, then?"

"Aye, love. But he'll need rest. So will you. Strong one you are, yes, strong and strange and with a handsome face and hidden song behind whetted lips . . . but not a god." Suddenly she turned to me, eyes widening slightly. "And perhaps you'll need more than rest. A place to hide from eyes who'd see? A place to wait for storm clouds to pass?"

I hesitated, but as she saw my face she just smiled crookedly and nodded, continuing her tuneless hum. Probably harmless, and a bit . . . enthusiastic . . . but her level of insight was troubling, and I had long ago learned not to go by the external. "I don't know what you mean," I replied after a moment. "We were just passing through . . . the last thing we want is to linger."

She hummed for a while longer as she wove, acting as if she had not heard me, but I saw her eyes narrow again.

"Don't misunderstand me. I appreciate what you've done for us. If I can repay you I'll do so, as soon as I can, but—"

"Repayment's expensive," Alarene said, her voice suddenly harsh. But she did not look at me, and as I watched her face, it seemed more soft and sad than angry. Finally she took a deep breath. "Not for you, love. Don't usually save people so's they can pay me." She peered at me. "But I don't much like snippets when I ask for stories. No one passes through the Bloodmarsh unless they're looking for something . . . or leaving something behind."

"Is that what you did?"

Alarene's gaze grew more intense, then melted into a smile. "As far as you know, love," she said, cackling. "But the question's not yet answered."

I paused. *If she meant to harm us, she could have left us there . . . unless it was information she needed first.* Then I considered where

we were: exhausted, injured, and in the heart of the Bloodmarsh.
Who knew how she would react if I refused to tell her why we
had come? And how were we to find our way out if we didn't have
her good will? *Again, the river.*

I considered a moment longer, then sighed. "We're headed
to Tellisar by the fastest route possible . . . and the most secret," I
said, watching her face for a reaction. "Getting over the Glacalta
is too risky, either by boat or by swimming. And traveling around
the Bloodmarsh would take too long, if I even knew the way. So
we went through. Running into a krellic wasn't part of the plan."

Alarene nodded, her expression again serious. "Aye, so it
seems." She turned back to her weaving and fell silent, letting the
crackling of the fire and creaking floor fill the space.

Finally I spoke again. "I've told you why we're here, but my
question remains. What brought you to the Bloodmarsh?"

Alarene sighed. "Not the same as what keeps me in it, love.
I've been here for a long time . . . haven't counted in a while, but ten
years, I think? Eleven? In here, the time comes and goes, comes and
goes as it will. I've learned not to mark it too close." She pulled a
reed around the side of the basket, which looked almost complete;
her weaving speed seemed almost supernatural. "It's not the kind-
est nor the cruelest place. But it suits me now, and I it."

"You never venture out, then? To one of the nearby cities, or
farther?"

She cackled. "What's out there that I can't find in here, love?
Are people still fighting each other for money, for power? Farmers
still growing their crops?" Her smile vanished. "Lies still selling
as truth?"

I smiled thinly. "Only when there are people willing to buy

them." Alarene nodded but did not reply, and I saw the faintest twitch in her cheek as she closed her eyes for a long moment . . . a moment in which I might have an opening. "Then you haven't heard of the war between Calarginn and Arginn?" I asked.

"No," she said, opening her eyes and smiling wanly. "But fights don't much interest me anymore, love. I've seen enough of them to know what the end'll be. Tellisar, though . . . now Tellisar's a place to see. Have you been there?"

"No, I'm from Cohrelle. This is as far as I've ever been away from that city, in fact."

"Cohrelle?" Alarene repeated, raising a dark eyebrow. "Haven't heard much about Cohrelle for a long time . . . before I came here, even. You've walked quite a way if you started there, love. Most don't bother to leave Cohrelle at all."

"Or Tellisar," I replied. "Was that your home?"

Alarene shook her head. "More a prison," she said at last, staring at the basket. "My home's here now. Don't get bothered by anyone, unless I want to be."

"Not even krellics?"

She grinned. "Not when I know enough to stay away from their nests, my love." She pulled another reed through, tied it off, and laid the completed basket on the table next to her. "After a time you see the signs, and know to steer clear. And there are lots more than krellics." She stood slowly, curling upward into a standing position like a cat stretching after its nap, and went to the fire, where she took a padded cloth from near the fireplace and carefully removed the pot. "You'd not want to cross paths with a callisk here, no, you wouldn't," she said, turning and putting the pot on the table, waving the steam away from the top. "Look at one of them straight on, and you'll spend the rest of your days as one of the trees they like to perch on." From another shelf she took a battered metal mug and placed it on the table, then poured some of the liquid from the pot into the mug. "Or a wisp. All bright and beautiful it is, real light instead of what comes from the mallin and your own lantern. But follow it, and sure as fate it'll bring you to a bad end—a boghole, or a krellic nest, or worse. And then, the people." She brought the mug to the pile of furs where I was sitting and knelt down. "The people are the most dangerous things of all. The ones who don't come to see me." She winked again. "But I've learned to get by." She smiled thinly, then held out the mug. "Drink up, love. Krellic didn't bite you, but you've got just as much hurt as your strong friend there . . . and harder to fix, too, I'll guess."

I took the mug. "Why?"

Alarene shook her head, her expression gentle. "Worst hurt of all's the one that comes from inside you. Not so easy to heal that." She sighed, then gestured toward the mug. "Drink. It will help."

"What's in this?"

"Answers to questions," she cackled. "Answers to questions you haven't even asked, my love."

I hesitated. I'd already revealed things I wouldn't have wanted to if it could have been avoided; if this was some sort of truth potion, I'd end up telling Alarene even more, things which could endanger Kraes and her soldiers, maybe Rillia and Caron . . . not to mention me.

"There's naught in there but help and comfort," Alarene said, frowning. "I don't poison people in my own home, especially when I bring them here myself. Even strange ones." She leaned back, waiting.

The scent wafting from the mug was earthy and slightly sweet, reminding me of old days in the taverns of Cohrelle, and after a long pause, I drank. It tasted like a heady blend of cinnamon and honey, and as I swallowed I felt a delicious warmth spreading from my chest through the rest of my body. It was a soft, comforting warmth, coupled with—drowsiness?

Alarene's eyes glittered in the firelight.

I tried to jerk forward, but the best I could manage was a slow rise ... which itself came to a halt and reversed as my body felt increasingly heavy. I turned my head with a tremendous effort. "What—what did you ..." I said thickly, my head swimming.

"Relax, love," she said softly. "I gave you a dream you'll want to have, for a change. And I'll be with you."

I tried to move again, but it was hopeless, and my vision was already darkening. There was just enough light for me to see the lighter streaks in the woman's hair as she leaned over me. "Let go. And trust for once."

Something about that reminded me of a conversation I had a long time ago, but I couldn't place it. Then everything faded.

———————◆———————

"It's pretty," she said.

I started and looked around. I was standing on the top of a narrow shelf of rock, bitten by the cold wind which whipped both my cloak and the dry, powdery snow around my ankles. I was only a few feet from the edge; to my left and right, mountains soared high above me, their peaks shrouded in clouds. And I was not alone; a woman stood next to me, staring out at the land beyond, cloaked but with her hood thrown back, revealing lush, wavy hair which fell past her shoulders. Memories quickly rolled back to me: I had been in a hut in the middle of the Bloodmarsh; I was now high in the mountains. Then this was the dream she'd promised. But the cold felt real enough, the dry snow stinging as it blew into my eyes, and I felt the hard rock below my feet. "How are you doing all of this?" I said at last, facing the cloaked figure.

"The distance is what surprises the most," she said, her voice steady and even. "So many things to see, and this only the tiniest fraction; towns and countries and continents beyond, out there, through the clouds and ice and snow." She turned to face me, and my eyes widened as I saw her. Alarene, perhaps—but Alarene much younger, fresh-faced and brown-eyed, with no streaks of gray in her hair, which rippled gently in the breeze.

"This is illusion?" I asked.

"Does it seem like it?" she replied with a smile. Her grin was perfectly symmetrical here, her rustic accent gone. Perhaps not a younger Alarene, then: a different version of her, an alternate image of who she was in real life.

"I don't know. I've learned not to trust what seems to be real. The truth is usually deeper."

She laughed, a tinkle of light bells in the high mountain air. "Your enemies could learn to exploit that in you, Grayshade. If you trust only the opposite of what you see, you're as predictable as those who accept only their senses. Especially in a dream."

She turned away, gazing again over the landscape. "But even in a dream, you should be able to recognize Silarein."

I turned and, despite my skepticism, took an involuntary breath as I saw the sweeping vista laid out before us. Below and to our left I could see the Bloodmarsh's dark green and brown canopies, and beyond that, lighter swaths of verdant sand, bleeding into the dark blue of the Glacalta. A width of low buildings which must be the city of Arginn stood to the right of that, then a distant yet towering patch which must have been the great city of Tellisar, further down the Glacalta's northern edge. The Scales, on which we must be standing, continued to spike forward as far as I could see, as did the endless blue of the Glacalta. Across the water was a distant sprawl which I knew to be Calarginn, and far beyond that the rolling fields and gentle plains of the Glacal basin.

I turned again, toward my own path, toward Cohrelle, but clouds obscured the view. Hiding the first pang of true emotion I'd allowed myself to feel, I turned back, allowing my eyes to rest on the deeply glittering Glacalta.

"Pretty," she repeated, chin straight and body steady despite the cold, which I could already feel seeping into my bones despite my cloak ... which I noticed was as new, without seams of mending.

"Beautiful," I answered with a nod. "But reality is much uglier, and more permanent."

"Because of what you choose to look at," she said with a faint smile, not shielding her eyes from the blowing snow. "There is plenty of beauty to be found in reality, if you seek it out." She glanced at me. "But you doubt your choices quite often, don't you?"

I frowned. "I don't think I requested a priest, nor a doctor. My choices are my own, not to be shared with strangers."

She nodded, looking away again. "Yes. But you share your fate and fortunes with a panther, a creature of the wild who seems to follow you without question or resentment."

"He shared his fate with mine several weeks ago, and we have been companions since, yes. In part because of his silence. He doesn't ask questions." I drew my cloak closer around me. "So—if this is part of the dream you've created for me—why? Why have you brought me here?"

"For answers," she replied simply. "In the waking world, it would be difficult for you to trust me, and my own doubts and uncertainties plague me likewise. Here, we can build a bond which will extend from the dream world into the waking one." She turned to me. "Here, we can learn to be friends."

I snorted, despite the situation. "I don't typically befriend witches and sorceresses who give me strange drinks of drowsiness."

She laughed again. "I'm not surprised. We don't typically befriend anyone, a consideration I'm also unsurprised you've missed. Though I'm neither a witch nor a sorceress . . . I'm as you see me, here or in the real world, as you like. A foolish one alone, where she can do little harm to others who happen to wander into the swamp."

"And yet you saved us," I replied. "Why? And why drug me?"

"You haven't been 'drugged,'" she said, her face falling. "I told you what it offered, and you drank it. This is meant to help, not harm. Here I can give you something you need."

"Which is?"

"Hope," she said. "I've been in the Bloodmarsh for a long time, and have few visitors. I—prefer it that way. But you're heading to Tellisar, and from Cohrelle ... and both you and your companion are strange indeed. I'd be happy for you to stay for a time, to search the depths of that strangeness—but as you don't seem inclined to do so, I would at least know more of your journey, and its purpose."

"That's exactly what I cannot provide," I replied. "Even if I did trust you, I couldn't explain our presence here. It could put us, and you, in needless danger. It's enough to say that we need to get to Tellisar as fast as possible, and without attracting attention. I thought the Bloodmarsh was the best way to do that."

"It's a difficult place, but that's what makes it valuable," she said, nodding. "So you mean to cross over the River Carrtish, trace the Scales, then approach Tellisar from the north?" She pointed with her finger, as though outlining the route.

"Yes," I said. "And you seem to know an awful lot about that city ... and about me."

She shook her head. "I only know your strangeness here, and your aura. It is ... unusual. Focused, in a way. And there is a darkness which follows you ... a shadow, a hunter of some kind." I glanced at her sharply, but there was no sign of malice or subterfuge. "I have not felt it before," she went on, "but it's uncomfortable, and in truth I'd like it to be gone as soon as may be. If you won't stay and let me find it, then I will help you, and it, leave my home sooner ... within a few days, I hope." She smiled. "I mean no offense."

"None taken. Then what is this?" I asked, gesturing to the landscape.

"A dream, created by a special tea from herbs found in the Bloodmarsh. We share that dream, you and I." She looked up as the wind picked up in intensity. "But it will pass soon, and we will wake again in the real world." She turned to me. "You must make your own decisions. But I ask that you do so from your hopes, not your fears. I brought us here to offer ... perspective. This is the place through which you travel: Silarein, and the Glacalta, and the Bloodmarsh, and the Scales. All are beautiful in their own ways, if you can lift yourself out of the shadows long enough to see them." She smiled, her eyes, still glittering as they had in the firelight, fixed on mine. This time, I held the gaze. "But even if you don't want to do that now, I hope you'll remember this sight. This view comforts me when I feel crushed by the weight of my own burdens."

I nodded. I did not understand all that she was trying to say, but having this view of my path could be a crucial asset in my journey. "I'm grateful. And I'll help as best I can." Suddenly the wind began to howl in earnest, and the blowing snow swirled into a solid curtain of white; then I felt the cold give way to warmth again, and saw my vision again beginning to fade.

"Good," her voice came from beyond the white veil. "I'm pleased to meet you, Grayshade. May you lift yourself above the shadows again."

I did not reply, for my consciousness was leaving me. My last thought before slipping into darkness was of a dream, a shadow, and the fierce yellow eyes within.

CHAPTER THIRTEEN

AS Alarene had predicted, my strength and clarity returned quickly, but Caoes was in no condition to travel that day, or the next few. Despite its small size, the krellic bite was serious, and the panther spent many hours lying in half-slumber on the pile of furs near the fire. I did not want to linger; I had not forgotten the splash I had heard when we crossed the Glacal, and the dread I had started to feel made me wary of this place, even if that dread was much lesser here. But trying to force Caoes to move before he was ready could land us right back where we started, and I wouldn't leave him behind.

So I was forced to wait . . . but not idly. Gathering plants and herbs had never been my line of work, but Alarene described them in enough detail that finding them was relatively easy. "Not the ones with four berries, love—those'll poison you if you squeeze them," she cackled good-naturedly. "Three berries is the goal: three is free, four death's door, five not alive, that's the rhyme for you!" At first I resisted these nonsensical poems, but over time I began to appreciate their value. Picking the right plants by moss and lantern light was no easy task, especially when I also had to keep my eyes open for the other denizens of the Bloodmarsh. More than once I thought I had found what I was looking for, only to remember the rhyme just in time to avoid grabbing something deadly. Soon, though, I was becoming expert at differentiating not only between different herbs, but different times of their cycles—in some cases an herb with strong healing capacities when first visible above the muck would become deadly poison if picked several days later, or would lose its effectiveness altogether if not picked at the exact right time of day. I quickly grew tired of being laughed at by Alarene, even if meant kindly, after these failed excursions. Still, there was a certain peace in the process, a kind of comfort in the simple act of seeking and finding and returning again.

After a couple of days, Alarene sent me to trap small animals, first fairly close to her home, then further afield. I expressed discomfort at first; I avoided killing when I could, but Alarene had only laughed. "Do you think they offer themselves for sacrifice, love?" Annoyed, I had grumbled but set to the task.

There were some ordinary creatures within the Bloodmarsh, toads and snakes and fish, but the bulk of what I was tasked to get were unfamiliar beasts: the annid, an amphibious creature which slithered in shallow pools during the day and returned to its nest in overhanging branches at night; the jark, a thin bird which slept while standing and whose wings were almost as wide as it was tall; the kellen, a vicious little predator which could easily bite off a finger if you allowed its placid demeanor and innocuous furry face to fool you. I didn't hear another krellic on these trips, for which I was grateful, and short of that, the challenges posed by these creatures were minor. But Alarene's gratitude, and the delicious stews she managed to make from some of what I retrieved, was more worthwhile than I might have imagined.

"That tea you gave me," I said one evening several days after our arrival, holding the bag of herbs open as she sorted through that night's haul, cackling at my inability to find the right kind of fireweed. "How difficult is it to make?"

"Not difficult, love," she replied. "But that tea would cause much worse than dreams if you added fireweed in flower."

"Death?"

"Delusions."

"I'll pass on both, thanks," I said dryly. "It's hard for me to understand how you avoided either when you first got here. Did you have training back in Tellisar?"

Alarene's expression immediately shifted, her smile falling away. "Not enough," she replied shortly, grabbing a handful of brushweed from the sack and throwing it into a pot of boiling water behind her.

I could see from the tightness of her mouth and her narrowed eyes that she was displeased; not a common state, but one which I already knew was not easy to shake. But I was tired of being put off about her past, and irritated at having wasted my time collecting the wrong plant. "So afterward, then? It couldn't have been trial and error that gave you such herbal lore, Alarene."

Alarene did not reply, but the water splashing out of the pot as she stirred with her wooden ladle told me all I needed to know about her level of irritation.

"You're not being fair," I said.

The ladle thunked as she stopped stirring.

"We can't just communicate in dreams, and I've told you a good deal about my travels. It's only fair for you to return the favor—"

"There's nothing fair about it, love," the woman said, turning on me abruptly. "Nothing that happened to me in Tellisar, or for a long time afterwards, was fair." She turned away again, more slowly, but the intensity of her stirring did not diminish.

"I can't know what you went through, Alarene," I replied with some heat. "But I doubt very much you'd want to compare notes."

Alarene set the ladle on its rest, and for a long while simply stared into the fire. Finally she sat down heavily on the seat of the rocking chair and shook her head. "It's not about figuring who's had the most pain. Some might not have learned how to live with it as well as you have." I said nothing, and after a minute she sighed. "I was—a healer, in Tellisar. Would have stayed one if all went well. But . . ." She trailed off and closed her eyes. "Well. It didn't. That's all." She stood and peered into the boiling water of the pot, breathing deeply of its fragrance.

I nodded, feeling slightly guilty. "It's fortunate you held onto some of your knowledge, in any case." I looked over at Caoes, still sleeping. "How much longer do you think it will take him to recover?"

"Another day or two. He's strong, but if we hurry it, the body won't ever be as strong as it used to be. But don't worry, love," she said, glancing at me and winking, her earlier anger apparently forgotten. "You'll be out of my lovely marsh soon enough."

I smiled and nodded. But inside, I wondered. Not that there was much about a small shack to hold my interest. Could I imagine myself, former Acolyte of Argoth, honored member of the Service, greatest assassin of Cohrelle, wasting the years of my life away in a swamp, eating stew and drinking dream tea and forgetting any other responsibilities? Perhaps I could be like Alarene: help the poor fools lost enough to wander near my home, bring them into the shack, ask for news of the outside world, cackle at the stupidity of the powerful . . .

And yet—there was something to it. For the dread I had felt before began to slip from me, hour by peaceful hour; the routine of a simple life sinking into my bones, settling there like the mud and muck of the ground outside. For the first time in many years, I would do my work during the day and sleep peacefully at night . . . for if my dark dreams had not wholly lost their power, they were muted, their impact transient. My heart grew lighter with every conversation I had with Alarene, strange as she might be. She had learned songs in her time in Tellisar, and she would alternate singing and humming them for many hours during the day as she puttered about the shack, which seemed as welcoming now as it had seemed small and constricting at first. Some of these songs reminded me of ones I had heard in Cohrelle: ballads about sailors lost at sea, mourned by their wives and children who stood vigil on the shore waiting for their return; shanties about sailing the Westing into the Waves, watching The Clouded Isle standing foreboding against the horizon; even bawdy songs about taverns and their workers, their brusque language somewhat out of character for the gentle woman. But she sang these as lustily as all the rest, cackling at my (apparently) bemused expression.

Then there were the stories: tales of young men encountering the mists, how they were twisted into beasts and worse for the encounter, if they ever came back at all; narratives of the Imperator and his origins (he was a demon, said one story; an orphan from the streets of Tellisar, said another; not one person but a whole group of people, said a third); epic poems about heroes from Relevas, across the sea. We would exchange these stories over the fire, the creaking sound of the rocking chair accentuating the beats of the words as Caoes slumbered near the hearth. After a time I grew used to my tasks outside the shack, more confident in my searches and more certain of the paths to get to and from the various harvesting areas, and my speed finding the items I was told to deliver increased steadily. Within several days I was bringing back more plants and herbs than Alarene knew what to do with, piling them on her small table and waiting as she combined them into multiple recipes, all nourishing and delicious ... and each one with some kind of catch that made eating them exceedingly risky without the proper preparation. Her knowledge of herb lore seemed well-nigh infallible, and we discussed the making of tinctures, poultices, and elixirs, though she did not again suggest drinking the dream tea. "Healing draughts are easy, love," she told me once. "It's the love potions that are hard to make, and harder to take."

"Because they taste terrible?"

"Because they're delusions," she said with a wink. I never quite knew what to make of these folksy sayings, which sometimes seemed too perfectly homespun to be real. But Alarene seemed as comfortable with her eccentricities as she was with her tiny home, and soon I learned to accept what I was seeing from her as legitimate—odd, quirky, but true enough to who she was.

So hour passed to hour, day passed to day, and soon a week or more had gone by. Caoes was now more or less recovered and capable of travel, but still I could not bring myself to leave. The environment was oppressive, the work tedious and boring, the company bizarre ... yet I knew now that a part of me had longed for peace, steadiness, the regularity and certainty of a life like this.

To vanish forever into the Bloodmarsh would be a better kind of end than the one I had anticipated for myself, after all, and I now felt guilty for thinking of this life as a waste. For her part, Alarene said nothing more about wanting me to leave, despite her earlier statements. Perhaps she also enjoyed our conversations, or perhaps she appreciated the help I provided her around the home. Perhaps she was simply happy not to be alone.

Either way, we seemed as settled into the marsh as the shack itself, embraced by the soft soil below us, and as I left that morning on my daily foraging expedition, I found myself smiling as I clambered over one of the large tree roots nearby and passed around the fallen log, covered in the faintly glowing moss which Alarene referred to as mallin. Caoes was at my side again; for the last couple of days he had been accompanying me on my journeys, his leg seeming no worse for wear, though he was still a bit slower than normal. Otherwise his expression had its usual placid quality, yellow eyes glinting in the half-darkness as he took a parallel course to mine, climbing over stones and padding through shallow water as we went. I was glad to have him; something about his still presence steadied me, and I was pleased to see him standing again.

Alarene had asked for dellens, dark mushrooms, for a new stew she was planning—"just a fungus and a fool's guess, love," she had said, cackling loudly—and told me where it might likely be found, underneath rocks near the expanse of shallow water which, much further south, led to the krellic nest into which Caoes and I had stumbled. But I was no longer concerned about the krellics, signs of which I had learned to look for in my previous explorations; besides, they almost never came this far north.

So I felt safe enough to head somewhat to the southwest, through the light marsh to the hillocks which marked the beginning of the shallow water. The trip was surprisingly smooth; behind a tree in the distance I once thought I saw the waving, eerie light of a wisp, but it did not follow, and we stayed on our course. As we arrived at the hillocks and began our search, me lifting rocks as Caoes sniffed underneath them (I had brought a lantern to aid in the search), the Bloodmarsh seemed quiet, almost as if it slumbered as we sought its secrets. The haul was not large at first—one or two small shoots of the dark, woodsy fungi Alarene craved—but soon we started to find more of them, and then several full clumps, springing to life as we removed their stone blankets.

An hour passed as we labored in the fetid water, the flickering lantern and the dim mosslight providing the only illumination, but when I finally stood straight, back aching, I had a grin on my face. We had collected a full sack's worth of dellens, enough for thirty pots of stew at least. "That's good work, Caoes," I said as the panther blinked his yellow eyes slowly. "Enough even for Alarene to be happy, eh?" And so we set off for the shack, stepping carefully through the last of the shallow water before treading more confidently on the solid ground beyond. The Bloodmarsh was a curious place: threatening, intimidating to those on the outside, but with treasures to be found if one was patient: quiet, solitude.

Peace.

I had spent almost my entire life traversing alleyways and streets and tavern rooms, working in man-made shadows; here I was in shadows of a different kind, rounded and haphazard and organic, driven not by the desire of man to control but the imperative of nature to be free. It was a difference I could finally appreciate.

As we made our way around a half-fallen tree, not too far now from the shack, we saw a minor miracle: sunlight, and not a little of it. Somehow, shooting down between the tangled branches and leaf cover of the trees overhead, a shaft of perfectly placed sunlight had landed on a dry, grassy piece of flat ground next to a relatively straight tree trunk lifted above the muck below. I hesitated for a moment, then made my way onto the spot, blinking as I entered the bright sun—almost noon, I guessed from the direction of the shaft of light. It had been less than two weeks since we had entered the Bloodmarsh, but it felt like a year since I had seen something other than fire or mosslight, and almost without thinking I lowered the sack of dellens to the ground and sank down next to the tree, spreading my cloak under me and leaning my back against the trunk. Caoes lay down as well, head between paws, the barest hint of a sigh escaping as he closed his eyes.

Yes, there was peace here. It was an uneasy and imperfect one, but then, when had my life ever been anything but imperfect, at the best of times? What could I expect out there—there, where the world still sold death as faith and blind obedience as devout service? "Maybe just a few days more," I murmured, closing my eyes against the brilliant light. "Just a few more, to catch my breath." In the far distance, I heard the slightest sound of splashing, drifting lazily through my languid thoughts.

I made my slow and cautious way down the hallway, musty and damp despite the stone walls. The light when I had first entered through the trapdoor above had been a dim but steady blue, but as I went on it grew brighter and soon changed hue to a yellowish-red ... though I could see no obvious sources of light. For several minutes I had crawled, using my cucuri to feel ahead of me for traps, but as the light grew brighter and the way clearer I became increasingly confident. Perhaps the way had indeed been as secret as Caoesthenes had implied, and I might be able to find what I needed to after all.

After a few more minutes I came to a dead end, a stone wall blocking my way. But the now-bright light illuminated the symbol of Argoth's Hammer embedded in the middle of the slab, and I placed my hands on the symbol and pushed ... and immediately had to catch myself from stumbling forward as the wall crumpled beneath my hands. I pulled myself straight and stared in shock at what I was holding: a huge piece of yellowed paper, which even now dropped from my fingers in bits and drifted to the ground.

"What in the Hells," I breathed as I looked up ... and then breathed in again at the sight. I had come to the Repository, the sacred room which stored the collected wisdom of Argoth, documents, treatises, sermons, histories, and most important of all: the Writ of Argoth, the truth and meaning of all our faith. For anyone but the High Prelate and the ruling Council of Argoth, viewing the Writ brought an immediate and irrevocable sentence of death. The room certainly looked the part: books were stacked everywhere, and piles of yellowed, cracked papers sat on several ancient wooden tables. But most notable was one small stone pyramid, sitting on a dais in the center of the room; the light which flooded the room seemed to be coming from there, glowing out of the cracks in the pyramid's surface. I stepped forward, overcome as much by fascination as fear. But as I came alongside it, something nagged at the back of my mind, a voice both familiar and strange: *This is not how it happened*, it said.

There was a rush of wind, and as I looked around I saw the piles of books had disappeared; all that remained was the pyramid on the dais, its top now open, revealing a single large book inside, blinding yellow light pouring from underneath the cover of the book. On its cover was the same symbol of Argoth's Hammer I had seen on the wall outside the Repository . . . no, not quite the same, for the hammer here was shattered and broken. Shivering slightly, I reached my hand toward the book. The cover was made of leather, old and worn, but it was as light as air as I opened it to the first page. The light blinded me for a moment; then my vision adjusted, and my eyes widened as I stared in shock. It was a black page, totally black—except for two baleful yellow eyes from which the light poured.

This is wrong, Grayshade, the voice echoed in my head. *Beware the hunter, and remember!*

There was a snarl, and as I turned around I saw Father Jant, my old superior, striding toward me from the corner of the room. He was grown nearly to giant-size in his wrath, and as I took one trembling step back he drew out his blade, glittering in the yellow-orange light.

"Contemptible fool," he said, but his voice was guttural and croaking, and as he opened his mouth I saw he spoke through rotten teeth. But I had no time for questions, and I barely had time to bring up my cucuri to block the downward sweep of his weapon. The blades clashed, and I fell backward from the strength of his blow.

"It is a shame," Jant croaked, drawing his blade back. "To let your foolish pride bring you to this. To fail your mission. To willingly walk into your own death." His blade fell again, and again I parried it, but the vibrations of the blow rippled up the blade of the cucuri into my arm, and I winced in pain as I staggered back. As I drew my blade up, I saw a huge notch in its center.

"This—a lie," I said, my words oddly familiar even as I said them. "All a lie."

"I warned you about the price of disobedience," Jant said, his voice a hiss. "Your defiance has consequences, Grayshade."

The hunter wants you to forget, the voice in my head said. *It needs you to forget what happened.*

The light was beginning to grow in intensity again, but now it was not coming from the book, but from Jant's eyes, and I had to squint to see as he brought his weapon up. "Why did you lie?" I stammered, my voice thick and dull. "Why did you—" But I could not finish the sentence as his blade came down again. As it struck my cucuri the blade split, and like the wall outside the Repository, the pieces of it drifted away even as I watched. I fell back again, defenseless, stepping back as he pressed in on me inexorably.

"Contemptible fool," Jant said again. "Angry because you feel your faith has betrayed you. Angry because everything you touch dies, Grayshade; everything you touch dies. Everything dies. Everything." He grinned, his smile a horrible collection of impossibly shattered teeth.

"I'm not," I panted, back against the wall, barely able to make out Jant's silhouette against the painful, relentless light, "I'm—I'm not—I—"

"Contemptible," he said again, and his mouth opened as he raised his blade. I stood helpless as the stroke fell. But it did not fall on me—for some shadow flashed in front of him, and Jant's blade pierced it. It gave no cry, and suddenly the blazing light dimmed rapidly until I could make out the face of the one who had taken the attack meant for me.

Grayshade, said both them and the voice in my head.

It was Caron.

There was another snarl, and their lifeless body toppled over into my arms.

I gasped as I lurched forward, but as my eyes opened I saw I was not in the Repository. I was still in the Bloodmarsh, on the patch of dry ground next to the tree. The area was dim with mosslight again; the sun had vanished, and for a moment it seemed that Caoes had too. Then I saw him standing, turned away from me, a low growl in his throat.

"Caoes," I said, shaking my head to clear it of the nightmare. "Caoes, what is—" But I stopped as he turned toward me, for I had never seen him look like this, teeth bared in a twisted mouth, yellow eyes narrowed. He stared at me for a moment, then snarled, turned, and bounded away. "Caoes!" I shouted, then stopped as I saw where he was going.

He was running in the direction of Alarene's shack, vanishing even as I watched into the shadow of the trees ahead. And as I stood stupidly for a moment, in the far distance I heard a high, keening shriek, suddenly cut short.

Gods, no.

In an instant I was after him, the sack of dellens forgotten, leaping over roots and ducking branches as I went. We were still a good ways from the shack, probably ten minutes under the best of circumstances, but I'm not sure I ever moved faster than I did that day, somehow avoiding the tree roots and the logs in the dark patches of deeper water as I drove myself onward, the echo of the shriek and Caoes's snarl still lingering in my mind. I had no time to think of eventualities; when we got there, we would find—

Nothing. Just Alarene humming as she hovers over her pot, I thought, a child's desperation filling me. *That's all we will find.* But whenever I tried to summon her image, all that greeted me instead was the Jant of my nightmare, his blazing yellow eyes . . . and the dead face of Caron as they fell into my arms.

Within ten minutes, having traversed the ground of the Bloodmarsh faster than I could ever have thought possible, I pulled up short as I saw flickering firelight directly ahead: the fire from Alarene's shack, from the two torch poles she kept lit next to the path leading to her front door. I almost laughed in relief. My nightmare had been just that, the shriek I had heard no doubt coming from one of the denizens of the marsh. But as I drew closer, I saw the front door of the shack was open; a dim, low light shone from inside.

I drew my cucuri and bolted forward and onto the path. But just before I reached the front door, I saw something glinting from within. I tried to slow down, but heard an audible click as I stepped on the threshold of the shack. From pure instinct I threw myself backward a split-second before something exploded with a roar below me, kicking mud and wood high into the air. I landed heavily on my back, though the mud cushioned my fall, and covered my head as debris from the explosion rained down. After a moment I looked up to see the door of the shack caved in, a large hole where I had stepped just a few seconds ago. I pulled myself to my feet a bit unsteadily, ears ringing and a bit stunned but otherwise unhurt, and stumbled around the hole and into the shack.

The inside looked like it had been as destroyed by the explosion as the front had, but even as I struggled to process what I was seeing I knew it was impossible . . . as powerful as it was, the explosive radius of the trap which had almost claimed my life had been too small to affect much beyond its immediate location. Someone or something had wrecked the inside of the shack, ripping the herbs from the ceiling, throwing the furs about the floor, and spreading the wood and ashes over it all. The dim light was coming from a lantern, one of the extras I knew Alarene usually kept by the door for foraging expeditions. It was tipped over, and its light illuminated, twisted as if thrown there with the furs . . .

Hells. And suddenly an unbidden memory of the last time I had seen Caoesthenes flooded into my mind.

It was Alarene, eyes closed, breathing shallow. But even in the dim light I could see the blood on her face, her leg twisted at an impossible angle below her . . . and the huge rent in her side, wide and deep.

I bent down next to her. "Alarene," I said. "Alarene, I'm here."

At first she had no reaction. Then her breathing caught, and her eyes flickered open. They stayed unfocused, but she smiled. "Hello, love," she whispered. "Didn't . . . didn't hear you come . . . in."

"Alarene," I said, swallowing my grief. "Who did this?"

"Cloak," she said, coughing. "Cloak like—like the one you . . ." She lifted her hand to the edge of my cloak, only able to brush it before her hand fell back and her eyes closed again.

"Alarene!" I said, sadness warring with my need for information, but I fell silent as she opened her eyes again and, with an effort, shook her head.

"Much for . . . you to do," she said. "To find who you are. They'll . . . come for . . . you. Run, now, love. Find them. Don't . . . hurt . . . your . . ." Her last word trailed off, and with her smile fixed, she drew a long, shuddering breath and was still.

I stared for a long moment, then gently closed her eyes and lowered my head. Suddenly I heard a growl outside, and springing to my feet I ran to the destroyed door.

Standing there, a piece of ripped cloak in his mouth, was Caoes, sides moving with apparent exertion; nothing else stirred within eye or earshot. Wordlessly I knelt and took the fabric from him.

There are many kinds of cloaks in the world, but only one kind of cloak I knew used material like this: dark fabric, thick and warm while also flexible and light—and in the ripped piece I held, the remnants of an inner lining which had once been a pocket.

The cloak of an Acolyte of Argoth.

CHAPTER FOURTEEN

THERE was a time when I wouldn't have bothered burying a body. Death was a normal state of affairs for Acolytes, and unless we had to make a target disappear entirely, we usually just hid the corpse well enough to buy us time to escape. And in some cases, we were instructed to leave the body to be found . . . a more effective weapon at spreading the word, the Order thought, than propaganda and direct threats. But here again, I had changed. I would not allow one of the creatures of the Bloodmarsh to come across Alarene's body, nor would I allow it to slowly rot into the ground. So after I scouted the area for any sign of a continued presence, I took the small spade Alarene used for extracting dellens from particularly troublesome areas, and Caoes and I spent an hour or so digging a hole not far from the shack, in the driest area I could find.

I emptied my flask onto an unburned scrap, and cleaned the blood from Alarene's face. I lifted her body, surprisingly light, and walked to the waiting hole, Caoes waiting there, sitting upright and unusually still. He did not approach as I laid her body into the grave, straightened her limbs and smoothed out her stained garments. The positioning of her hair felt unnatural, and so I gently lifted her head, bringing out the long locks, realizing that the wild way they had fallen had not been unkempt, but natural—free. The wavy strands felt soft in my fingers as I loosely combed them out, and in the seconds before I rose, I allowed my hand to linger. As I gazed at the lifeless face, I decided to remember another one instead: the face on the mountain, and Alarene's eyes glittering as she looked out at Silarein.

I rose, shoveling the adjacent pile of soil over her until it met level. It was a shallow grave, and I did not know how long it would protect her rest . . . but it was the best I could do, especially when I dared not linger again.

I kneeled by the grave and bowed my head. I could not summon to mind the words for a true prayer of rest, and the Prayer of Repayment seemed inappropriate here. I was silent for a while, then raised my head again and looked at the gentle rise of soil. "Gods bring you to a better rest than you had here, Alarene," I said at last, my voice halting. I stood, turned and took a few steps, then looked back. "And I am sorry I brought this darkness upon you," I said, feeling twisted and empty. "I am sorry I lingered too long." Next to me, Caoes lowered his head, his face somehow somber, and blinked his yellow eyes slowly.

Finally I exhaled. "All right, Caoes. We delayed for too long here, and it cost us . . . and her," I said, nodding at the mound of dirt. "From now on we go at our pace, and we slow down for nothing." I set my jaw and turned away.

We took little more than what we had brought with us when we had first arrived at Alarene's shack, though we restocked our food and filtered water, and filled a small sack with herbs and other ingredients. I considered burning the shack down, but quickly decided against it—there was no telling what attention a fire might bring, and besides . . . something about the thought of destroying all that Alarene had been, as simple as it was, was uncomfortable. So I left her home dark and open, and walked away without looking back.

Accustomed now to the Bloodmarsh, I could sense directions easily within it; knowing the mallin grew mostly on the southern side of the trees, we set off northwest. If I properly understood where Alarene's home was located, it would only take us about a day to reach the flow of the River Carrtish–finding a path across now seemed a simple task—then head west toward the southern edge of the Scales, giving Arginn a wide berth as we went, before heading directly south into Tellisar.

But we would no longer walk in the shadows, seeking to avoid detection at all costs. I knew now that I had made a mistake in thinking I could hide away from the world, sinking into the still waters and mud of the Bloodmarsh. The outside world would never be content to let me hide away; it had sought me out, and punished my lethargy by killing my host. Alarene had paid the price for my selfishness; now I would take recompense for her loss, no matter what it took.

I kept a wary eye out as we slogged through the muddy water, both for unexpected residents of the Bloodmarsh and for unwelcome visitors, but as hours passed I saw nothing more than moss and marsh, with the occasional distant cry of a krellic or something else I was only glad to have left behind. But I knew now that someone was on my trail, and had managed to follow it even into the heart of the Bloodmarsh. What I couldn't understand was why they hadn't pressed their advantage when given the chance. Why not follow me when I left Alarene's shack to go foraging that morning, and strike when I was asleep? Of course the assassin might just have found their way to the shack a couple of hours ago; not wanting loose ends, they interrogated and mortally wounded Alarene, but I arrived before they could finish the job with me or at least set a more effective trap for my return.

And in fairness, they *had* tried to finish the job. But of course, there was Caoes. That was the random element, the part which no one, including me, could have predicted. Caoes was there while I was sleeping; he had been the first one to arrive at the shack; and he was the one who had found the piece of cloak, either lying on the ground as the assassin escaped or taken directly from it, ripping it off as the killer ran. Whoever was following me had to know Caoes was traveling with me, but had left him alive—why? Perhaps Caoes had gotten the jump on the attacker, who had no idea how to handle him, or both of us at the same time. Or perhaps they had let the panther escape—sending a message, after it was clear the bomb had failed to eliminate me, that I was still pursued and marked for death. Yet Caoes had been laid up for days while recovering from the krellic attack, and for at least a day or two of that time I had not been in much better shape . . . why bother to send a message when the assassin could simply have attacked then?

Unless, of course, the Bloodmarsh had been as inhospitable to my would-be killer as it had been to us. And the more I thought about it, the more it made sense; the splash I had heard when we had crossed the Glacal might well have been our pursuer, though there had been nothing else for days afterward. Perhaps they had some trouble with the crossing, or perhaps the assassin had fallen afoul of a krellic themselves. It would also explain the lack of follow-through at the shack; perhaps they hadn't adjusted quickly enough to Alarene's presence (and my absence), and were uncertain how to react, given the hostility of the environment and their own circumstances. With Caoes and Alarene, after all, I had allies; the assassin was almost certainly working alone.

But who are they working for? I thought, stepping onto and over a tree root as Caoes slid underneath. In truth, that was the only question which mattered. Almost certainly the Order of Argoth had decided that I was a threat which needed to be eliminated, and instructed the Service to make it happen . . . but from Cohrelle, or Arginn, or Tellisar? How many branches were there? How far did the Order's reach extend? For if the branches were so easily connected—if Cohrelle had alerted Tellisar, and they had sent an Acolyte to kill me . . .

Then there was nowhere I could run. Even if I fled to the Scales, they would find me eventually. And any hope I had of finding out the truth of what had happened, and who had ordered it to happen, would be forever lost.

To turn, then; to change from hunted into hunter. This had been my intention to begin with, and at least this attack had refocused me on that mission: to seek answers, to discover what was at the root of the events in Cohrelle, and to respond. Acolytes were not driven by vengeance, at least directly; we cloaked our activities in order, infused them with ritual and devotion. We served the Just God. But strip an Acolyte of their faith—remove the rules and strictures which dominated their life—and you would find what beat in their chest was the heart of a killer. That was who I was, and I could not escape it.

The Order knew this. The Order knew that Acolytes outside of their control were dangerous, and took rapid steps to silence them.

Fortunately for me, they occasionally failed. And now I was on my own, working for myself . . . free to indulge my emotional urges if I so chose. Even if I chose to take them all the way to wherever the heart of the Order's power lay—even if I were to stab that heart with all the fury I felt.

As Caoes jerked his head in my direction, I realized I had growled under my breath. "Mind your steps, Grayshade," I murmured as Caoes and I climbed up and over a raised hillock of grass. My rage fit me in that moment, but no payback would be possible if I blundered into a trap. So yes, I had to hunt—but with calm and precision and care, not wild anger. And that meant I needed to head to Tellisar, while watching my back. My mind on my mission, and nothing else.

As the hours passed, the air became less humid and the water less omnipresent. The glow was lower now, for the moss which produced it was increasingly sparse. And the cries of the marsh creatures grew quieter and more distant. All put together, it meant we were nearly through . . . and as I looked overhead and saw the leaf cover beginning to thin, the tree trunks growing straighter, I breathed a sigh of relief. After another hour, treading on ever firmer and drier ground, we heard the distant call of a bird—perhaps a hawk, or something similar. And another twenty minutes or so after that, we saw glittering ahead.

Pushing through a last set of bushes and branches in front of us, we emerged on the bank of a river, its water twinkling in the bright moonlight overhead. I drew my cloak around me, shivering at the touch of the cool night air on my skin; it had been some time before I had felt even a breeze, let alone a chill, though I would take the open cold to the oppressive warmth of the marshland. We were on the southern bank of the Carrtish; looking to my right, I could see the river wind down from a gentle incline, while to my left it widened and deepened as it meandered westward, before dipping south to reach the Glacalta. That was my ultimate course, but not on this side; I needed to head to the edge of the Scales first, and that meant crossing the Carrtish.

The river looked simple to cross here, but I didn't trust it . . . I had enough experience with water, and some of the creatures who lived in it, to last a while. So we turned east and trekked uphill along the southern bank for a while, until a widened patch of river spread over a low waterfall. I slogged across the smooth rock in water barely up to my knees as Caoes half swam, half crawled over the expanse. We climbed up on the other side and looked back, down the hill. There lay the Bloodmarsh, an ominous wall of dark green, silent and threatening in the moonlight; and inside it lay Alarene's shack, and near that, Alarene herself, resting in the shallow grave that was all I could give her. And elsewhere, perhaps not far from the marsh's edge, lurked her killer—and mine, if I wasn't careful.

I looked down at Caoes, who was lapping at the shallow water he had crossed. His leg seemed fully healed; even the wounds were somewhat difficult to spot in the dim light, and he'd showed no signs of distress during our journey out of the marsh. But as I turned and peered west, where I could just see the dark, somewhat indistinct shape of the closest mountain of the Scales, I wondered a bit how he would handle this next stage of the journey. I wasn't planning to take us far into the mountains—we had neither the time nor the equipment—but almost certainly we would be in the foothills, and that would mean climbing. How would his leg hold up under the strain? Under the best of circumstances Caoes was not demonstrative; how would I even know if he was in pain? And what could I do about it? Maybe I could carry him again, but . . .

I sighed as he looked up at me, licking his lips and blinking his yellow eyes. *Solve the next problem when you come to it,* I thought. *Right now we need to get away from here and to the Scales.* "Time to go, Caoes," I said. "No more swamps to deal with for a while, I think . . . but we'll have some hills to climb. You think you're up to it?" He tilted his head, observing me solemnly. "Close enough to a yes," I said with a small smile. "Then let's be off. I'd like to get clear of the river before we try to make camp for the night." And with one last look at the Bloodmarsh, we turned and set off toward the mountains.

We traveled for about an hour. We had come out of the marsh much further north than I'd intended, so as long as we kept west, we would avoid the northern sprawl of Arginn. I didn't know how far city patrols would wander, but even if Arginn had the upper hand in its war with Calarginn, I doubted they had the resources to send soldiers this far from the conflict. I finally had us stop in a small wooded area—barely a grove of trees compared to where we had been for the past fortnight, the ordering of the trunks suggesting a manmade planting from many years ago—and set up camp on a grassy mound, only a few feet above the land around it. The ground had grown progressively drier as we went, and the air cooler; despite the need for caution, I knew we needed a good rest, and that meant having enough warmth to keep from shivering uncontrollably through the night. So I built a small campfire from fallen branches nearby, with leaves for kindling . . . not much better than a couple of torches side by side, but considerably better than nothing. We had a meal of candied dellens over leftover bread from Alarene's shack, listening to the wind blow by as the trees surrounding us swayed gently back and forth. *Like me,* I thought; *back and forth with the wind, no matter how much I try to stay on the path.*

Of course, I *hadn't* always tried to stay on it, and Alarene was dead as a result. I couldn't expect to predict everything . . . but I'd had the warning of the splash, of the hunter. I should have prepared for the possibility of an attack, instead of wallowing in self-pity and delusion, driven by doubt and relatively peaceful slumber. I pursed my lips, looking down at Caoes, who had finished his last bite of bread and now had his head between his paws, eyes half-closed. I had never dreamed much during my time in the Service, or at least I had never remembered them, beyond a few fragments here and there. Since arriving in Elskeg, though, my dreams had been both vivid and memorable . . . and disturbing. They were focused, for one thing, specific memories of particular moments in my life. Even more troubling, they were . . . wrong. And of all of them, the dream of my attack on the Repository, the one where I had finally learned the truth about the Order, the one where I had killed my Apprentice Ravel and Jant, the Head of the Service—this was the one which bothered me the most. It was Rillia who had pulled me from the room, saved me from the ultimate act of despair, but in the dream, Caron was there. In fact, Caron had been in every dream, a curse or warning on their lips every time. Why? Coincidence? A warning?

An attack?

I shook my head and frowned, chewing and swallowing the last of the bread. I no longer believed in prophecies or displays of supernatural power; it was people who made the delusions to which we desperately cling for comfort or counsel or direction, people who understood the power such delusions gave them. *We are the gods you thought you prayed to*, Jant had said, just before I had ended his life in a rage of fury and hatred, and he had been right.

Yet there were Caron's words again: *Just because one god is false doesn't mean all of them are.* Typical innocent optimism, the philosophy of a child. But then, that child had saved me, there in the Governor's mansion where the High Prelate had intended to stake his claim as ruler of Cohrelle. Perhaps I couldn't afford to ignore the signs, even if I couldn't understand what they all pointed to. Perhaps . . .

Hells.

I shook my head again and kicked the dying fire, hearing the sparks crackle as the wood fragments shifted. Such thinking would lead nowhere in the end. First Tellisar, then the Order, then the answers I sought: this was my only path now, as uncertain as it was. I slid back onto the ground, half of my cloak piled underneath my head for a pillow with as much of the rest as I could manage draped over my body, and closed my eyes. The sighing of the wind through the trees was not loud, but it stayed with me as I drifted into sleep, hoping it might take me with it—blowing over the land below, caressing the surface of the Glacalta as it went, and from there to the Waves beyond.

The philosophy of a child, I thought just before awareness faded.

When I woke up to shafts of sunlight crisscrossing the grove, the wind had mostly died down—a good thing, as the temperature had also dropped. The campfire had long since burned out, and I shivered as I sat up, pulling my cloak around me. Caoes was already up, facing away as he stood near the edge of the clearing. "You're ready to go, eh, Caoes?" I said as I got to my feet. "That's good, but first we should probably—" Then I stopped, for Caoes hadn't turned at the sound of my voice, and as I looked more closely I could see the hackles on the back of his neck were elevated. Then I heard the unmistakable sound of his low growl.

By now I had learned not to question Caoes's instincts, and immediately I drew my cucuri as I lowered silently to his side. The panther was staring into and past the single line of trees which separated our campsite from the land beyond, grassy and gentle hills sloping down toward the Glacalta, and as I came alongside him and knelt down I followed his gaze. At first I saw nothing but the same grass and hills over which we had traversed the day before, and I opened my mouth to ask a question; then I saw the source of Caoes's attention, and let my words drift away unspoken.

Some distance away, a line glittered in the morning sunlight, but not the Glacalta. This was smaller, and it was drawing gradually but inexorably closer as we watched—and the light was fragmented, split, as if reflecting off of a number of different things.

Hells.

I waited for a time, staring as if my gaze alone could change what I saw . . . but this was no dream, and my vision not mistaken. The light was glittering off of metal: the metal of spearheads, swords, and helmets. It was a patrol, and unless the war had seen a massive shift in direction over the past month, it had to be a patrol from Arginn.

I had been wrong, then: apparently, Arginn *did* have the resources to send patrols this far afield. But why bother? The war being fought was a hundred miles away, on the other side of the Glacalta. What could a patrol possibly find this far northeast?

"Well, us, for one thing," I muttered, glancing down at Caoes, whose soft growl had been as unwavering as his stare. "All, right, Caoes," I said, sheathing my cucuri. "Whatever they're doing here, we're in no condition to deal with thirty well-armed soldiers." I looked over my shoulder; there, past the line of trees on the other side of our camp, the foothills of the Scales rose toward the ominous wall of sharper, snow-covered peaks beyond. "I didn't want to do this," I said, looking back at Caoes, who had finally shifted his gaze to me, "but we don't have a choice now. We'll need to get further north, into the foothills of the mountains. No matter what they're aiming at, it'll be a lot harder for them to get up there than us. Head west once there, and keep an eye out for Tellisar." I was grateful, again, for Alarene's vision. While Kraes had assured me I would not miss the city from the ground, having seen its array of spires from a distant peak of the Scales, I was certain I would recognize it from any vantage I might reach. I took one last look at the approaching patrol, then stood and sighed. "And hope we've used up our share of surprises by now."

It was quick work to scatter the remnants of our camp and

head north; if the patrol had somehow seen signs of our campfire the previous night, covering every trace would have been super-fluous. In any case, it would have taken too long; if the Arginnians spent time puzzling out the signs of a man and a panther in a lonely, deserted area of northern Silarein, so much the better. We headed directly toward the hills, the land rapidly sloping upward as we went. As the Scales drew closer, rough and threatening in the shrinking distance, I began to understand why I'd heard their name so much since arriving in Silarein, sometimes reverently, sometimes in the form of a curse. The mountains not far from Cohrelle, between which I had passed to enter Silarein several months before, were hilltops in comparison to these peaks, jagged as if they'd been ripped from the surface of the land by an angry god. The immensity of their scope dominated everything else near them; for a moment I remembered the Cathedral, soaring over the other buildings in the Church District in Cohrelle. But that was one structure; all of the Scales led to towering heights, with no one peak dominating the others. It was a massive wall, well beyond the abilities of mortals to breach.

As imposing as the sight was, I took strange comfort in it. At least something, somewhere, was beyond what humans could do to affect it, more permanent than our small struggles and petty hatreds. I thought again of the dream I had with Alarene, the two of us standing high in these mountains, looking out at Silarein and the land beyond. There, the machinations of the Order, the war between Calarginn and Arginn, the political maneuverings of Tellisar—even the loyalty of Kraes to her soldiers and city, or the anguished hope of Ress for the return of his son—all of it seemed unimportant, tiny. Perhaps that was all any of us needed: the chance to see our world from a different place, to view our problems standing on the foundations of the world, where centuries passed like seconds, and where stone and rock taught patience and wisdom.

I snorted, causing Caoes to glance up at me as we trudged on. I had fashioned myself a poet, now? It had been a dream, and the person who created it dead at the hands of the same people I fantasized as being insignificant. Neither Alarene, nor I, were made of stone and rock. And in any case, I didn't plan to go that far, gazing upward at the wall of mountains in front of us . . . or at least I hoped not. But even the foothills were steep enough, and as we climbed, our pace was beginning to slacken. The trees were short and growing shorter here, the grass becoming sparser and giving way to scrub brush and rock, and as I paused and turned, I could see that we had already ascended a good distance in several hours, gaining a better view of the land below.

The sun was now well into its ascent toward midday height, and the warmth of its rays was welcome in the growing chill of our own ascent. We were now on the edge of a kind of plateau, carved into the side of the hill like a massive step. In the distance, I could just make out where our campsite of the night before might have been, though I could no longer see any glittering light from the armor and weapons of the patrol—perhaps they were inside the grove of trees and blocked from our vision, or perhaps simply too far away to be seen. This was a comforting thought, for I felt exposed here, naked against the white-gray backdrop of the mountains behind us and highlighted in the morning sun. Of course it would take superhuman vision to see a cloaked man and a black-furred panther in all the expanse of the foothills of the Scales, but I had overestimated the level of my concealment before, and I dared not make a similar mistake now. Yet there was hope, for in the distance to the southwest, I could see the sparkling waters of the Glacalta, and—perhaps only driven by my desire to see it—a dark streak along its coast. Tellisar? My goal, at long last?

We trudged on for several days this way, though not with much complaint. The terrain was rough and unwelcoming, but the sun warmed our shoulders, and I could see that its touch was as welcome to Caoes as it was to me.

From time to time, Caoes would peer over the ridges as we came close to them, and I knew his mind was on the patrol we had seen, or others like it. Each time I awaited his growl, relieved when he padded back to my side instead, selecting our path forward as often as I did.

When the first growl came, it was behind me: a yowl and a bark of challenge. But the voice was not Caoes's. As I turned, I saw Caoes on the other side of the plateau, low to the ground, ears flattened and teeth bared. Facing him, body in a similar position, was a creature so white I blinked several times to make sure I was not seeing some bizarre reflection of the panther. But no; it was taller, its fur more bushy and prominent, its face contorted in an angry snarl.

It was a large white wolf.

For a moment no one moved. Then the wolf leapt, jaws open, snapping at Caoes's neck. The panther jumped upward, raking his open-clawed paw across the wolf's face. The wolf yowled and fell back, tilting and shaking its head, then put its ears back and charged. Caoes attempted to dart away, but the wolf's speed evidently surprised him, as the body of the wolf slammed into the panther and knocked him onto his back. The wolf raised its head and howled, drops of saliva dripping from its mouth, as Caoes twisted and squirmed underneath the larger creature's weight. But before it could latch on to the panther's torso with its open jaws, it jerked back, its howl cut short—for I had gotten to the side of the beast and slashed down at its exposed flank with my cucuri. It staggered off of Caoes, and with careful aim I kicked it in its wounded side, driving it further away from my companion. It snarled at me, then whimpered in pain as it stumbled. I held my blade loosely, ready for its charge. But suddenly it snarled again, then turned and loped off, limping badly as blood dripped from its retreating form.

"Leave it. If it's got a pack somewhere, we'll be in worse trouble if we follow it," I said before glancing at Caoes. He was standing slowly, sides heaving with (I supposed) the surprise of the sudden encounter . . . but I could see no obvious wounds on his body, and I exhaled in relief as he padded forward a few steps before looking back at me, apparently no worse for wear. I knelt and stroked his fur, gently in case of any bruising, feeling both pleased and foolish as Caoes made no move to shy away.

The white wolf had vanished into a scattered maze of rocks on the opposite side of the plateau on which we stood, and after watching for a minute to ensure it was truly gone, I looked back at Caoes. "I don't know much about wolves," I said, "but I don't understand what would lead it to be that aggressive, unless we somehow stumbled near its den. Either way, the behavior is odd . . . and dangerous." I glanced back toward the edge of the plateau. "But in any case, we can't stay here," I went on. "If that patrol *is* following us, it almost certainly heard the sound of that thing's howl, and the way it was cut off. We can't keep dodging patrols and fighting animals in the wilderness." Caoes blinked slowly, his breathing normal again, as I stood and walked back to the plateau's edge, looking back at the dark circle at the edge of the Glacalta. "A minute to catch our breath," I said as Caoes padded up alongside me. "Then we head down as best we can."

Somewhere in the distance behind us, the ghostly howl of a wounded wolf drifted through the air.

CHAPTER FIFTEEN

✦

THE descent down the side of the foothill was considerably more difficult than the ascent had been, especially with the need to keep a low profile. I still felt all too exposed here, with few bushes or trees available to hide our advance, and what freestanding rocks there were lay in unstable-looking gatherings; I had no desire to slip and tumble, even if I trusted Caoes's steadier footing. So we kept low to the ground, holding our balance with difficulty as we continued downward in a roughly southwestern direction.

We neither saw nor heard any further sign of the white wolf; now that we had departed its territory, I assumed it wouldn't bother to follow, especially in its wounded state ... though Gods knew I had been wrong before. But my greater concern was for the patrol. We hadn't seen or heard them either since beginning our descent, which worried me more than if we *had* caught sign of them; patrols weren't particularly easy to conceal, especially on difficult terrain like this. If they had decided to parallel our course, planning to cut us off when we reached the bottom ...

I looked down at Caoes, clearly laboring as his paws slipped and slid on the loose gravel. Though he had healed remarkably quickly, he had taken a grievous wound in the past three weeks, and the fight with the wolf had been rough, if not very long. Up against a fresh opponent, a conflict could be difficult.

So strange, I thought as I placed my hand down for balance, my right foot slipping slightly. I had always worked alone, always found the presence of companions to be a distraction, an irritant. But now it was difficult to imagine my life without Caoes in it, difficult to imagine not taking him into account. I was thinking about him more than me at times, which, given my past, was probably a welcome change.

Still, there were obstacles ahead. Even if we did make it down without further incident, how was I going to get him into Tellisar? Even with the reported size of the city and its prominence as a trading center, I doubted they had much experience with panthers strolling through their front gate. It would no doubt invite questions, and those were questions I wouldn't feel like answering. Perhaps in a cart, if I entered while posing as a merchant . . .

"Bah," I muttered, letting myself slide down a few feet to the next space of relatively rock-free ground. Until we got there, speculation like this was pointless. For all I knew, Tellisar had been dragged into the conflict between Calarginn and Arginn already, and who knew what entry protocols would be in place then. And if—

Suddenly I caught sight of something below us, and I held up my hand. "Stop, Caoes," I hissed, watching as the panther scrabbled to a halt and turned his yellow-eyed gaze to me. I narrowed my eyes against the glare of the early afternoon sun. There in the distance, rising from a small stand of trees, was a thin but clearly visible strand of smoke.

A campfire. Not a large one, but a sign of life, and directly in the path we had chosen for ourselves. If we were to avoid it, we would either have to alter our track to head straight across the hillside—and it had been difficult enough to maintain our balance on the treacherous, angled ground when we were traveling with the angle, let alone cutting against it—or go down directly here, straight south, and pass by the fire's eastern edge. Neither was a promising prospect, but heading right for the source of the smoke seemed even less wise, especially if it was coming from the same patrol we had caught sight of before. Looking up at the hillside we had just traversed, I knew going back up wasn't an option either.

I sighed. Directly south it was, then; at least it would get us off this damned hill. With luck, we'd clear the stand of trees quickly, and then could stick close to the bottom of the hillside. We turned and began to make our way carefully down our new path.

Despite my fears, we went much more quickly on the direct descent, and soon after, the gravel gave way again to the grass and dirt of the lower regions, making our footing much easier. I kept my hand near the hilt of my cucuri and my ears primed for the sound of booted footsteps or metal on metal, but other than the gentle blowing of the breeze and the call of some birds far overhead, we heard nothing beyond the sounds of our own passage. It only took about twenty minutes for us to reach more level ground, and a few minutes after that we were essentially on flat terrain, walking through gently waving grass. The stand of trees was still a good ten minutes' walk to our west, but nevertheless I stayed crouched as we went; any lookout worth their job would be looking for variations in the landscape, including standing figures. But it would have been tremendously difficult for anyone to see a panther and crouching man from this distance, and I was inclined to feel somewhat pleased as we cleared the southern edge of the stand of trees, the glittering expanse of the Glacalta's water laid out before us in the further distance. To the west, the streak I had seen from the hillside had now expanded into a visible line of buildings—perhaps with spires above them, though I was not close enough to be sure—and again, I pictured Cohrelle's Church District and the Cathedral towering above it. Now that I was in sight of my goal, my worries about entering the city seemed somehow less important. One way or the other, I was drawing close to the answers I sought.

And then, something whipped past me, jerking my cloak back as it went. I grabbed my cloak and blinked stupidly at what I saw there: a small hole, jagged around its edges.

It had been made by an arrow.

I whirled in the direction of the shot, Caoes growling as he turned with me, just in time to see a large pile of what looked like ropes land on top of his body. He ran forward, but stumbled and fell as the ropes contracted around him, leaving him in a struggling heap. *A net . . . but . . .* I drew my cucuri, but a second later another net landed on me from behind, and I was suddenly aware of something sharp poking me in the back between the interconnected ropes.

"I'd let that blade drop if I were you," a familiar voice said from behind me. "A spear would be much more useful; and fortunately for us, we have one."

Hells.

I hesitated, but the sharp object in my back pushed forward insistently, and with the surrounding net ensuring I had nowhere to go, I lowered my cucuri to the ground.

"Good," said the voice, sounding pleased. "You haven't lost your sense of caution, I see, Grayshade. It's good to see your foolishness isn't total." Whatever was in my back was removed, and I slowly turned to see the voice's source, though I already knew who it would be. There, flanked by several leather-armored men holding spears, stood the figure of Captain Merynne, an unpleasant smile on her face.

I swallowed a curse. "So they've got you on patrol duty now, Merynne," I said, standing as straight as I could inside the net. "I thought you'd have gotten a promotion after tearing up the Calarginn company and getting control of the Depths."

Merynne's smile vanished. "Maybe I was wrong about your stupidity. You're not in a position to be clever, Grayshade. If you've wandered through swamps and up mountains trying to stay alive, I'd suggest you don't throw your life away now that you're finally caught." There was something off about her demeanor, but I couldn't quite place it. She glanced down at the prone figure of Caoes, yellow eyes still visible through the net, his growl low but audible. "And if you don't give a damn about your own worthless skin, maybe you care a bit about this animal. Maybe I'll show it what we do to cats that don't play nice." Suddenly she drew back her boot and kicked the net; Caoes jerked back, but made no sound.

My stomach twisted a bit, but I kept my voice level. "I'm not interested in threats. If you've got something to say to me, make it swift."

Merynne's eyes narrowed as she stepped closer, staring at me from barely a foot away. "I've got plenty to say to you, *assassin*," she hissed. "My superiors are very interested in the actions of an

Acolyte of Argoth, especially when they get in our way." I tried to keep my expression steady, but the sudden return of Merynne's wolfish grin told me my eyes must have widened a bit at her words. "Oh, yes, they're very interested," she went on. "And so am I. We've got unfinished business, you and me—about the camp, and what you were doing there. And now I want to know just how you escaped, and how you got your little kitten to help." Yes, there was something different in her face, for certain ... something tired about her eyes, a kind of hollowness to her cheeks. She stepped back from the net. "We have a lot to discuss ... but not here. You'll have a bit of time to think about how cooperative you want to be as we go. Use the time well; when we reach our camp, the questions will begin, and how you deliver your answers will decide how long you'll stay alive." She turned and strode away. "Take them," she said without looking back as she passed the spear-wielding men. "As long as they're alive, conscious, and mobile when we get there, I don't care what else happens to them."

The sneers on the faces of the men as they strode forward suggested they didn't care either—and it didn't take long for me to learn exactly how little regard they truly had for anyone, human or panther.

✦

Much of the travel to Merynne's camp was a blur of beatings and threats, with more than a few references to the imminent end of my existence. But the Arginnians were much quieter now than the first time I had encountered them. I expected jokes and comments about finishing the job they had started back in the camp; certainly at least a few of them knew of my previous time there, and I doubted they remembered either me or Caoes with fondness. Yet they said nothing about our previous encounter, and as time went on I began to wonder a bit about what had led them here. Presumably Arginn had no interest in keeping Merynne out in Elskeg once the Calarginnian company had been destroyed; any vaguely competent officer could babysit the miners while the real combat played out closer to their enemy's main city. But Merynne and her troops must have left the Greenmark not long after I did; even with my delay in the Bloodmarsh, she would have had to take a fairly direct route back to Arginn to report and be reassigned, though of course they could have commandeered horses. And in the end, it wasn't her group that attacked the remainder of Kraes's company, but Acolytes of Argoth . . . so why—

A punch in my side knocked the wind from my lungs and my thoughts to the present. I had my hands bound behind my back, connected by a rope to one of two leather-clad soldiers between whom I was walking and who had obviously taken Merynne's advice about being as free as possible with "correction" to heart; I didn't think I'd said anything out loud or slowed my pace, so I presumed they were simply enjoying the control. "Move, gray-cloak," said the man on my right, a sneer twisting his greasy face. "You're plenty strong enough to go faster than the crawl you're at now. Unless you feel like joining your pet there." He jerked his head over his shoulder at the two men behind him; they had placed their spears in between the ropes of the net which had snared Caoes and were carrying him between them as they went. I could see him gazing out of the net as he lay quietly, but I knew they had been none too gentle with him either, and I wasn't sure how much of his current state was due to his usual calm and how much because of the abuse he had taken.

"I don't think so," I said, a wave of anger passing over me. "You can't have all of your targets trussed and ready for beating so easily."

A punch, this time in my stomach, nearly doubled me over, and I stumbled forward a step or two before regaining my balance. "Shut your mouth," the man growled. "You're lucky Merynne said to keep that heavy lump alive, and it's her orders that we follow. But his time will come, and yours too—sooner than later, if you don't step lively."

Something stirred in my mind at that as I stood straight and, ignoring the new aches in my stomach and side, picked up the pace of my walking. Their cruelty was genuine, but the speech seemed—off, somehow, forced, as if this wasn't the man's usual way of speaking. In my experience, bullies came by their roughness honestly; Kester certainly hadn't sounded inauthentic, or any of the other Arginnians I had met. This felt like a ruse . . . but to what end, even if true? And perhaps I—

Suddenly I felt the rope being jerked, and I came to a halt along with my captors. Over a small rise ahead of us I could see the dark expanse of the Glacalta, much closer now, and in front of it the city of Tellisar; we were only perhaps two hours' march away. Ahead of us, Merynne whistled three ascending notes, and nodded as three descending notes responded. She walked back to me, taking in my form with her searching gaze as she came close.

"Well, did they survive?" she asked as she stopped a few feet away, looking first at Caoes's motionless form before peering into my face. After a quick inspection she smiled thinly. "Good. I didn't expect you'd be much hampered by a bit of a stroll."

"And a few beatings to help my pace," I said, and a second later jerked left as one of the men next to me punched my side.

Merynne held up a hand. "That's enough. Remember, I need him functional enough to answer questions. Don't want him losing consciousness," she said as she turned and walked away, "yet."

I stumbled forward to follow as the man pushed me in the back, heading toward the small rise. As Merynne reached it, she disappeared over the edge, and as we got to the same spot a few moments later I understood why. This was not a hill descending gently toward the flat land in front of Tellisar, but the leading edge of a ridge which surrounded a tiny valley—almost a depression in the land, maybe four or five hundred feet in diameter, a few short trees and wide bushes scattered here and there around the perimeter. Several cloaked figures, mouth and noses masked, were positioned just below the ridge, gazing out at the space beyond. In the middle of the open area, a handful of bedrolls lay around a small campfire, unlit but with wood piled high for the evening, near which a few more soldiers in leather armor and cloaks with hoods thrown back were talking in low voices. Counting the members of the group that had captured us, there were perhaps twenty people all told in the circle . . . a far cry from the number Merynne had commanded when I had last encountered her.

What in the Hells—

The men pushed me down the slope, and I only just managed to keep my balance as I staggered down the hill and came to a stop not far from Merynne herself. Those near the campfire stared, but quickly looked away as they saw Merynne's expression—tight and serious, the smile on her face gone. "Sit," she said, jerking her head toward a small patch of grass near the pile of wood. "And get rid of that rope, Arnnis; we're not walking this dog any further today. Leave his hands bound." Arnnis, the same man with whom I had exchanged pleasantries a few minutes before, complied—none too gently—and took up a position near me as I sat in the indicated position. "Bring the cat to the other side of the wood," she said to one of the two men bearing the net in which Caoes hung. "Lay him down. He can watch how well his master does tricks for a change." She waited as the men dumped the net and the panther on the ground; Caoes's eyes were narrowed, and I could see his mouth working a bit as if in pain, but otherwise his expression remained as inscrutable as ever. Then she turned her attention to me. "I don't think you need any more time to decide if you're willing to talk," she said, folding her arms. "I gave you enough of that the first time, and we both know how much respect you provided my . . . hospitality."

"We have different definitions of that term, Merynne," I said, wincing in spite of myself at pain from the various places where her men had applied correction.

Merynne did not smile. "We have different definitions of a lot of things, apparently," she replied. "But we both know what it means to be out of patience, and I'm well past that now."

"Do you really want to ask more about Calarginn? Because I thought—"

"I'm not interested in that little adventure now," she said, cutting me off. "I'm more interested in where you've been since we last parted ways."

I shrugged. "Traveling cross-country. After you wiped out the company in the Greenmark, there wasn't much reason to stay. So I headed west, toward the Glacalta and then north to the Bloodmarsh."

Her eyes opened a bit at my last word . . . but with less surprise than I might have expected. "Lovely place, the Bloodmarsh, if you're looking to vanish," she said after a moment. "But most people who go there don't come out so quickly."

"Complications," I replied, pushing aside the memory of Alarene before it could surface on my face.

Merynne nodded. "And then?"

"Then I headed north."

"You have a lookout in the Scales?"

I smiled. "Something like that."

"A place which might be of interest to your masters, perhaps?" she went on. "I'd like to know about them. I'd like to know where they come from."

"I've told you everywhere I've been—"

"Your beginnings, Grayshade. At the start of it all." She leaned in, her expression hard and set. "I'd like to know all about Cohrelle."

I stared at her a fraction too long, and as she saw my expression she smiled. "I thought you would have been trained to be a bit less obvious in your reactions. But maybe you're not as good now as you used to be. Oh, don't worry—you haven't betrayed any secrets, despite your incompetence to this point. We have ways of getting information we need ... and quickly, when we need it."

I shook my head, pushing away my surprise, and my questions, for the moment. "The war must be going very well if you can get it that quickly," I said. "Doesn't Arginn have better things for its commanders to do than track down rumors about unimportant strangers?"

"Oh, you're not unimportant," Merynne said, leaning back. "I think you were very important—to the Order of Argoth."

A chill began to creep up my back. "I don't understand," I managed.

"I think you do. I think you know what it's like to throw a whole city into chaos. I think you know how it feels to be on the run, Grayshade. You've been that way for a while, haven't you?"

The chill rose higher, and I stared at Merynne. *Her speech pattern—she—*

"A long while," she continued, as if not noticing my reaction. "Looking over your shoulder all the time ... not a moment's peace. And something driving you on for ... what? Redemption? Answers?"

What?

"And no companions ... none which you can protect, anyway. A soldier from Calarginn. A strange panther." She paused, then looked right at me. "An old woman in a swamp."

Suddenly the warning from my dreams came back to me with a vengeance: *beware the hunter*, it had said. In the depths of the net, Caoes growled, his yellow eyes glittering.

Suddenly the chill spreading through my body exploded, and I felt my heart freeze in horror. "You—" I started, then stopped, unable to process the full sentence. And then, seeing the slightest twitch of her eye, I looked around the camp and realized what had struck me as strange. There were no golden trees of Arginn here, no military equipment, no tents; I recognized none of the people from before. The cloaks were familiar, though—but not from Arginn.

I stared up at her, mouth working. "The laquevoxes at the camp," I said. "You knew what they were, how to defuse them . . . because you've used them."

Merynne stood straighter and looked at me steadily, face expressionless.

"You're not from Arginn. You're an Acolyte of Argoth," I said as if in a dream. "All of you are." And as if in answer, all of the people who had turned away now looked back at me, expressions serious, bodies held in that tense readiness only an Acolyte can truly perceive as their own, like the words and import of a ritual only the faithful can truly remember.

"Slow," Merynne said after a long period of silence. "But now you understand." She turned to face the others. "Yes, we are all Acolytes of Argoth—but not from Cohrelle."

"From Tellisar," I said in a whisper, grasping on to what was left of my world. "Tellisar sent you—"

"As if," Merynne said with a sneer, "Cohrelle was the only place where Argoth's will was enacted. As if you could run from Him, or your own crimes."

"You were following me," I stammered, my head spinning. "You were tracking me . . ."

"Not until Elskeg. I had been with the Arginnian company for some time when word came that you were in the area, and to track you down when I located you. For a time I didn't know exactly how I was going to do that, actually . . . I was too busy playing nursemaid to the Arginnians, pretending I gave a damn about their silly squabble. Their little war." She laughed. "As if anyone outside of Silarein would know or care if both cities slid into the Glacalta and vanished forever."

I thought of Ress, pining for his son gone to the war.

"Then you pulled your business at The Mountain's Heart, and I knew who I was dealing with. I assumed if I was patient, I'd find a way to catch you." She chuckled, turning back to me. "I didn't expect you'd cast your lot with the Calarginnians and come right to me that night, of course. I'd heard you were much smarter than that, in the old days." She frowned. "But I had been told to get information before killing you, and assumed it would be easier to do so if you still believed I was an Arginnian soldier. It was a foolish mistake. And I hadn't planned on your cat, either," she said with a glare at the still growling Caoes. "I thought I might smoke you out when we attacked what was left of the Calarginnian rabble, but that attack didn't go as well as I hoped. Still, I managed to set the two companies at each other's throats while I slipped away to find you, and it didn't take long to pick up your trail."

Now the tiredness of her eyes, the hollowness of her expression, made sense. "The Bloodmarsh . . ." I said softly.

"Even after I ran into some trouble in that cursed mudpile, I thought I had you there," she replied. "But that cackling bag of bones got in my way, and I didn't have time to set a proper trap. And there was this *animal* again," she said, spitting on the ground near the panther. "Still, I knew I was close. The other

Acolytes from Tellisar were waiting at their station when I left the Bloodmarsh, and then I knew it was only a matter of time." She grinned. "It took longer than it should have, but in the end, it was worth the wait. Now I get the information I want, and then I get to pay you back for the dirt and grime I've had to wade through, all the bodies I've had to climb over to reach you. I'll even get to bring this thing to heel while I'm at it," she said as she shot a look at Caoes. "And I'll take my time doing that, believe me." She leaned in, lowering her voice to a whisper. "Maybe I'll even start with him."

I felt a surge of rage replaced almost immediately with despair. In the end, nothing I could learn had mattered. In the end, the darkness would always return.

Merynne's grin grew wider. "You think I don't know your training? You care nothing for yourself. But that, ha! Look at you, in love with your kitten. Grown soft, Acolyte." Merynne drew her short sword and turned to the panther. "Yes, you first, kitten," she hissed. "Let's see if I can teach your master the price of disobedience." She took a step forward, and just before I surged forward in a fruitless attempt to stop her, I heard a familiar sound of rushing air and a soft *thunk*. Next to me, Arnnis grunted and toppled over, and Merynne whirled as she heard his body hitting the ground. "Who—" she snarled, right before the man on my right fell in the same way. I stared down at him.

In the back of his neck were four kushuri darts.

Looking up again, I saw, silhouetted against the rapidly fading light, two cloaked and masked figures standing on the top of the ridge—one short, one tall. Then a yell, and leather-armored soldiers leapt over the ridge and poured into the camp, and as the area erupted into chaos, I caught a glimpse of the soldier at their front.

On her chest was the silver and blue of Calarginn. She had no helmet, and her hair fluttered in the wind.

It was Captain Kraes.

CHAPTER SIXTEEN

AS soon as I saw the Calarginnians charging into the camp, instinct took over, and I threw myself onto my back and brought my bound hands down and around my bent legs. Even tied, I could do a lot more with them in front of me than behind, and as I rolled into a crouch and got back to my feet, I saw I would need every advantage I could find. Combat had broken out through the entire camp, with Calarginnians engaging with Acolytes everywhere I looked. Caoes was still netted, growling fiercely from inside, but his carriers had rushed to join the fray. Freeing him with my own hands still restricted would have been no mean feat as it was, but with the conflict raging there was no way I would be able to attend to it in any case—I'd be an easy target with only a moment of inattention. I just had to hope that Caoes would be enough out of the way that he'd survive until I could reach him.

Still, it was going to be hard to be particularly useful; I was bound, had no weapon, and no amount of training would help avoid a blade I couldn't see.

Hmm—a blade one cannot see.

I turned to find two Calarginnian soldiers locked in combat with an Acolyte, sword against sword. These Acolytes didn't seem to use cucuris as we had back in Cohrelle, but the swordplay was familiar enough, and even against two opponents the Acolyte was more than holding her own, blue eyes wide as she parried the first soldier's attack and drove in on the second. He dodged her thrust, but it had been a feint; as he tried to regain his balance, she dropped low and swung her leg through his, sweeping him off his feet. He hit the ground with a groan, his sword slipping from his nerveless fingers, but the Acolyte was already moving, bringing her sword up in a diagonal slash as she spun to her feet. She cut across the front of the other soldier, evidently stupefied by her speed, and he went down clutching at his neck—maybe not enough of a strike to pierce his armor, but she had connected somewhere. I had no time to see where, though; I was already charging forward, and I threw myself into the Acolyte's back as she was turned. She grunted in surprise as I connected, plunging forward, and as we hit the ground I heard the wind being knocked from her. I brought my elbows together and down on the back of her neck, and with a quiet sigh she lay still, her blade underneath her.

I looked around, but the battle was raging too fiercely for me to see anything in particular, and I decided I needed to take a risk: leaning forward, I started to slide the rope binding my hands back and forth on the exposed part of the Acolyte's sword blade. It was freshly sharpened, and the ropes none too sturdy, but the angle was awkward and the room limited. "Come on, Hells take you," I muttered as I bore down, hoping the added pressure would speed the cutting process. Every second that ticked by seemed like an hour as the fight raged around me.

Suddenly I heard a yell next to me, and I only just had time to flatten before the body of a soldier went flying over my head, followed by an Acolyte, face sweaty. The soldier didn't move after hitting the ground, but the Acolyte did, turning to face me with an angry expression on his features. He looked younger than the previous Acolyte had—perhaps recently promoted, or even an Apprentice, though I did not know whether the Service in Tellisar trained its Acolytes differently than Cohrelle's did—and as he strode forward, I knew I had run out of time, my hands still held together by the remnants of the rope. I stood and backed up several steps, but his sword was already drawn, and as he raised it above his head my heart dropped—until I saw his stance, too open, too forward.

He's going to bring his sword right down on my head.

And that was exactly what he tried to do. Except instead of my head, his sword hit the half-cut rope between my hands as I raised them to meet his strike. The sword cut through the rope with ease, and as it did I dropped my left arm and turned swiftly, allowing his momentum to carry the sword past my head and to the ground. His eyes widened in surprise as he spun back to me, but I was on him before he could bring his sword up again, and I drove my knee into his midsection, doubling him over in pain. I grabbed the sword from the unconscious Acolyte on the ground and, reversing the hilt, raked it across the head of the other, still struggling to stand. Without a sound, he fell forward.

I now had a weapon, but as I turned to survey the scene, I was hardly in better shape. A few Acolytes were down, with more Calarginnians—I couldn't tell for certain how many more of them there were, but it was clear that even with inferior numbers the Acolytes' skill outmatched the soldiers'.

But it would not, of course, outmatch mine.

I launched myself forward into the heart of the combat, slashing the exposed side of one Acolyte, then swirling forward to undercut the legs of another, then diving underneath a slash and ramming the hilt of my blade into the side of my assailant's neck. After a minute the Acolytes began to notice the battle had shifted, and the encounters more difficult. But it was clear that despite their training, these were almost all young Acolytes, limited in their ability to improvise—especially when confronted with someone with far more experience.

We'll see whether I'm as good as I used to be, Merynne.

I parried another strike from an Acolyte, but had no need to return the blow as the Calarginnian soldier engaged with him took advantage of the distraction to connect with a violent slash to the Acolyte's midsection. Again, I did not stop to see the result. I was looking for one person in particular, and as I moved past another skirmish between three soldiers and an Acolyte, I saw her. There stood Merynne and Kraes, bodies of Acolytes and soldiers at their feet, locked in combat. Kraes was taller than Merynne, and wielded her longsword with skill and precision; yet Merynne was an Acolyte of Argoth, and clearly more experienced than those under her command. She parried Kraes's strikes with her own shorter blade, seeming content to wait for an opening rather than launching an immediate counterattack; Kraes's face was covered in sweat, her eyes narrowed and mouth set in a determined line as she rained blows down upon Merynne.

As I strode forward, Kraes grunted in exasperation and leaned forward into her next stroke. But she had overextended herself, and swifter than a snake, Merynne spun away and brought her sword around toward her exposed arm. Kraes gasped in pain as the blade bit deep, and stumbled backward. But Merynne's following attack never connected, because my blade was already there, and with a clang the swords met and parted.

I stepped in front of Kraes as she clutched her injured arm. "Get back and keep them from us, Kraes," I shouted without looking back. "This isn't your target, Merynne," I said, my expression steady as I regarded her. "You were sent to find me, and here I am."

Merynne grinned nastily despite the obvious exertion in her face. "Still the Calarginnians' pet," she sneered. "I've never understood what possessed you to do what they say you did back in Cohrelle, Grayshade. I've never understood what could cause someone to betray his faith and his oaths."

"You don't even understand your faith, Merynne," I replied. "You don't know how many things you have to abandon for it, in the Service of Argoth ... morality, friendship, love. Truth. The Order takes it all, and you along with it."

Merynne's grin vanished, replaced by a scowl. "Don't talk to me about sacrifice, heretic," she hissed. "Argoth's will is stronger than your petty desires, your pitiful defiance. I am the hand which bears His Hammer, and through me it falls upon His enemies ... including you." And with a yell of challenge, she brought her sword up in an arc toward my face. I stepped back to avoid the upward slash, but didn't trust it and turned completely to the side—wisely, for a split-second later she threw something from her sleeve, a spray of kushuri darts which came so close I could hear the slight *whoosh* of air as they passed. I turned to face her again as I brought my sword across in a vertical cut, but she parried the attack with little difficulty and, stepping forward into the space created as she pushed my blade aside, kicked my exposed waist. I saw the attack at the last second and pulled away, yet even without full force the blow was well aimed, and I winced in pain as it connected. Immediately she was upon me, attacking my midsection with a series of slashes which I only just managed to parry. The exertions of the past few days and the beating I had taken en route to this camp hadn't helped matters, yet even taking that into consideration, against Merynne I felt sluggish, uncertain. Her fighting was quick and agile, a mix of the style I had seen from Acolytes in Cohrelle and something else—more angular, shorter, movements more compact and unpredictable. I was holding my own but giving ground, and any minute one of her Acolytes could join the fray … and one mistake would end the battle, and my life, for good.

I took another step back as she aimed another slash at my side, turning away to let it pass. *Don't just react, lad; set the tempo of the music you would play,* Caoesthenes once told me many years ago, and I felt the wisdom of his approach now. Merynne was controlling the fight, wearing me down bit by bit; she knew I couldn't continue at this pace for much longer without making an error, and all she needed to do was bide her time. Roaring as if addled, I ducked low and jabbed forward, hoping to bait her into a block—and as she brought her sword down I thought I had succeeded. But when I began my counterattack, she let her sword fall and spun away, and as my blade flew up, she grabbed my hand and drove her forearm into my wrist. Fire shot up my arm, and I dropped my weapon, staggering back.

"You fight well, Grayshade," Merynne said as she kicked away my sword, a savage snarl on her face. "But not well enough, I'm afraid. You should have spent more time honing your craft."

I laughed at that, in spite of my pain. "Or more time not taking a beating at your command, Merynne. Is that Argoth's will, too?"

"Whatever allows His will to be achieved is acceptable in His sight," Merynne said with a scowl. "And in this case, your lack of faith will be punished. Goodbye, Grayshade. May you find mercy in His sight." She raised her sword aloft—but as she stepped forward, a confused expression came over her face. "What—where are you?" she said, looking around as if searching for something. "Why—" Merynne now spun in place, her expression growing frightened. "Who is speaking? Show yourself!" Suddenly she began to swing her sword wildly, as if trying to fight off unseen enemies. "Get out of my head!" she screamed.

I tottered forward, though even now, in my pain there was probably little I could still do to her. Then I heard a low growl from behind me, and I turned to see a streak of black charging my way. Merynne also turned in the direction of the growl, eyes wide and staring—but far too late. She only had time for one shriek, cut short, before Caoes had leapt past me and landed on her ... and before I could say or do anything, a strangled cry sank to a gurgle and then silence.

As I swung toward the direction from which Caoes had come, I saw the net in which he had been trapped cut open on the ground. Kneeling next to it was the taller of the two figures I had seen at the top of the ridge, the shorter one alongside. And as they saw me staring at them, the short figure drew back the hood to reveal a young, brown face, no longer masked; after a moment's hesitation, their companion threw back the hood, beneath which was a black-haired woman. Neither was smiling, but their eyes were alight, their appearances familiar.

"It looks like you still need some looking after, Grayshade," the woman said quietly, her slightly husky voice steady.

"*Rillia*," I whispered.

"You have an interesting group of friends," Kraes said later, unsmiling . . . but her voice was light. She sat cross-legged on the ground near the pile of wood like the rest of us, her arm now bound in a makeshift sling. Around her, most of the remaining Calarginnian company—still two thirds of it, about forty soldiers or so—was searching through the Acolytes' camp, while several soldiers stood over a few bound and sullen-looking Acolytes. Caron sat by the prone form of Caoes, stroking his fur occasionally.

"It seems that way," I replied, wincing as Rillia moved her fingers up and down my injured wrist, expression serious. After a few moments, she sighed and looked up at me.

"Your luck hasn't abandoned you completely," she said with a small smile. "I don't think it's broken . . . sprained, probably, but nothing that won't heal given a splint and a bit of time. A few days, maybe a week."

"I can probably afford that," I said, unable to stop staring at her face as she sat to my left. It looked much the same as it had three months ago, though perhaps more worn, more tired, a few worry lines visible around her eyes. "How have you been, Rillia?" I said more softly.

She shook her head, still smiling. "Worried," she replied. "But glad we made it here in time. We wouldn't have had a chance without Venner."

"I could say the same," Kraes said with a chuckle. "And it wasn't much of a chance even then."

"I assume someone will explain how you all ended up

together?" I said, feeling somewhat in the dark. "Did you manage this somehow, Caron?"

The leader of Varda's people smiled and shook their head. "Not most of it, Grayshade," they said in their high voice. "I felt more like baggage than a useful traveler."

"Most useful baggage I ever saw," Kraes cut in. "I could do with a lot more exactly the same."

"But what are you doing out here at all? What's going on in Cohrelle? Who's managing—"

"Easy, Grayshade," Rillia said as she held up a hand. "We'll explain everything . . . or as much as we know how to explain."

I pursed my lips and settled back. "All right. You can start with what's been going on at home."

Rillia sighed, her smile vanishing. "That's—complicated."

"And we're not completely sure ourselves," Caron put in. "We've been away for a while."

"For the first few weeks after you left, Cohrelle was in as close to complete chaos as I've ever seen it," Rillia began. "The Order itself was in total disarray, from what I was able to find out . . . but one thing everyone could agree on was that they were angry. For a few days there were random killings in the streets . . . the Service's work. No one was safe, but city guards were the ones in particular danger, especially the ones in the Government and Merchant Districts. The Church District was fairly quiet, with the Cathedral completely shut down, no one allowed in or out; it was more like a fortress than a religious building."

"A logical progression," I murmured.

Rillia nodded. "After a week or so the murders died down, but the city was on a razor's edge. Rumors flew: some said you had wiped out the entire Service, and Governor Jarrett had replaced all of the Acolytes with his own loyal guards; others claimed the Service had killed Jarrett and installed you in his place. A few of the more outlandish ones said the whole thing was a plot of the Sewer Rats to take over the city."

"There were some really imaginative ideas," Caron said with a smile.

"One way to put it, yes," Rillia said. "No matter what the theory, everyone agreed that things had changed massively . . . which was a good thing, because it gave Jarrett room to maneuver. You had the right instincts about him, Grayshade; he's a brilliant politician, as shrewd as you like, and somehow with a bit of integrity left over. He immediately started rounding up Acolytes, carefully, in ones and twos, always making sure the capture was ensured and the results kept quiet. I helped a bit there; his guards aren't actually as bad as you had thought them to be. Just needed a bit of training, and a bit of understanding about how an Acolyte thinks. Within a week he had at least gotten the Order to back off—all while making them angrier than a ralaar, but he didn't seem to care about that."

"He's brave, too," Caron said.

"So are you, Caron," Rillia said with a smile. "Caron helped with all of this, especially as Jarrett began to rebuild his Circle. He started with the two of us, but gradually he added a few more here and there, one from his personal guard, one from the merchant class, one from the religious circles. The Order couldn't have been too happy about that."

"He had me there when he talked with each of them . . . to get a sense of what they were feeling. I could tell him whether they were upset, or angry, or lying. I've been practicing, too . . . I can do a lot more than I used to," Caron said with what might have been a proud smile.

"It's true," agreed Rillia. "Without them, I don't know how Jarrett would have managed it. But even with them, it was a big task, especially when we turned to the ruling structure itself. I don't think anyone knew how far into the government the Order had gotten, but they have spies and informants everywhere, and flushing all of them out was a bigger job than cleaning the sewers. Which, by the way, has been changed in favor of the Rats, just as Jarrett promised; they know a great deal more than even I had expected. They're becoming a source of information no one else in the city can match." Rillia took a breath, leaning slightly back.

I nodded. "So far it all sounds promising."

"It is, as far as it goes," Rillia said. "But Jarrett also sent his own people outside the city to ask questions, and the answers they got weren't good ones. Soon enough news started to filter in from abroad—about Silarein, the civil war between Arginn and Calarginn, Tellisar acting strange . . . and the Order, though no one knew exactly where they were, or what their influence was. The more we heard, the more nervous we all became."

"Especially Rillia," Caron said.

Rillia shot a glance in their direction and sighed exasperatedly. "It was my job to be nervous, Caron, and I had reason to be. After three weeks or so, I told Jarrett we couldn't stay; the Order had been badly weakened, but was still a threat, and as far as any of us knew they were still after Caron and me. Jarrett could protect himself, but us . . . well, we were taking our lives into our own hands, unless we were going to stay hunkered down in his house for a year or more. And I wasn't going to do that. Finally I convinced him to let us go. Well, I convinced him to let *me* go, actually," she amended, looking sideways at Caron again. "I wouldn't have taken Caron . . . too much of a risk."

"But they wouldn't stay," I said, keeping my expression as serious as I could.

Rillia glared at me for a moment, then nodded tightly.

"I wanted to come," Caron said, "and the Governor didn't need me anymore, at least not as much as at first. I need to learn everything about the Cloud, and I can't do that just in Cohrelle. And there were—the dreams," they said as a troubled expression clouded their normally smooth features. "I needed to do something about them, too."

"The dreams?"

"They can explain more about them in a minute," Rillia cut in. "We followed your trail into Silarein; it was a pretty good bet that you had at least wandered through Elskeg, and sure enough, when I got there a few questions led me to a friend of yours: a miner called Ress. He told us you were working with the Calarginnians, or at least you were at first . . . I couldn't understand all that much of his story, really, but at least it seemed obvious we needed to make our way to Calarginn. We managed to track down a couple of horses, and that sped up our journey—we made good time, especially since we encountered almost no one on the way. Lots of destroyed farms and houses, though, and a feeling of . . . dread?"

"Despair," Caron added, scratching Caoes behind the ear as the panther tilted his head in obvious enjoyment. "A lot of despair."

Rillia nodded. "When we got to Calarginn, we couldn't find anyone who knew anything about you—but we did hear about the war, and the company which had just returned, almost destroyed. That's when we met Venner."

I glanced at the watching soldier. "I'm surprised she would have anything to do with you when she found out where you were from," I said. "Acolytes of Argoth from Cohrelle aren't her favorite."

"Aye," Kraes agreed with a wry smile. "But I'm not fool enough to turn down help when I can get it, and when these two arrived and explained their story, I saw a way they could do just that. As it happens, that ambush you helped break up at the farm had one benefit: it helped convince the higher-ups that something was very wrong, and that Tellisar had something to do with it— and your Order of Argoth too, although the Tellisar connection seemed more important to them. In any case, Gods know the war against Arginn isn't going well, and the commanders are getting desperate. So I asked them to give me a group—half a company, the best I could ask for—and track down the rest of the Acolytes who had attacked us. Find them, and we'd have information we could use against Tellisar."

"You must have been convincing."

"Not much," Kraes snorted. "If it had been my word alone, they would have told me to go break rocks. But Rillia knew what the Acolytes were about, and her word meant a lot . . . and then there was them," she said, glancing at Caron. "They've got a way with words. It was hard for anyone to say no after they spoke."

"I just reminded them what was important for their city," Caron said frankly. "I could tell they weren't bad people."

Kraes shrugged. "Might be, but not being bad isn't the same thing as being sensible. But these two convinced them somehow. They gave me a week, told me they'd have my rank and my hide if I was wrong, and sent me on my way. I didn't think we'd make it to this side of the Glacalta, but luck was with us—and your Acolyte, who knows something about the art of distraction," she said, nodding toward Rillia. "Even on the other side, I still didn't think we'd find you or the Acolytes. But Caron here helped on that score."

I looked at Caron. "You could—sense me, then?"

Caron nodded. "My abilities have expanded, Grayshade . . . a lot, actually. My teachers say this is how it usually works: a sensate of Varda's people slowly develops until a certain age, and then jumps forward. Especially in a different environment, something which challenges what we can do." They smiled. "I've had a lot of challenges lately."

I understood that. "You started to feel this with the Rats, then . . . back in Cohrelle." I was mostly reminding myself, but Caron nodded enthusiastically.

"Yes. And over the last three months, ever since I entered the Cloud, it's grown. I can sense emotions from great distances now . . . and even send messages, sometimes, at least to people with whom I have a strong connection."

Beware the hunter, I suddenly thought, and my jaw dropped. "My dreams—was that you? Those were warnings?" Caron watched me silently, and after a while I shook my head. "I should have realized," I said. "You knew what the dreams were, then?"

"No," they replied. "I can't control how you experience the messages I send, and I don't really understand all of how it works anyway. My teachers say that I can connect with people's emotions—send them fear, caution, uncertainty, hope—but not how they receive those emotional messages." Suddenly they looked concerned. "Did they frighten you? I was trying to help, not make things worse."

"It was my fault anyway," Rillia said, resting a hand on my uninjured arm, the one beside her. "As we were leaving Cohrelle I got word that someone from the Order had been sent to find you; there were no details, but the person definitely wasn't coming from Cohrelle. I knew you had at least a month's lead on us; you could be dead weeks before we found you." She looked at Caron, face still clouded with worry. "Caron had been talking about the growth of their abilities ... and I thought they could ..." She stopped and swallowed. "It might have been foolish."

"It wasn't," I said. "But I almost misinterpreted it, when Caoes showed up. He wasn't your doing too, was he, Caron?"

We looked at the panther, eyes closed as Caron stroked his fur. "No," the sensate replied. "I can't reach animals who aren't people, and I wouldn't control anyone who wasn't hurting someone. But I told you there would be others who would want the best for you, you know."

I nodded. "You did. He's still a mystery for the moment, then, but it's good to know not everyone wants me dead." I turned to Kraes. "And you?"

Kraes shrugged. "Now we go home. With this information, and these Acolytes, I think there's a good chance Arginn's leaders will want to have a long talk with Calarginn's. They may have the upper hand in this war—but with clear evidence that Tellisar is playing both sides for fools, waiting to jump in as soon as we've torn each other apart, I think we could get our cities to unite against them . . . especially if we get some assistance," she finished, looking meaningfully at Rillia and Caron.

Caron hesitated and looked at me, as if waiting for my response. Rillia's hand still rested on my arm. With each second, it had released a tiny bit of the tension I hadn't known I'd still held, and though it made me feel childish myself, I hadn't yet turned to face her since she'd done it. Now I did, to see her staring directly at me, a new expression on her face—calm but a little strained, an unspoken request written into her features—and again, childishly, I looked away. I saw Caron sitting next to Caoes, who had opened his eyes and was now regarding me solemnly. I thought of Alarene: *You must make your own decisions,* she had said, *from your hopes, not your fears.*

I knew what my fears were. And my hopes?

I said nothing more for a long time. Finally I took a deep breath. "Captain, the Order won't be stopped with the loss of a few Acolytes, even if Arginn and Calarginn can make peace with each other. I need to stop the Order, and to do that I need to go to them, in Tellisar. That's my path . . . and if there's anything I've learned, it's that I can't tread that path alone." Rillia gently squeezed my arm, and I looked at her, Caron, and Caoes, then back to Kraes. "My friends and I are going to Tellisar. All of us."

EPILOGUE

"Do you think Captain Kraes will be able to convince Calarginn to stop fighting?" Caron asked. It was two days after the battle, and we were standing on the top of the ridge overlooking the campsite with our cloaks drawn closed against the chill, watching as the Calarginnian company slowly disappeared into the night, making their way west with their captives in tow.

"I don't know. But Kraes is no fool, and she's as stubborn as it gets ... maybe even more stubborn than Rillia," I said, letting a small smile play over my features as she rolled her eyes. "And the evidence is pretty strong, especially if they already believed her enough to send soldiers with her in the first place. Of course, even if she does convince Calarginn, there's no guarantee that Arginn will want to go along. But when they find out they've been set up ... well, who knows."

"And us?" Rillia asked. "Your wrist needs to stay splinted for another few days at least, and rested after that."

"I know," I replied, turning to face Tellisar, the sparkling light of lanterns and torches visible even from this distance. "We'll move away from here, find a vantage point to observe any movement, and wait for a day or two. That will give us enough time for my wrist to heal ... at least enough for me to hold a blade again." Rillia shot me a look. "Just in case we need it, Rillia. And we still need a plan to get into the city. I might be able to figure out how to explain the three of us, but Caoes ..."

I glanced down at the panther, still staring at the twinkling city in the distance.

"But he has to come, doesn't he, Grayshade?" Caron asked.

Rillia opened her mouth, but I spoke before she could object. "Yes, I think so. He's become sort of ... attached to me, at this point."

"And you to him," Rillia said, shaking her head. "I wouldn't have imagined you wanting a pet."

"He's ... not," I replied. "He's a friend. And I wouldn't have imagined you to be a political operator, Rillia. Convincing the Calarginnians to help was no mean feat, especially after Kraes's first company was practically wiped out."

"I might have been something of a novelty to them," she replied. "I never wanted to return to the identity of an Acolyte ... but I'll admit it helped when I needed to convince strangers of the threat. And of course, Caron was a huge help, as usual."

"I know some people who will be grateful," I said, thinking of Ress and his son. "Including me." Rillia and Caron looked at me with surprise, and I cleared my throat uncomfortably. "Well— we'd better get moving. I'd like to find a more secure place before daylight, if we can ... perhaps down the hill and over to the west a bit, closer to the water."

We shouldered our belongings and turned to go, shivering a bit as tiny white flakes began to blow past us on a light breeze.

"The moon's rising," Caron said, looking up at the sharp crescent. "Some light for our path."

I looked up, then turned to Caron, then Rillia, then Caoes. I smiled. "For once, I don't mind a bit of light," I said. And turning, we set off toward Tellisar, the Order, and whatever fate awaited us in the greatest city of Silarein.

ACKNOWLEDGEMENTS

Most milestones seem obvious from the beginning, events and accomplishments which one can list ahead of time as being significant steps along the road. But sometimes you reach a stage in your career where something turns out to be more important than you thought it would be, and finishing this book was just like that. It's my first completed sequel, and marks two thirds of the journey through what will soon be my first completed trilogy—and as I've learned, writing Book Two is just as challenging as Book One. But it's also the first book I've had to complete under difficult personal circumstances; health is something I've tried never to take for granted, but I was reminded many times how important it really was both when I began writing this book some time ago and over the past year as I was completing it. So when this was done, I felt a bit like Grayshade himself—tired, a little world-weary, but also relieved, proud, and grateful.

Speaking of gratitude: I remain grateful to Marie Bilodeau, the editor of the original book, for her support during the first difficult period when it was being written—her understanding was important and greatly appreciated. But of course, the editor for this book, Emily Bell, has again shown not only a keen and sensitive critical eye in helping shape the manuscript, but equal levels of kindness and support of me, and I remain deeply grateful for her editorial insight and personal friendship.

Besides the editors, this book had a smaller group of people involved in its creation, with each member that much more important. Jeff Nelson, a long time reader of my work, was as thoughtful as always with his feedback, and Kelly Swails continues to be not only a good friend and gifted author but a wonderful critiquer of my work; it's nice to have someone really "get" your style, and Kelly has always been that way for me.

Beta readers Brandon O'Brien and Dimitris Tzellis were both thoughtful and encouraging, and I'm deeply grateful to both of them for their insights into and support of this series. I'm also thankful for the proofreading work of friends Tren Sparks, whose audio version of *Grayshade* continues to be an inspiration for me, and Patricia E. Matson, whose attention to detail and continual support is enormously valuable and appreciated.

I remain thankful to Brad Beaulieu and Mike Underwood, authors and friends, for their friendship and support of this series, to Chris Bell for more wonderful work on layout and design, and to Peter Tikos for another amazing cover image. Thanks are due to my students for helping me learn even as I'm teaching them. And for the viewers on my Twitch channel who saw some of this manuscript coming together—thanks, everyone. A sympathetic audience is always good, even when accompanied by a healthy dose of Kappa emotes.

As always, I'm most thankful to my friends and family who support me in everything I do—especially Mom and Dad, whose presence in my life remains even with them gone, my wife Clea, from whose calm understanding I've always drawn strength, my wonderful daughter Senavene, who continues to be a personal inspiration, and son Calen, who has a smile to match his spirit.

And I want to make special mention of my oldest friend Ewen Ross, who passed on earlier this year, much too young. He left behind loving family and friends, and as someone who gave me the earliest bound version of the first book in this series as a gift, he holds a special place in the history of this work and for me personally. Not farewell but fare forward, my friend.

Finally and as always, I am thankful to you for reading this book. It is still a great privilege to be able to publicly share a world I have long imagined privately.

Connecticut
2023

GREGORY A. WILSON

Gregory A. Wilson is the author of the novel *The Third Sign*, the award-winning graphic novel *Icarus*, the award-winning first novel in this series, *Grayshade*, and the 5E adventure and supplement *Tales and Tomes from the Forbidden Library*, along with a variety of short stories, academic articles, and books. He is also Professor of English at St. John's University, where he teaches courses in speculative fiction, creative writing, and Renaissance drama. He is the co-host of the critically acclaimed podcast *Speculate!*, and under the moniker Arvan Eleron he runs a highly successful TwitchTV channel focused on story and narrative.

He lives with his family in a two-hundred-year-old home near the sea in Connecticut; his virtual home is gregoryawilson.com.